BAD BREAD,
GOOD BLUES

RONAN J. O'SHEA

This paperback edition first published in 2019

Cover design by Gary Ogden

ronanjoshea.com

For Jambo Connor

Bad Bread, Good Blues

The plan was to go to Primrose Hill with a date, but then my date cancelled. So I changed my plans and went to a quiz night at a local pub and nothing much happened at all. That was good.

I planned on dating another girl I used to know, when I ran into her after a five-year gap. The bit just before the gap had involved a night of what I doubt she'd describe as passion, but when I bumped into her I got the impression she seemed interested in rekindling whatever passion there had been, and so I asked her out. She didn't reply. That was so-so.

When I was four my family planned on moving back to the rural town in Ireland where my father was born. He'd never much liked the city, but remedied that by loving us, us and the sea. We planned on moving back to Ireland. Then he died out in the same sea he loved. That was bad, luck and otherwise.

I planned to work hard after the Christmas of 2015. I'd had a fever throughout the holidays but started the year with steely resolve. The company I'd been working at for nine months or so was finally gaining some momentum. I'd become editor of one of its websites (by default), and it looked like we might start making money. And then I was told there was no money, and the website was being taken down and I was being made redundant. That was all right. It wasn't too much of a surprise, either, despite my recent motivation. But then it was bad, really bad.

I planned to marry Jana despite my youth, and to have children around the age I am now. That plan became problematic when I started living in London and she stayed in Prague. Sperm does not travel as far as yearning.

It remained the plan, though, because I loved her and did want it all. Then she left me, but only because I'd left her. That was bad, inevitable, and just how it goes sometimes. Worse, though, is how it didn't hit me for six the way losing the job did, not at first. That's because I was stoic, something often better described as numb.

Before there was Jana, I'd never been one for plans, unless you count dreaming of one day being a rich, famous and (importantly) revered writer. That was my plan. I didn't really do planning, didn't know how. Life had been quietly chaotic enough as it was to be thinking about plans and whatnot. That was either dumb or it was smart, and I haven't figured that out yet.

I never planned on being saddled with debt or living alone or having regrets by the time I was thirty, which suggests that maybe plans are not the smartest of things to have after all, or that they should be planned well well well in advance.

Thinking about it, I made a vague one once, a half-plan you might say, telling myself that if I'd not succeeded by the time I was thirty, I'd give up. I failed in that endeavour, though I did reach thirty, if that could be called success. It's more than Hendrix achieved. Or James Dean. Or Egon Schiele, for that matter. Pocahontas too, though it's fair to say era and luck and everything in between were against her.

But anyway, plans or no plans, there are truths in all that happened. I never intended to stay in Prague as long as I did. That's true. Prague didn't end too well. That's also true.

My aim was never to be so aimless out there, but I did do and see things others could only dream of, for the sole reason of being in the right place at the right time, in a world that just turns, always turns, axing on its axis, around and around with me in the right spot when it was needed.

Your plans to read on may have been affected by what I've said so far. That's neither smart nor unsmart. It just is.

I will say now that I've plans to talk about a lot of things, about everything that happened after Jana, and some of the bits in between as well as a little before, but as you have probably picked up on, I'm not much good at making or sticking to plans, and may well veer. But I promised her once that I'd talk about it all: us, Prague, my life as a monkey, my life as hers, my life in the city and my decision to leave.

So, before anything else, before the coffee granules and the bad dreams and the beer and the no-frills adventures, there's Prague.

*

If I met Hemingway I'd tell him he was wrong, that it's Prague which is a moveable feast, not Paris. He'd probably punch me. That would be fine, and as good a way of stating his point of view as I can imagine.

I lived in Prague as a young man. I'm still a young man, but today it's an extremely young person's world. Well, they have the run of us at least, and when we tell them otherwise, they tell us we're mad, bigoted or outmoded. That's horseshit, straight from the mouth of a generation that does not know what it means to be wrong, or even considers the idea. But anyway, Prague.

I'm not suggesting I lived Prague the way Hemingway lived Paris - far from it. I didn't drink Martinis like him, fall in love with nurses like him (I didn't know any) or get into any dingy barroom brawls, like him. A skinhead did once beat me up on a train for reasons I've never learned. That was fine. It just happened, as things do. But I didn't live like Hemingway, not at all.

I did go to many bars, though, pubs mainly, getting drunk often and with enthusiasm. I had blackouts, Sundays spent mostly in bed, and Mondays where I felt like shit, resolving to be a different man that week. But by the end of the week I'd feel refreshed enough to do it all over again. That was the circle of life.

It wasn't just drunken things, though. There was other stuff too. I worked as a teacher, floating between classes on the city's public transport system, went to cafés, ran in parks and shopped in shops, filled out tax returns that nearly destroyed me and invoices that I actually found kind of calming. I did my groceries at Albert, a supermarket chain a little like Tesco, where I sometimes shopped too, always irritated by the way Americans (I was friends with many) called it Tesco's, as if Mr Tesco were some sort of kindly Colonel Sanders-like figure, something itself fraught with connotations I've not the time to go into now.

Saturdays were spent watching football and also Sundays, because my team, Spurs, weren't very good. As they weren't very good, they played in what's called the Europa League, which was on Thursdays. That meant they'd often play Sunday instead of Saturday, to give their legs more time to recover. That's good science.

The Europa League is kind of like a B-side on a record, but not a B-side like 'R.E.S.P.E.C.T' was a B-side that ended up making it big, just a regular B-side that no one really has want or need of, not really.

I spent a lot of days and evenings watching Spurs, and if you think that's wasted time you may well be right. That's subjective and it's important to be subjective, particularly nowadays, when it's almost a crime. Watching football might have cost me one girlfriend early on in Prague, but it also kept me calm and sane on Sundays as I didn't have to *think*. Of all my plans, it was the least interrupted.

Weighing up whether I ever planned to fall in love in Prague, I'd have to say yes, which is about as non-committal as you can get from a man who had nothing but commitment on his mind. That was me.

I didn't plan to fall in love with anyone in particular, but upon running away to Prague at the age of twenty-four, I probably, somewhere within me, planned on meeting a beautiful Czech girl. I met many. That was wonderful. Most didn't fall for me. That was understandable. I met a few girls I liked and who liked me, some Czech, some not. That was just par for the course in youth and young manhood.

One time I strung a girl along. Another time a girl strung me along to improve her English. That was funny, really funny, even as it happened. Another time a girl broke my heart. I'd started making big plans surrounding her. That was dumb.

Another time I broke another girl's heart. That was necessary, but it didn't leave me feeling good.

A third time, there were two hearts of equal breakability and I broke them both, one being my own. That was love.

And amidst the sub-zero mornings and the language barriers and the conflicts of opinion and value, Prague was, in its way, love.

But of course, there was also the problem with the bread.

*

I once argued with friends over where the best view in Prague could be seen. It wasn't a full-blown "we're not talking again" kind of argument; more like the kind you see in a bad film, where unctuous, insufferable people bicker over bagatelles whilst drinking wine, eating bread and using big words even they're not sure the meaning of. In this case, I was one of those people, though I don't think there was any bread. Good bread wasn't easy to come by in Prague.

My friends believed Letná had the best views of Prague. Letná is a huge park in the north of the city which stretches for what seems like miles. At its edge is a hill overlooking the Vltava River with its river cruise boats and the bridges and all the pretty buildings either side. It's picture-perfect, which is why many postcards from Prague are shot from Letná, which is itself pretty.

Letná has a huge mansion often used for weddings. There's a beer garden in front of it. I went there a lot, the mansion not so much. Not far away there's a metronome which clicks back and forth all day long. Before the metronome, there was a statue of Joseph Stalin.

When Khrushchev decided the Czechs needed to love Stalin a little less than they already did, it was brought down. Now there's a metronome, and there is also a bar. It's called Bar Stalin. That's tongue-in-cheek. The Czechs did that well. That's also opportunistic, and it's smart too. Sure, the views from Letná are impressive. You can see some of the best sights, like the TV Tower, which has large steel babies that climb up its shaft. That's a sentence I never thought I'd say.

But to my mind, the best view is somewhere else, in Riegrovy Sady. That's a park maybe half a mile from Wenceslas Square, and that's a square, though not really.

People gathered in Wenceslas Square in 1989. They jangled keys, called for the Russians to leave, demanded the communists go. I say communists. I mean the communist government. There are still communists in the Czech Republic, of course, well-meaning and disaffected communists. Not everyone was going to win when things changed. Yins must have their yangs. They're misguided, insane or just broken (usually a mixture of the three), but their disaffection is not. That's something we don't like to recognise now. Those broken by the loss of what we might call bad.

Riegrovy Sady is a park named after a famous Czech nationalist. There's a statue of him at the bottom of the hill where teenagers meet at night to drink two per cent fruit beer, smoke weed and negotiate naked exchanges in the shrubbery. That's one way to be remembered.

The part of Riegrovy Sady I refer to is a little further up the hill, just to the left of where sunbathers lie in the summer. From there you can see Petřín, which is like the Eiffel Tower, and the opera house, which is like an opera house. You can see the Barandov Hills too, which is where the rich live, because rich people like to live on hills. We can destroy villages from thousands of miles away now at the click of a button, yet height advantage retains its appeal. That's funny. Ha-ha funny.

I liked looking at Petřín and I liked the opera house, especially at night, but it's the bits between the landmarks I always liked; the dysfunctional, unevenly erected housing blocks that really make up the city, buildings that sprung up at different times, storing all the lives and their stories.

The rooftops are red like African mud. At one time I planned to someday live in one of those buildings, beneath an African mud-red roof-tiled flat.

Of course, it never happened. Hey and ho.

*

I was twenty-four when I moved to Prague. That was young, though I'd no idea at the time. It was the summer of 2011. I knew that. It was a hot summer, knew that too.

A weird thing happened a few days after I arrived, completely unrelated to this story. I'd told someone months earlier that Britain was different to France, said that you would never see the kind of things you saw in France happen in England: riots, people getting set on in the street, that kind of thing. There had been riots in France in 2005.

I can't remember how the conversation began, but began it did. Sure, we had problems, I said, big problems with race and police and poverty and everything in between. But we would never get riots in London like the ones France had in 2005. That would never happen.

Then a few days after I moved to Prague there were riots in London. That was funny. Not ha-ha funny, just, you know, funny the way people say *that's funny* when something's disconcerting or just *is*, something that doesn't hit you for six but does put you slightly out of kilter. It was that sort of funny then; now it seems like ha-ha funny. Not that it happened, just, well, it was naïve, wasn't it? That was good. Naivety is good.

I decided to move to Prague on a whim. My original intention was to go to Germany. That was the plan. But it turned out it wasn't so easy to teach English in Germany. You had to have experience I didn't, and good German, and I didn't have that either. That was state education for you. I'd had three German teachers at secondary school: one from Northern Ireland, one from Truro and the other, well, I think she *was* German. That was third-time lucky, or it would have been if she'd not been the middle of the three.

Anyway, with Germany off the cards I still had to find somewhere to teach. There weren't any jobs in London, and there was a recession too. I figured it was smart to get out as quickly as possible. That was impatient, but fuck it. "Good things come to those who wait" is a thing said to sell beer made from fish eggs.

Go fish.

Prague came out of nothing, a conversation. A friend of mine was seeing a girl and that girl recommended I look at Prague. And that's how I ended up in Prague. Go figure.

The biggest decision of my life was made on the recommendation of someone I hardly knew then and don't know a thing about now. They split. That's young love.

I'd never been to Prague before moving there, but had been to other places, like Cyprus and Crete and Portugal, and even Denmark after a nineteen-hour boat ride when I was two, during which I threw up a lot. That's to be expected. My father did not. He was a sailor. Sailors are expected not to throw up, on boats at least.

When I was fifteen, my mother took me and my sister to

America, which was great, even if the American dream seemed to remain in a nascent, oneiric phase. That's dreams. At sixteen, I visited Thailand. My mother didn't earn a lot of money in her job as a library assistant, but my father's death years earlier did. That was circumstance.

My first girlfriend was studying in Lyon the year after I graduated. I'd left university without having made any kind of plan. That was dumb or smart or fine or not. I don't yet know, and won't for a while. I went back to university a year later. That was following my dreams, but following my girlfriend also, which wasn't so smart maybe. In February I was picked to go to Milan for three months to be tutored by a novelist out there. My girlfriend planned to visit. We booked a night's stay in Rome. Then I caught her in an alleyway with a guy a week before I was due to go. The fella's hosepipe was back in its can before you could say "oh me oh me oh my", and that was the end of that.

In Milan, I wrote and smoked and drank and sometimes saw the famous novelist for an hour or two. At the end of it I travelled round the Balkans a little, watched the World Cup in pubs and looked forward to being home again. Back home I didn't find work, and wanted to leave again. That was running from your problems.

And that led me to Prague.

*

I moved there on August fifth. It was overcast, but it was warm too, and humid. When I arrived, there was supposed to be a taxi waiting for me. I was doing a course at a language school, where I was going to learn how to teach English. The taxi was included in my course fees. It wasn't there when I arrived. That was a taste of things to come.

I walked from Terminal 1 to Terminal 2 then back again, and back and forth once more after that. Eventually, a middle-aged man with a paunch pitched up, carrying a placard with my name on it. We got in his car and drove towards the city. Close to the centre, the driver pointed to a girl with long red hair, a short silver skirt and heels. She was pretty. That was something we agreed on.I had high hopes that my existence was about to be full of colour and life and love and laughter. I hadn't been in the best of shape for the last year or so. I'd been depressed, and ultimately introduced to Messrs Citalopram and Fluoxetine in their red and yellow suits and green and white skirts. That was an inconvenient reality but a reality nonetheless. I was much better now, though. I'd done therapy, I was over it all. That was naïve.

I was looking forward to my life in Prague, where I
planned to be happy, and healthy. I wasn't going to drink too
much or smoke at all. That was naïve in the extreme.

A moveable feast, remember, is also a banquet.

*

The driver dropped me off at my hotel. The other people on
my course were staying elsewhere. I checked in, put my stuff
in my room and walked across the road to a pub, where I ate
my first lunch in Prague, a simple meal of sausage, bread and
horseradish.

There are things you get used to when you live in another
country, but bread is not one of those things. When I did teach,
students often moaned about English bread, which they'd eaten
in the UK. They said it was terrible, the worst. Why it was
English bread and not Scottish or Welsh, I don't know, but they
hated it either way. Back then I didn't get it, but I do now. A
person's view of bread is gospel. It's a belief set handed down
through the generations and you're as likely to see pigs fly as
you are Czechs changing their view on bread. It's an opinion,
and opinions are often valid.

But when it comes to the Czechs' opinions about bread,
it's also bullshit.

Czech bread is heavy. The crusts are soft but incredibly
hard to chew. The smell and taste of yeast are palpable and
it leaves a gassy residue in the mouth. It goes well with beer,
but only because it dehydrates you so much as to make beer a
necessity. Water isn't possible. It softens the bread too quickly,
or at least that's the justification the Czechs give. That's
convenient.

As for horseradish, well, that was a surprise. While we eat
it as a sauce, they shred and put it in ramekins, but the taste is
just as strong, maybe more so. Nostrils flare from the heat, and
it should probably be eaten even more sparingly than the British
equivalent. That would be wise.

I ate my first lunch with a beer. The waitress was surly, the
waiter I paid at the end friendly. After nearly overpaying him, he
saw that I wasn't from round here and showed me the coin I'd
given him.

—Remember, this is fifty, he said, before holding up
another one.

—This is twenty.

That was kind.

I walked to the Metro, bought a ticket, stamped it, and made my way to Muzeum, a station just two stops away. There, I planned to walk around Wenceslas Square, a plan that didn't quite go to plan. Why? Well, for starters, it wasn't – and isn't – a square. It's a rectangle, a long, shitty rectangle. It starts up by the National Museum and glides down towards Old Town like an alpine slope. In between there are countless shops and restaurants aimed at tourists, serving familiar foodstuffs and brands like Nike and Adidas and Dior. That's people for you.

As I said earlier, this is where the Czechs decided it was time for the Russians to leave after outstaying their non-existent welcome.

Today, the square is where any event of note is commemorated, including the revolution. Today, most of the buildings in that square are owned by wealthy Russian businessmen. You can decide if that's ha-ha or just ain't-that-funny funny. The National Museum is a beautiful, ornately decorated building with a green roof. It was surrounded by scaffolding the entire time I lived in the city. It sits beside the National Museum, where the taxi driver pointed out the pretty girl with the red hair. That's apropos of nothing.

When I said the National Museum was beautiful, that wasn't quite accurate. The museum is split between a few buildings, and opposite the main one is the other National Museum, an extremely ugly, communist-era structure built with no regard for aesthetics. They'll probably tear it down one day, and try and forget what once was. That's a shame. The Wenceslas Monument is at the top of the square, opposite the museum, with a three-lane motorway in between. Parallel to that motorway is another, and the two lead out of the city in opposite directions. That's commerce, or weekend plans, depending on whether it's Monday to Thursday or if it's Friday. One road goes to Liberec, the other to south Bohemia.

That's where the word 'bohemian' comes from.

When I lived in Prague, I'd often wake on Saturday mornings without plans, except maybe to get some writing done. I would get up, and make coffee in a small Moka pot. After my first year in the country, I moved into a flat with two strangers, one of whom owned but rarely used the Moka pot. It was small, just big enough for a cup and a half of coffee. That was inefficient. I always drank two cups of coffee in the morning, but not three.

Three was excessive.

After drinking my coffee and writing a little at home, I usually went to Kaaba, a café, not the place in Mecca. It was my favourite place, and was just a three-minute walk from my flat. I'd get breakfast, usually the farmer's breakfast, which now strikes me as odd, given that it was rather bread heavy, with a rectangular slice of rye that wasn't dissimilar to Wenceslas Square, and a small piece of French baguette that wouldn't have known France if France hit it in the face with a horse's dick. I think it was the croissant that pulled me in each time. That's pastries for you.

Anyway, I would write in Kaaba for a while – I'd been working on a novel for some time – but of course I'd then get restless, or run out of ideas, or I'd have my third or fourth coffee before ten and not know what to buy next. I couldn't bring myself to sit in a café without a 'live' foodstuff or drink in front of me. It felt like I was taking up precious space. So I'd get up, pay and go, and that would leave me with a whole unplanned day to get through. At weekends there was too much time to fill. That was dangerous.

Still, I usually went home and watched TV, wrote more if writing was going well, or prepared Monday's classes. I'd have lunch, and count the hours down 'til around two-thirty before walking to a pub called The Lion to watch Spurs play at four. Sometimes when I walked through Wenceslas Square I'd see protests: for the president, against the president, for Palestine, for Israel, for Communism, against Communism. I even saw a protest about Assad once, though I can't remember if it was for or against. That's right, even Prague, with its near total white hegemony, was a melting pot of angers and cultures, gripes of every shape, size, colour and hue.

I saw it all. The scorching summers, the seemingly unending winters. The boredom and the joy. The ha-ha funny and the kind of funny that makes you shake your head. I saw it all.

But before all that, there was the hotel.

*

From the get-go, the staff at the hotel looked upon me with disdain, even though I largely kept myself to myself. I did ask to use the kitchen facilities, as the language school had promised I could. When I told the receptionist, she looked at me like I was crazy, reasonably so.

In the end they gave me access. It was in the basement, a cupboard-sized room with a small window that looked out onto the back of an Albert supermarket, where cashier ladies smoked cigarettes as quickly as they could because they were not – I later learned – allowed cigarette breaks. They weren't paid to be smoking, and in fact if they were idle at any moment it was believed they weren't worthy of being paid at all. That was insanity.

I could only use the kitchen after 07:30 in the evening but was rarely back from the language school before then. Using it before breakfast was out of the question. I had a fridge in my room, and took to eating ham and cheese on rolls made from the same sickly bread I described earlier. I got by. Ham and cheese can mask many of life's shortcomings, a cup of coffee and a Lucky Strike even more.

Yes, I was smoking again, just days after my arrival.

On my Wizz Air flight, I had promised myself I would quit forever. That was called going back on your best intentions, and I would become regularly acquainted with it over the years.

On the first day of our course I woke up early, ate a simple breakfast of bread rolls with ham and cheese, and had a cup of coffee. It was bad coffee, sachet Nescafé with peel-back pot milk, but it was coffee. I had my Lucky Strike after leaving the hotel. I would have preferred to have it with the coffee but didn't want to risk trouble with the hotel staff by smoking in my room, and so opted to take it as a digestif on route to the station.

Though the course didn't start 'til nine, I left the hotel at eight, even though the station was just two minutes away and the school two stops after that. I was nervous with both fear and excitement. I was going to start my new life now. Soon I would be a teacher, with regular free time for writing. I could turn my ideas for a novel into reality. But first, I'd be a teacher, with a normal job from nine to five – something that proved to be woefully naïve.

I wanted to be special in life, to be unique. But at the same time I wanted normality, to feel like everyone else. In that regard, teaching was ideal. But it kept me busy too.

On the first morning of my course, it was extremely hot, even at eight in the morning. I stood outside the hotel and lit my Lucky, knowing full well the heat was going to kill me that day. I was wearing a shirt, tight jeans and shoes.

It seemed smart to dress smart on day one, even though I'd met my new classmates the previous evening at an ad hoc get-together arranged by our tutor. My getup the previous night had been vastly different. I had dressed to impress: denim jacket, denim jeans, a white T-shirt and winklepicker shoes. Walking into the restaurant, I hoped to give off the cool swagger of a man that didn't give a fuck about anything, for the very reason that the polar opposite was true. I didn't just want to be cool, I wanted people to associate it with me in every sense. I'd been an agitated outsider my whole life; now I wanted to appear the captain of equanimity. That was bad, but I was worse.

Sadly, I overdid the denim. When I said I liked Bruce Springsteen during the meal – for reasons I'll never understand, I thought this would make me seem cool – a group of American girls started to laugh.

—That explains the Canadian tuxedo, said Charlene, the tallest, lithest, blondest and most outspoken of the three.

—What's a Canadian tuxedo?

She pointed to my legs and, from a distance, led her finger up to the nape of my neck.

—That's a Canadian tuxedo.

I looked myself up and down.

—Why Canada?

She shrugged.
	—It's Canada.

That's how Americans explained Canada. They laughed. They thought it was ha-ha funny. I guess it was. Not to me, though. I'd come with such determination to be cool and confident, everything I wasn't before, but quickly realised that in moving to Prague, I'd brought myself with me. That was a shock to the system.

*

Our course was the largest the school had ever had. There were sixteen of us: twelve Americans, a boy from Omagh, a girl from Northamptonshire and a Czech named David who'd recently returned after nearly a decade in the States. He was enthusiastic to the point of nausea and spoke at length about the many charity marathons he'd run to provide children in Africa with clean water. That was good of him.

There were those people, and then there was me, a man born in London, insistent that he was from Ireland, a country

I'd never lived in then, as I've not now. That must have been confusing for everyone.

On the first day of the course, we learned a little grammar before being taken on a tour of the city by one of our tutors, an American woman named Tessa. She gave us a rundown of Czech history, but I switched off sharpish when she referred to Charles the Fourth as 'a super awesome guy'. That didn't seem accurate, though perhaps she was right. Later that evening, the tutors took us all to dinner, where I had pork knuckle with more of that horseradish and a couple of Pilsner beers. That was nice. On the second day, we started teaching English. That was not.I'd anticipated having at least a week of settling in before being unleashed on Czech students, but I was wrong.

Before I knew it, I was planning lessons every evening. For the first time in my life, planning was the beginning, middle and end of my existence. I had to plan speaking and reading exercises, a listening activity, and of course some writing too, all in one class. I had to plan for the fact that Czechs could be taciturn, and, given that we were meant to stick to a strict ratio of eighty per cent student-to-teacher talking time, planning for this was difficult. Within my plans I had to have eight to ten words I wanted the students to remember, which required an Activation, a short summary which would make clear to my assessors that my students were fully on board with the plans.

Oh plans, they were going to be the death of me, now that they were tangible. It wasn't that I'd not had plans before, but they had been vague and illusory; plans to be rich, to be famous, to be understood, to be loved, to give up, to go on, to be here, to be there, to be elsewhere. Suddenly, plans were everything. That was stressful.

Each night, I studied the grammar we'd been told to remember and prepared my lessons, all the while trying to memorise the rigid lesson plan we'd been instructed to follow. I didn't use the kitchen as much as I'd planned. I'd no time. Instead, I ate slices of pizza from a nearby pizzeria at thirty crowns a pop, about a pound. They knew how to make pizza. So why in the name of God couldn't they make bread?

The Wi-Fi didn't work in my room, so in order to plan lessons or check the news to see what else I was wrong about or contact friends, I had to sit in the hotel lounge. Sometimes I took a break to see if anyone missed me, or how the riots were getting on, which, it transpired, was well.

Though I didn't like having to plan lessons outside my bedroom, it did allow me to smoke freely, flick, flick, flicking a

Zippo lighter a friend had given me just before I left. My plan to quit smoking had failed, but I hoped the lighter, which was gold-plated and bore a touching, highly personal inscription, would add an allure of mystery to me. It didn't. I'd undone all my good work with the double denim. That's fashion for you.

The weeks passed, the course progressed and the hotel staff continued to be unfriendly even though I rarely got in their way. There was a pretty, short, blonde woman on reception who I said hello to each morning. I was lucky to get a curt nod by way of reply, though I may have been overly sensitive to her unfriendliness because she was a pretty, short, blonde woman and I desperately wanted her to like me.

Worse than her was the guy in his mid-forties who sometimes manned the desk. A balding man with unkempt stubble, he would say hello if I said hello, with a sneering smile, as if he suspected I was up to something, which, sadly, I never was. One Saturday, I asked him for directions to a nearby shop. He shook his head, like I'd requested a knee trembler behind the bins, and pointed at an out-of-scale map. I couldn't wait to get out, and on with my plans.

The course came to an end after a month.

We had a big blowout to celebrate at the flat of one of our tutors. It got out of hand – someone fell through a glass table – and we moved or were moved onto a bar.

It was there that I started kissing a girl who I'd barely spoken to during the course.

It was left-field and surprised everyone, including the two of us. She was pretty, short and blonde, but also a staunch Republican, the American kind. I didn't let it get in the way. That was nature.

During the course, I'd had my eye on her taller, leggier, blonder, slightly less Republican friend. That was nature times four or maybe even five or six. That was Charlene, the one that introduced me to the concept of the Canadian tuxedo. I kissed the Republican girl in a club, then beside a tram stop, then several times on the way home, which turned out to be my hotel, where we were greeted by the male receptionist.

—I see you have a guest.

—Yes, I said.

I walked through the lobby nonchalantly, holding the girl's hand. That was a façade. The heat of his eyes were on me, and I didn't know what I'd do if he tried to stop us. That was *my* nature.

Nothing happened. We walked into the lift, kissed, then walked to my room. For the first time, I noticed just how large it was. Until now, I'd only had a TV, a Joseph O'Neill novel, and my half-unpacked suitcase for company. We slept together – me and the girl, not the suitcase – and in the morning, left together too. I needed to pack. I was moving to a flat with three boys from my course. Brad, Thomas and David (an American boy from Virginia, not the altruistic Czech). Living with Brad was an adventure. I'd never met a Brad before. That was nice.

The Republican girl smiled as we left the hotel, she to her apartment, me to the supermarket, where I would think of something to buy.

—See you later, she said.

I couldn't tell if she was happy or sad, if she was glad what'd happened had happened, or if she was now a well of regret, something I couldn't figure out in myself either. But I was done with the course, done with the hotel too. I went upstairs, packed my things, brought them down and went up to the desk. The male receptionist was there.

—Hello, he said.

—Hello.

I smiled. —I'd like to check out, please.

He looked at his screen.
—Room 120, yes?

—That is correct.

He typed something into his keyboard.

—Thank you for your stay. That's everything.

—Have a lovely day, I said, and walked towards the station to meet my friends for lunch.

*

Sleeping with the Republican girl had never been in my plans, and I knew a few things as soon as it happened. Firstly, Charlene would never go for me now. Not that she would have before, but I was young and delusional and selfish and yet more delusional still with that in mind.

I also knew I'd opened a can of worms, of feelings and thoughts, hopes and wants on the part of the Republican girl, myself too.

I knew it would complicate matters and feelings might get hurt. All of that came true. I don't regret any of it, though. Feelings got hurt, but they got felt too. That's something.

I don't plan to talk about her much more and never really intended to in the first place, it just happened.

It's not that it's uninteresting or irrelevant or that she's long since married and made a life for herself. It's simply a story for another day or year. Which leads me back to the views.

Why? Well, it was in looking out on the city that I had time to ruminate on it all, think about the life I'd led and the things that happened. And when I think of Riegrovy Sady, where I spent so much time looking, it's happiness, and it's sadness too. That bit to the left of where the sunbathers bathe, with the views of Petřín and the hills and the opera and red-tiled roofs, it's all wrapped up in that view, my three and bit years in Prague which were then called my life.

To be honest, yes, Letná does have the best views of the city. The panoramic is more vast, the number of iconic buildings on display greater. But a view's as subjective as anything else. Riegrovy Sady won't mean a thing to you. You probably can't even pronounce it right. That's okay, there's nothing wrong with that. It's such an English thing to laugh at the way people pronounce words or names. It gives them comfort, helps them make sense of a world they half covered, never conquered and completely lost. It's funny (ha-ha and otherwise).

When you think about it, even Matthew, Mark, Luke and John would confuse someone somewhere. Italians don't use 'k'. Try telling a Czech John is said with a hard 'j'. And Matthew? Don't even bother. Outside our tiny little island, our staunchest, safest names don't mean shit, and yet the English still like to think things that aren't English are silly. That's the price of history. It's also a digression on my part. I will endeavour to avoid them as I go on. But, well, I'm not much good with plans, as you can see.

*

Riegrovy Sady is a park. In that park I kissed four women, at different times, obviously. I am not a four-mouthed monster.

That much is true.

I kissed three on New Year's Eve, one in autumn and the other I kissed New Year's Eve and then New Year's Day too.

That was a plan, an ad hoc, on-the-hoof plan that happened when we woke up together and decided it'd be nice to go back to the park with its fresh snow in the fresh January air. She was my girlfriend by this point and her name was Jana, still is.

Me and Jana. We made a whole host of plans and did a whole lot of kissing too. We kissed all over the place: mountains, castles, restaurants, even the pub I'd had my first ever kiss in, we kissed there once. That was ha-ha funny, but of course I never told her about it.

Jana was working in Kaaba when I met her. I didn't say much about Kaaba, did I? That was rude of me. And stupid, as I have to go back and do it now. But stick with me. I promise to try and be less of a backtracker from here on in. Notice the use of the word 'try'. That's a get-out clause.

Kaaba had '70s décor and lots of antique furniture, with stainless steel coffee machines, cake displays and tables. I'd been going there a long time before Jana ever pitched up, maybe a year. I went most Saturdays to write my book, as I said. I went every Thursday for my Czech lesson, talking to my teacher for an hour with the sound of coffee machines and children and sometimes a barking dog in the background. It was a terrible environment to learn an almost unlearnable language, but it was Kaaba. I liked being there. I also went most weeknights to drink solid, good beer, alone, or with Brad, who came along regularly. We would talk about philosophy. Well, he'd talk; I'd throw in the odd opinion here and there. He spoke about the one per cent, a term that was doing the rounds at the time. We would talk about women, a topic of conversation that was and remains popular among men.

When Brad wasn't around – unlike me he could translate talking about women into talking to and then dating them – I would sit alone reading. I read a lot of Norman Mailer, lots of Sir Arthur Conan Doyle too, and Tolstoy. That's a mélange. I think. I thought ceviche was a vegetable 'til two months back.

Me and Jana didn't get together right away. I was too craven to ask her out. In the end a waiter gave me her number, saying she'd left it for me.

That was a lie.

She was pissed at him, but happy too, and then her and me became *we* and *us* not long after. I loved Kaaba after that, thought it was just about the best place in the world; beer, a girlfriend, Mailer, it'd given me everything.

The thing is, with everything that happened later, with it all having gone to shit, I still think it's the best place in the world. That's good, and gives me hope, but it might be a little foolish also. Who knows?

We had our first date in a pub about a mile away. She wore pink trousers and was a little shy. I wore denim jeans and was a lot shy. She told me about her hometown in the country.
It sounded idyllic.
Our second date was in a place called Big Lebowski. It was a tiny bar, really tiny, with a ladder between the upstairs and downstairs. You paid what you wanted for beer because they didn't have a license, they could only 'give' it away. That was great. Big Lebowski got shut down after locals complained about the noise. That was tragic.
Our third date was in December. Jana wore a red jumper that may or may not have had something to do with her excitement for the coming Christmas. It was cold. It was also a Friday, and that helped me out.

—Would you like to come upstairs, she said, unlike the previous week, when she said thank you, that was a nice evening.

I said yes. That's the beauty of Fridays.

We got to know each other. I became relaxed around her and she didn't go away. I acted like myself, a fool. She didn't mind that, liked it even.
I stopped worrying about Canadian tuxedos and notions of being cool, and while I still wrote in cafés, it wasn't important to me if anyone took any notice. I acted the fool, making impressions of monkeys because they made her laugh.
Soon I became known as Opičko.
That's Czech for monkey.
I put socks on my ears and pretended to be a Cocker Spaniel and she found that funny too. I'd never planned on making someone laugh so much, and that, that was sublime. She had a good sense of humour. Sometimes she didn't get the things I said and that made her laugh; sometimes she got exactly what I meant and that made her laugh too. Sometimes she just didn't get it and I thought that was language barrier, but no, that was just me.

When Jana laughed, she laughed kind of like a kid, with
an infectious giggle. But sometimes she laughed hearty, for
minutes on end, at things I'd done or said. That was the greatest
thing ever.

We fell in love in winter and it felt like summer. We went to
restaurants and we went to bars and we even went dancing.
That had never been a plan of mine. We went to the farmers'
market in Jiřího z Poděbrad –a square, like Wenceslas, but more
accurately named, with a large church and green spaces.

It has a children's playground with swings and
roundabouts. The children's playground has pictures telling
people what they can and can't do inside, pictures which include
a gun (with a cross running through it), a dog taking a shit (with
a cross running through it) and a needle (with a cross running
through it).

The sign doesn't say which kind of drugs are banned, but
if you ever need to shoot insulin, make sure your dog's taking a
shit at the same time. That's the lesser of two evils.

Us expats called the square JZP, and in my three-plus
years in Prague, I spent a lot of time there as a single man and
a not-so-single man, watching football, drinking beer, walking
through farmers' markets, that kind of thing.

That was humdrum a lot, but lovely sometimes too. That
was Jiřího z Podebrad.

I told her once in a wine bar that I was going to get help
and everything was going to be okay. That was a lie, but in my
defence, I didn't know it at the time.

*

I recently met a man who'd never been to Prague. He said
when he thought of it, he imagined cafés with writers working
out their frustrations and thoughts over cigarettes and wine or
coffee. I didn't want to disabuse him of this notion, and didn't
need to. That's nice.

Prague was exactly that. Of course, it wasn't all like that.
There were the high street stores and places like Mr Tesco's and
McDonald's and H&M, which I've gone over and won't again.
But put simply, it wasn't all writing by candle in cafés with pen
and paper or laptops, and glasses of red wine in hand.

It was getting up at 5:45 to go to industrial estates on the
edge of the city, to teach an engineer idioms that went in one
ear and out the other with the sound of circular saws whirring in
the background. It was cold, dreary weekends watching football

in dark pubs, because as much as you wanted to be a writer
you also wanted to unwind after a long week. It was language
schools thanking you for all your hard work, saying you were
one of the best teachers they had, only to cut your wage at the
yearly review.

It was bitterness. It was trying to communicate with
staff in state offices. It was frustration and disappointment. It
was students who said they didn't want to learn grammar and
complained that there wasn't enough grammar three months
later. It was hope and love. It was winter and summer, cold and
heat. It was all that, but it was also the writers in their cafés.

That's true.

And it was Kaaba, where I wrote, where I felt alone a lot, where
I found love. I wrote, I read Mailer and better male writers too.
That's misleading. They weren't better writers, God no. They
were just better males.

Kaaba was writing and reading and drinking alone, but
it was also where I met Jana, too dumb to notice her at first,
too pig-ignorant and stupid and self-loathing to take note. Still,
don't ever plan to fall in love at first sight. That's hocus pocus.

It was a grey spring day. The café was busy, and Jana was on a
trial shift with another girl who caught my eye, a brunette with
a slender jaw, acute eyes, and thin hair that went down past her
shoulders. I was smoking outside with Brad. Kaaba was both
smoking and non-smoking. Non-smoking in the day, smoking at
night after nine when there were no kids around. That was logical.

The girl shook my hand, then Brad's, the chronology of
which I thought telling.

—Do you come here a lot?

—Yes, most days, I said, waiting a moment, hoping Brad
would add that I went there to write.

I was a serious writer, she needed to know that. I planned
on becoming world famous. That was idyllic, and foolish and
important. She stubbed her cigarette out on a bin beside her feet.

—Well, I better get back to my
shift, she said. —Hopefully I will see you both soon.

That was that.

*

After that was that, I got to know Jana. She was short, blonde and pretty.

She had a friendly smile. She seemed shy, but quick behind the bar and was chatty with colleagues if less so with the likes of me. I started to notice her more often, but it wasn't until later, when I got to know her name, that I really paid attention. And then she was all I could think about day and night. Two syllables and a soft 'J'. It would never happen in England. That's the glory of travel.

Sometimes I think about what life would have been like if I'd never gone to Kaaba, or planned on going out with Jana when I started going there even more than before, solely in the hope of asking her out even though I never did 'til someone forced her number on me.

Maybe I'd have left Prague earlier. Probably. I never planned on teaching for three and a half years and certainly did a year longer than I should have. Perhaps I'd have met someone else in another café if I'd only gone to Kaaba less.

There's no answer to that.

I wonder if it would have been better had I drunk and written elsewhere, but I know the answer to that.

It hurt and it ended in betrayal and anguish and confusion, and in the months leading up to when I finally did ask her out, a lot of money was spent on coffees I didn't really want with all the stomach troubles such amounts inevitably entailed. I would do it all again. That was love.

*

I never planned to stay in Prague and once I had Jana never planned to leave, quite the opposite. I planned to find a way we could live together, forever. I knew full well I'd regret leaving, but sometimes you have to plan to do something you know you'll regret.

I never planned to be so happy, and never planned to be so sad. I never planned to lose to the gods of circumstance, but hey-ho, there you go. That's life.

I was never much good at making plans, but at least now, with the air slightly clearer, I can say with confidence I did everything possible to tend it and let it thrive, to keep it too, even if it did all fall apart.

But first, Prague. Before I hash and rehash all that several times over again, Prague was tramps on trams in winter and people avoiding them like they were the plague. It was students bemoaning gypsies and English liberals bemoaning students their prejudices hewn over generations. It was tired eyes not ready for English in the morning or too tired from a day's work in the evening. It was frustration and culture clash. It was beer. It was a language I couldn't get my head round no matter how much I tried and, most definitely, planned to. It was sunny days in parks and beer gardens.

It was music with Brad; Hiss Golden Messenger mostly. It was nightclubs on boats or bars by the river. It was Lucky Strikes and Camel.

It was Nouzov, Jana's village about an hour away, a village that calmed then uncalmed me, and I don't know why except maybe I couldn't do it forever, much as I planned to.

It was Raymond Carver. It was chronic masturbation. It was bottles of red wine alone and, at sweeter times, in company. It was dumplings. It was dreary clouds and scorching night skies. It was thunderstorms. It was pink and blue and yellow and green, but very rarely red. That was the buildings. It was both ha-ha funny and isn't-that-strange funny and 'that's funny' the way you might say when you think what the hell happened, what in the name of God has or did happen or happened.

I'm not going to talk about Prague too much now, that's a story for another day, though I'm sure you've lost some faith in me. That's the value of empty promises. You may have planned to nestle in for a story about Prague but it should be quite clear now that plans are only for the making.

Anyway, just in case it hasn't been made crystal clear, Prague moves, but it stays, it stays with a man.

THE MOUNTAINS

In September we went to the mountains. It was autumn, 2014.
Back then I'd no idea I would be living in England again within
three months. That was good. I was still naïve enough to think I
would come up with a plan to make everything work out. That
was the best that could be hoped for.

We were on our way to the Konopište Mountains in the
north, Jana driving while I ate Haribo sweets, occasionally
handing her one or two on demand, the love hearts for effect,
the fried eggs for taste, the key rings for lack of an alternative.
We hadn't gone on holiday all summer, except for a brief trip
to Berlin to see the Arctic Monkeys, and I felt guilty. It was
my fault. That was bad planning on my part, laziness too, and
reluctance. If I had a free moment, I didn't do as promised
(holiday research), I worked on my book, the same one I'd been
working on since moving to Prague.

I'd finished it the previous year, sent it off in haste and
received several rejections. That was par for the course for
anyone who could write except Norman Mailer, who had nailed
it first time. He was also a man at twenty-three because they sent
him to war. That was just rewards. That was also how they saw
manhood back then. In reality, it's kind of how we see it now.
That's a shame.

Me and Jana had been together nearly a year. Life was better,
not so lonely or fraught with anxiety, or characterised by self-
love (physical) and self-hate (emotional), red wine in the week
and beer at weekends.

She was everything, and yet I still wanted to write, which
scared me, because I believed I wrote out of unhappiness. I
should have been able to give up writing, now that I was happy.
I was wrong, it was necessary to me. That I couldn't understand.
Writing was everything. And then there was Jana and she
became everything. Now I had two everythings. Naturally,
that was a problem. Jana wanted to be in the mountains, so we
went to the mountains. She loved the Nature, as she – and most
Czechs – called it. We had rented a room in a resort town named
Pec pod Sněžkou. That was a mouthful.

She'd been there before. I was excited for the trip. It
would be good to get out of the city. It would give me time to
work on my book, which I was close to finishing for the second
time. I just wanted to send it off now, even if no one picked
it up. I'd reread every sentence a million times over, put two
years of my life into it. I wanted it gone. Having cut it from the
original 641 pages down to 300, I'd altered the tone of voice and

added more swearing in the naïve belief that the book needed it. It was about a confused young man. Confused young men swore a lot. That made sense.

The agencies didn't get back to me. That was a lesson. Writing in desperation never worked. Things didn't go to plan with the book, which was inevitable. Important even. I didn't write because I was unhappy but because it was the only way I could speak my mind, the page the only place I could voice the things that scared me about myself. The drinking. The loneliness. The chronic masturbation. In digital ink it was all fine, good, gravy and hashtag fabulous.

I felt voiceless (I was white, middle-class and male). I felt misunderstood (I was white, middle-class and male). I felt maladjusted (the aforementioned). I was lost, that was all. But at the end of it, I still needed to write, just as crickets have to flutter their wings and ringers have to ring.

I was okay with being alone when writing. And then I was unalone. And unalone, a man starts making plans. That's dangerous. A good idea too.

Now, unalone, I still wanted to be published, but the plans were different. It wasn't about voicing the unvoiced. It was bigger. It was me and Jana. It was finding a way to earn money for the long term, earning enough to get by for the two of us. That was my plan, ha-ha, funny or otherwise, you decide.

My plan – sure, it was threadbare, but I needed something – was to get published, then get a job at Charles University, teaching English maybe, or creative writing. That'd do me just fine. Yes, it was strange that I planned to be a writer in order to stop being a teacher, just so maybe to become a different kind of teacher. That was topsy-turvy, but dammit, I was desperate.

Life was good with Jana. It was a man's life. I couldn't just walk around in my happy and sometimes unhappy little fug teaching, writing, writing, teaching, getting drunk, regretting it, writing, teaching, and occasionally going to the gym. I had to find a way to make our life viable. Because life was good. And because life was good, it required a plan. And here's why.

I could handle Czech breakfast.

*

That's right, I could handle Czech breakfast, even though it broke the routine of my weekends immeasurably and even though it featured Czech bread, or a form thereof.

For two years I'd followed more or less the same routine. Go home on Friday night, drink a bottle of wine or have a

couple of beers in Kaaba, get up in the morning, make two
Moka pot cups of coffee (occasionally three, despite what I
said) and write. That was ill-advised. By the time I got down
to writing I'd often be so restless that sitting still was barely
possible. I usually managed an hour or so before going to
Kaaba, which presented a problem, as it was either more coffee,
or buy a beer. Even I was loath to drink beer before the sun had
crossed the yardarm (noon).

My breakfasts generally consisted of peanut butter on
bread – yes, awful, raw, Czech bread – or maybe some cereal.
After that I could get on with writing or planning lessons. I
sometimes started Saturday mornings this way to reduce stress
later in the week, though I never, in three years, found myself
free of stress. That was life, or me, or both. I don't know.

When I moved in with Jana in May 2014, I had to adapt
to Czech breakfast, which proved surprisingly easy, including
the bread. Thankfully, it was sliced bread from the potraviny.
That could be compensated with ham, cheese and lots of coffee.
Potravinys were a kind of corner shop that sold everything from
fruit and veg and terrible Czech bread to cigarettes and booze
and kids' toys. They were almost invariably run by Vietnamese
immigrants, most of whom had moved to Czechoslovakia during
the communist regime to study.

Jana's approach to breakfast was at a polar opposite to my
own. Where she favoured nutrition and taste, I was all about the
means and the end, getting it out of the way so I could do my
writing. It usually went like this: bananas and apples cut into pieces
and mixed with yoghurt, several slices of that bread (toasted,
thankfully) with ham and cheese, tea for her and coffee for me.

Jana would make or have me make a pot of green tea,
and then leave her cup the whole day before drinking it. That
perplexed me. My triple-cup morning coffees perplexed her,
which leads me to believe that the differences between people
are often best illustrated via the bottom of a glass or cup.

And that was breakfast.

There was also lunch and there was also dinner, but it's
breakfast I remember best, most probably because it almost
always took place in the safe confines of our bedroom, that
haven in a heartless world, where until the very last weeks we
were happy, or at least the semblance of it.

But there was more to Jana and me than breakfast. She
was good with her hands. Ha-ha. I mean she was talented. She
made furniture, though sadly not for a living. That was a waste
of talent. I often bought her flowers, tulips, her favourite. That

was good, because tulips were cheap and easy to come by. We doted on each other. I said I loved her early on. She couldn't return the compliment for fear of what the future held and then she did it about two weeks later. That was sublime.

She was doting, she was jealous, she was talented, she was insecure. She was Jana. I was drunk and loving and funny and anxious and talented and insecure. We were us.

In September we went to the mountains.

*

The mountains snaked into view.

We'd been driving for around an hour. The Czech countryside, usually so flat, suddenly came to life; the houses, which were dotted on the hillsides, might not have been pretty close up but were pretty from a distance, nestled as they were in clusters between vast swathes of forest either side; the snow-capped mountaintops picture-perfect as snow-capped mountains invariably are; the sun hanging pendulously low and shining such a dull, yellowy-orange that you could almost stare into it, maybe even would if you were stupid enough, or simply hypnotised by its beauty.

It was true, the Czech Republic wasn't short on mountains and scenery, but as I didn't own a car, I'd only ever seen the flatlands, which seemed to control the middle of the country and any place within sight of a train track. That was irritating, because it really was a beautiful place. I could tell that just from the photos, and from what my students told me too, which was biased, yes, because they were Czech, but also no, because Czechs rarely had anything good to say about anything Czech, unless it was the mountains, of course.

That's the topsy-turvy world of the Czech Republic.

As we approached the mountains, I saw a number of desolate high rises which looked barely populated, a far cry from the alpine, Aryan/Kinder Egg vibe I'd expected.

Row upon row of communist-era buildings stood before us, each more alike than the last. Some apartments had balconies, others not. That must have grated for the have-nots. The blocks were largely grey with small panels of red and yellow and blue, which only served to make the scene all the more drab. Jana must have seen where my eyes were looking and sensed what I was wondering.

—This area is very poor.

—Why? I asked. —Doesn't tourism bring in a lot of money?

—Not here. There was a big paper factory, but it is shut now. These people aren't so educated. They can't do some other job.

—What happened to the paper factory?

—It moved to China.

That was a pity.
It was more than a pity, but whereas some things could be called funny funny or ha-ha funny, some things could only be described as a pity, because there weren't answers to such things, even though many were often given, both back and forth, forth and back. That was the way people ticked.She flicked her indicator. We turned into a new road for the first time in a long time.

—Some people moved up into Pec pod Sněžkou, the town *where are we going.*

I smiled. Where are we going. I could never bring myself to correct her. Right or wrong, I loved the way the words sounded from her mouth.

—But lots of these people worked in factories their whole life, she said. —They don't have the–

She tapped her forehead, looking for the right word.

—The mindset, I said.

—Yes. They don't know how to do anything else. When the factories closed, the only jobs they could get were really shitty, for worse money than in the factory. Or they couldn't find any work. The factory gave lots of people jobs. They were poor, but they had money for their families. There's nothing here now.
And for them, that was that.

*

Pec pod Sněžkou couldn't have differed more from the towns around it. It was sleepy, but there was life, a quiet hum of

29

activity, pockets of tourists in winter sports gear, bright pinks and oranges and blues, couples with dogs, older people with walking sticks, the sort designed for activity over balance.

We got stuck in a small stream of traffic snaking up the hill as we entered the town, giving me time to look inside a large hotel. The décor was European, with mirrored walls behind the bar, the spirits ordered in more or less the same way as any other hotel, the espresso machine huge, commercial and made of stainless steel. It was like something out of a movie from the '70s or, you might say, like something out of the '70s themselves, though there was a slight glitzy filmic kitsch to it that I could not quite put my finger on.

We moved up the hill. There were cottages, but also a few shops and restaurants, and one large building which looked like some sort of holiday community centre, a place where people who have never met before assemble to recreate the society they avoided in day-to-day life, where they force their children to mingle with other children they've never met, because making friends was important, even though they shunned their neighbours every day. That was ha-ha holiday time.

Past the community centre was a communist-era high rise. Unlike the apartment blocks, it appeared well looked after, save for the windows, which had a tawny sheen. While they were clearly cleaned often, they were well weathered too.

—That is the original hotel that was built, said Jana, pointing to the high rise, which stood above the town and all the quaint little cottages.

I pictured it as the kind of place where the moneyed few once went for vodka, slivovice and bad dinner, worth it only because it cost more than others could afford. That hotel held a strange kind of appeal to me.

We turned left and drove up another road. Jana stopped suddenly.

—Oh, shit of elephant, said Jana.

I loved this phrase of hers, an attempted translation of a common Czech expression.

It made no sense. It made every sense. And it was about elephants, and I liked that too, naturally.

—What?

—I went the wrong way.

—Hovno slona!

—Yes, exactly.

—Hovno slona!

—Yes, Opičko.

—Huuuuuuu!

She chuckled.— Opičko moje.

—Hu?

—Jo.

I nodded.

—Hu hu.

I put my arm and hand in front of my nose, imitating an elephant. She chuckled once more before concentrating on the narrow road ahead. That was called defusing the situation of the milk that had been spilled.

She turned the car back on itself, drove slightly further up the hill and turned left again to the cottage, which was roughly parallel to where we'd been moments earlier, the place of elephants and monkeys.

The cottage wasn't what I'd expected. For one, it was a house. I didn't care, though. The elderly couple who owned it greeted us, showed us our room on the top floor, said a few words to Jana in Czech and scuttled off. It was cosy. I was happy enough. I was on holiday with Jana, relaxing for a change, much happier than I'd been a few months back, when for the first time in what was then almost three years of living in Prague, I began to feel homesick.

Perhaps it was because life was more serious now that I wasn't simply writing and living alone. The pressure of the word 'future' began, for the first time, to build. I was happy, though, in the cottage, in the country. I'd successfully suppressed my homesickness. That was a recipe for disaster.

The previous evening we'd stayed at Jana's parents'
house, in Nouzov, the tiny village where she had spent her
childhood. It had only three or four houses and miles of wide-
open poppy fields which drew the odd bored local teenager here
and there into opiate addiction.

That's the illusion of the countryside idyll, but it was also
somewhere I flirted with living in for the rest of my life, despite
being utterly unsuited to the country.

That was called love.

I thought I could do it. I'd visited England in August
to see friends and come back thinking I could live in Prague
forever. I started to enjoy life again; changed my working
pattern, dropped classes at my language school and picked up
better paid private classes, which freed me up to write.

I could do it. I enjoyed the Saturday markets in the square
at JZP. I felt relaxed in my life. But after loving its smallness
for so long, Prague had started to seem very small. That was
predictable. For whatever reason, the relative ease of getting
around the city, the proximity to friends and pubs and the offices
where I worked, suddenly tugged at me. I felt caged, but tried
not to think about it. I still loved the city, and I loved her beyond
measure. But something was drawing me back to London.

Living there wasn't important, I told myself. Occasional
visits home would do me fine. Sure, I missed the pubs and even
the crowds sometimes, but I would be okay. Having Jana was all
that mattered. If it meant summers hiking in the mountains, so
be it. If it meant not understanding what my parents-in-law (or
anyone) said most of the time, then fine. I could understand her,
I'd get used to it, get used to country life too, perhaps, though I
was adamant I wouldn't live there.

I could visit often, however, because her parents were
kind, and even if the remoteness got to me, there was good beer.
Maybe I would take up skiing in the winters. That might be a
stretch too far. At the very least, I could decamp to the bar or ski
lodge while Jana (and maybe the kids) hit the slopes. Maybe.

—I love you, Opičko, she said, as we pulled into the small
apartment.

—I love you more.

She shook her head.

—Impossible.

—Hu!

We went inside the cottage.

*

The room was small. There were two beds, which was useful, as the cupboard wasn't big enough for all our things. I had as much stuff as Jana. I always over-packed for trips. I had two books because I might finish or not feel like reading the other, my laptop, a folder full of notes for my book, the first one hundred pages of that book printed and ready for editing, two sets of jeans, six pairs of socks, seven underpants, six T-shirts, and chargers for my phone and laptop.

I can't remember if I was seeing either of Messrs Fluoxetine or Citalopram at this point, but I believe it's likely I wasn't. Jana didn't like my happy pills. That was understandable. I didn't like the idea of being on them forever. That was understandable too. Within a couple of months, though, I wouldn't be able to live without the aid of a 20mg green and yellow pill. That was not.

Green's my favourite colour, to yellow I'm indifferent. That's just a thing.

Knowing I would overpack and badly pack, Jana had offered to help me. I had refused.

And as a result, I had forgotten my toothbrush. In the cupboard were three plates, a couple of mugs and a bowl which I realised we would have to share, including the spoon. I hated the thought of that, which was odd, given that we shared body parts and the like with healthy regularity.

Everything was fine with our small weekend cottage, except for the bathroom, or more accurately, the 'door'. The bathroom itself had a decent shower and a working toilet, but there was only a curtain hung over the entryway for the sake of privacy. Horror swept across my face.

—Oh no oh no oh no oh no, I said.

I couldn't stomach the thought of Jana being able to hear me going to the toilet, or vice versa. I didn't care how natural it was. I'd always been this way.

My childhood bedroom, or at least the one I spent most of my childhood in (we were nomadic in my house) was next to the bathroom, and whenever I heard my sister or mother going to the toilet before bed, I would bury my head in the pillow, hoping

33

not to hear. I did the same thing with my brother, but without
the same urgency. There was something about hearing women
answer the call of nature that created a sense of revulsion in me,
a prickish, childish revulsion I couldn't help. Thankfully, Jana
shared my worry.

   —Honey, I'll put my hands over my ears, I said, holding
them in position.

She smiled, with a look of relief, and hugged me, as if glad that I
held the same strange, antiquated position as she did.

   —Thank you, Opičko, she said. —I don't want you to
hear me.

I smiled too, kissed her, then helped unpack our things:
tomorrow's lunch and breakfast, our clothes, and my laptop
and cables, which I doubted were under any threat from being
stolen, here in the mountains. It was drizzly out, but Jana still
wanted to go for a walk.
   We put on our hiking gear. Her father had lent me an old
red fleece, as I didn't have outdoor wear of my own, and Jana
had bought me some hiking boots especially for the trip. I put
them on.

   —Honey, I said, tying up the laces. —I look like a tradiční
Czech man. All I need now is sandals and socks to go with them
and I'll be really authentic.
   Inexplicably, Czech men wore – and wear – socks with
sandals. That's a thing they do.
   She shook her head, and smiled.
   —Crazy Opička.

Satisfied at making her laugh, I giggled, then chased her around
the room (which required several laps, given the dimensions) for
about thirty seconds. She played along, and then we left for our
walk.
   On the way down, Jana poked her head through the old
couple's door, told them we were going, and said goodbye, as
did I. It was foggy and still drizzly. Small clouds were perched
on the mountainside, nestled between trees and atop rocks,
watching the valley below.
   The old hotel towered above the town. In its formulaic
style, it reminded me of the radio building in the centre of
Prague, and despite its ugliness I liked it, for reasons I couldn't

understand. The rain pattered against my cheeks, but I didn't
mind. I was happy, and besides, I was more than used to rain.
I came from the Island, after all. Jana hated rain. That was
problematic. I could tell she was happy to be here, in the
mountains, but disappointed by the muggy, miserable weather,
which at this time I believed didn't have any effect on me.

—It's lovely here, darling, I said.

That was true. She didn't believe me, of course. I looked around
again. It was very grey and drizzly, and there was something
about drizzle that was always more depressing than rain, like an
old person falling over in slow motion. I laughed.

—You wouldn't last five minutes at
Glastonbury, sweetie, I said, after she complained about the rain.

She flicked her head towards me without meeting my eye,
then back at the horizon, and scowled.—I wouldn't want to go
to Glastonbury. Too much people.

I smiled.
—True.

—And you have never been to Glastonbury, Opička. You
talk about it all the time.

I had said something I shouldn't have. I often talked of
my desire to go to Glastonbury. To my mind it was just a truth,
but Jana connected it to the things I'd said in recent months,
of feeling homesick, of wanting to return to England more
often. Even though I'd convinced myself I only needed to visit
from time to time, every mention of my country gave her an
underlying sense that there was a permanent longing. That was
true, but only she knew that at the time.

—Yes, I said. —I know.

I looked over towards the information centre. Our cottage
was at the end of a road, but it was possible to get to the centre
by walking down a steep stone slab path that had been laid out
on the grass.

—Come on, I said. —Let's go get the maps.

Jana wanted maps for the walks that we were going to be doing. That seemed like a good idea, and as the information centre was in the middle of town, it gave me an opportunity to stake out the pubs we'd be visiting, hopefully on a regular occurrence. That was serendipitous.

The information centre was an old, grand brick building with a wooden roof, or it was a wooden building with a brick roof, or it was neither of those things. I have an image of it, though, which won't shift. For all I know, it was grey and monolithic, though I'm fairly certain it bore some of the characteristics of what might be described as picture-postcard-perfect. We walked inside.

Jana went up to the information desk while I walked around peering at tat on racks and shelves. There were key rings and pencils and notepads and lots of tea towels with pictures of Snezka on it. Snezka was the biggest mountain in the country, and we were going to climb it in the morning.

There were also beer steins and nice mugs, but one of my favourite things was a huge candle of Konopište, the mythical, Santa-like figure the mountains were named after. My favourite thing of all, however, was a row of Konopište chocolate bars moulded into a vague simulacrum of him. They looked tasty.

After a few minutes, I noticed Jana walking back my way. I picked up one of the large candles of Konopište and held it to my face. That was my cue.

—Give me beer or I will destroy the mountain, I said. —Muuuuu!

She grabbed the candle from me, trying not to tear off his hosepipe in the process.

—Opička! You will upset them.

—Who is this Opička? I said. —I am Konopište, the mountain. Giver of life. Destroyer of men. Drinker of beer. Feed me.

I could tell that the women behind the desk were watching now, bemused yet smiling.

They were in their sixties, and while they must have been tempted to tell me off, I think they were amused, perhaps even impressed by the timbre of my impression. That was fun.

—We will get a beer soon, said Jana. —Please, Ronan, put

it down.

       That was foreboding, for she never called me Ronan. It was always Opičko or Opička (the Czech language did awful things to word-endings in a way I never understood) or Hontag. That was an approximation of the German word 'montag' and the English word 'honey' and was something that I had called her first.

       That was meaningless but it meant and means a great deal to me. Eventually, I put the candle down.

       —Blazen, said Jana, smiling through her ruddy, embarrassed cheeks.

       Crazy.
That was sublime.

I was weird. I knew that. It was okay, I knew that too, now. I'd always felt insignificant, incomplete and anxious, like I didn't quite fit in with friends who had normal jobs, or friends who had unusual jobs: the people in London who worked in construction or finance, or the teachers in Prague who had floated to the continent from North Carolina and Missouri and Ohio and Bristol and Leicester and elsewhere. I'd at times felt good around both kinds of groups, but never fully at ease.

       I felt that now. And that was good.

       —Look what I have, said Jana, holding up the largest key I'd ever seen, about a foot in length and several inches in girth, like a giant's hosepipe.

       —What the fuck is this, Janko? I said, gleefully, and loud.

       She enjoyed it when I was openly vulgar. It was fun. We'd reached a point now, however, where she barely noticed it, only making comment if and when I swore near people she thought I shouldn't, like the elderly. That was odd in my book, as elderly Czechs were the least likely to understand. I could have called a man feeding the ducks sugar-tits or an elderly babička taking a stroll shit-for-brains and they'd have been none the wiser. That was tempting for fun's sake, but I never did it. The shame I would feel was innate.

       —It is a key for the place where do we go tomorrow, she said.

—Are we going to Erebor?, I asked, smiling inwardly again at her phrasing.

—What?

—Never mind. Where are we going?

—There is some building in the forest that we can get into with this.

—Some building? Fantastic. What kind of building?

—I can't remember how to say it in English.

—Righty-o, I said. I didn't know what to say after that, so did what I knew how to do best.

—Hu!

A couple turned to look at us, and the women behind the counter peered over again. That was Jana's cue to make me leave the shop, after which we took a short stroll before having dinner and a couple of beers in one of the restaurants. That night, we watched *Locke* with Tom Hardy (on screen), had sex (off screen), and slept soundly in the small, uncomfortable bed which reminded me of childhood, just as the curtains and the cupboard and everything else in the tiny village did for some reason.

In the morning we woke up early, much earlier than I would have liked. I was an early riser by nature, but only if it was by choice. Most weekends, I woke between six and seven, much to Jana's annoyance, particularly if she'd worked in Kaaba 'til three or four in the morning. On weekdays I was worse. I would tiptoe around the flat, trying to find the various things I needed or felt I needed for the day. In much the same way that I over-packed for the mountains, I regularly, almost always, over-packed for work. That was bad for my back.

But I couldn't bring myself to leave anything to chance. I always had to have more than enough materials for the day. If I felt unprepared, the day ahead was filled with peril. Even after three years, each lesson was in some way a step into the darkness. What if something went wrong? What if my students didn't respond to my materials, of which I had plenty? What then? As in the English education system, there were no wrong answers to the question, largely because there were no answers at all.

Along with my teaching materials, I would carry around

whatever book I was reading and my laptop, on the off chance I had some time during the day to do a little writing. What's more, I sometimes took my gym gear.

Time was always in short supply. Even if I exercised after work, I didn't want to go home, change, go to the gym, exercise, then go home again. That was not a good use of my time. This meant that in addition to the book and the laptop and the folder with its thousands of teaching materials, I often had trainers and socks and jogging bottoms and a T-shirt, plus a change of underwear and socks and maybe, if I remembered, shower gel and shampoo. That was a heavy burden to carry, and I did it for about two years without the slightest hint of grace.

That's also, I'm sure you'll agree, another digression.

Anyway, on weekdays I would walk around our room looking for various things Jana had tidied away, playing my role in the constant battle we had between her practicality and my chaos.

It was wrong of me to leave items strewn hither and thither, but at that time of day I always felt righteously indignant that she'd tidied something away without informing me. How was she to know what might be important, and when? That was a hard position to justify, particularly when I forever left my large red teaching folder in the middle of our bedroom floor.

*

In the morning we got up, dressed and had Czech breakfast. Better than the usual Czech breakfast, it included several cakes Jana's mother had made especially for me.

After that, we made our way towards the hiking trail. I knew next to nothing about the day ahead. I also knew whatever Jana told me wasn't the full story. That amused me.

She thought I hated it all, the camping, the hiking, the outdoors. There was truth in that, yes, but it wasn't in itself true. We'd gone kayaking earlier in the year. That'd been a disaster. I wanted this trip to go better. I needed to believe I could acclimatise. Before Jana, I thought I'd lived in the Czech Republic, but I hadn't. I was an expat, who lived in a bubble, a beautiful bubble where I taught students in English and went to bars and clubs with friends from English-speaking countries, where I did my best to learn the language but never really felt any real pressure to do so. I was living in the Czech Republic now, though, with all that entailed. So it was important that I find ways to like all that that entailed.

Jana thought I could adapt too, perhaps even more than

39

me. That may have been wishful thinking, but I'm glad if nothing else that I wasn't afraid to try. I tried the world and it bit me. But I laughed a lot, loved too. And I made a girl love me by pretending to be an ape. That's more than most can say. Hu hu.

We walked past a large funicular. That was the coward's route of choice, and I watched the cowards glide up towards the mountain with envy. We carried on through a small woods, where I saw a goat in a clearing, and a few farmhouses interspersed with large buildings clearly built around the tourist trade. The land soon began to incline, and within five minutes we were – as far as I could tell – doing what was commonly known as hiking. That wasn't as bad as I'd feared.

—Are you okay, Opička, Jana asked several times, as we climbed the mountain.

I answered yes each time, or hu hu, and meant it. After a while, I stopped to take in the view of the mountains and forest and the blue sky. The weather had been foreboding in the morning, but it was beautiful now, and warm. It was a strenuous climb but pleasantly so, the sweat on my back a sign I was exerting myself, the slight strain in my legs a reminder I didn't exercise often enough, or at least not as hard as I should. After around forty-five minutes of walking up the mountain, we stopped for another breather and a sip of water.

—How far up are we? I asked.

—About halfway.

She furrowed her brow. —Are you okay, honey?

—Yes, yes, I said, with an eagerness I'd not expected of myself. —I was just wondering-

—We will get you a pivo when we get to the top.

I smiled.
—Hu!

I looked out across the land. Though we were only halfway up, we had climbed quite high.

—It is very beautiful, Hontag, I said. I turned to

40

her. —Like you.

    I kissed her on the cheek, but then, involuntarily, rubbed
my left eye, which had begun to smart.

            —You should put more sun cream on, Opička,
she said, and began fumbling in her bag.

    She had everything in there: medicaments, bandages,
water, snacks, fruit, everything.
    I was a lucky man. Why did I need to write?

We carried on walking. It felt good to be out in the open, away
from my writing and my coffee and my beer.
    For once, I didn't really desire any of those things
– except maybe the beer – and was enjoying the slight ache in
my legs, the fresh air and wide-open space.
    The relative difficulty of the climb surprised me. I thought
myself fit, but aside from jogging occasionally and lifting
weights in the gym, I never really exerted or pushed myself.
That was called sticking to your comfort zone.
    I hadn't done it in my work either, or my writing, not for
some time.
    Despite my supposed aversion to the outdoors, I was
doing just fine, often climbing ahead of Jana and scrambling
up the rocks. She asked every ten or so minutes how I was, to
which I replied with a guttural, primatial noise that told her I
was okay.
    In full swing, love created in me a sense of ease, where
I was able to think about more or less nothing, where I could
climb on rocks with Jana, pretending to be a monkey for her
amusement, and not worry that the world was watching, that I
was opening myself to embarrassment and ridicule and shame.
That was something they didn't tell you about love. It enabled
you not to care. That was good.
    Back in my day-to-day life, I worried about the future,
how me and Jana were going to forge this life we so very much
wanted to lead together; mutually satisfying, financially viable.
Happy. I worried my writing wasn't going to take me anywhere
after all and about how I still considered it important despite
finding Jana. I worried that I would be a teacher forever even
though I didn't like it, and that I might get sick again, really
sick. The few truly low periods I'd had in Prague I'd gotten
through in the company of Messrs Fluoxetine or Citalopram, or
simply by spending time with friends in the dingy but hallowed

basement bars of Prague. And I had written, of course. Writing had given me hope.

After the recent summer where I'd teetered on the brink, I worried about getting sick again, as the realities of life hit the two of us like bricks. But for the most part I suppressed the thought, letting delusion back into my life because I, we, needed it. Occasionally, I thought about how I was around Jana, how I responded to most questions with only an animal-like grunt. She always understood, simply from the tone, yes or no. In love, I didn't feel the shame, nor did I live life fantasising. I didn't have visions of being cool or calm or collected because in love I was those things, with the possible exception of cool. That was self-evidently not the case. It was easy in love, never more so than up on the mountain, where I knew I wanted to be for the rest of my life. Not the mountain itself – fuck no – but there, with her.

The shit of the world didn't matter in her presence. It was just the consequence of people's greed or ignorance or hate or arrogance; it was just stuff, bullshit that could be consumed, processed and ignored in the knowledge that I had her. It was simple, and that was good. It felt good, to wake up next to her. It felt good to know she was coming home, as it were. And it was easy, easy, easy. Until it wasn't so easy.

*

When we reached the mountaintop we ate our sandwiches, not talking too much. That was fine.

People around us took photos with phones and selfie sticks, and after we had finished our sandwiches we walked inside the cafeteria and got a coffee. After that, we looked at the views around Snezka, the mountains verdant in the last throes of a summer that had become prolonged through human intervention. That was no thanks to mankind, but thanks for trying anyway, Al Gore.

The view was stunning in every direction, the snow-capped mountains more numerous than on the drive into Pec pod Sněžkou the previous day, the peaks more jagged and starkly beautiful. To my left was Poland, my right the Czech Republic, but the beauty was equal in either direction. That was something people didn't like to admit.

After admiring the view for a while, we climbed back down the mountain, holding the weak chain link fence as we descended. A little further down, there was a long stretch of road, and another café sat just metres over the Polish border.

That was good and bad.

It was bad because it meant they served Polish beer. You could start a war saying Polish beer isn't as good as Czech beer out loud. But in reality, not even Andrzej Duda, jingoism in a hard-on, could argue the case.

It was good, though, because Poles were friendlier. That was undeniable, and of course utterly denied. The waitress smiled. She told me they accepted Czech koruna. That was fortunate. We had our drinks (Jana had a hot wine) and after that we went outside and I began to jump between the Czech and Polish border, demarcated by a large stone. Jana laughed.

I played the fool, jumping back and forth like a child. I looked the fool, but I'd chosen it, controlled it; it was my doing, it was fine. She giggled, and tried in vain to hold her phone still as she videoed everything. It was all fine. I was in control of the pointing and the laughter and the opinions of others. That was vital. It hadn't happened by accident. It wasn't part of the chaos, or shame.

—Grrrrrrr!

I woofed like a hound, and ran towards Jana and the camera. She began to run away, but was saved by a dog. The dog, a large chocolate brown Labrador, had taken my canine barking (which must have been pretty good) as either a threat or a come-on (I was both flattered and scared).

He began to chase me around while all and sundry watched on.

That was slightly embarrassing, but I still felt like I'd been the architect, and so that too was fine. Plus it was absurd. It was hard to be embarrassed amidst the absurd. Embarrassments only happened in the humdrum of daily life, which in itself is a little absurd. Eventually, the dog's Polish owners drew him back. I laughed, and walked back towards Jana.

—Jsou friendly, I said.

—Kdo, those people?

—Yes, they seemed nice, I said. —The Polish people.

She nodded, and we walked further on.

The land was flat for a couple of miles, and boggy. It was

marshland. Fortunately, there was a raised wooden platform
to walk along, and so we did, towards a large building in the
distance, which turned out to be another hotel. We stopped there
a while.

*

After spending an hour in the hotel, which resembled what I
imagined a ski lodge would up close and personal, we continued
to walk. The grass was yellowing as autumn set in. I'd first
noticed the difference in this regard to the UK a couple of years
earlier, standing on the top floor of Raifessenbank, a popular
(in investment terms, if not cuddliness) bank where I taught an
actuary or accountant or something. I can't remember. That was
so-so.

Peering out of the window and down the thirty-odd floors
one afternoon as I waited for him in the lobby, I noticed how
grey and yellow and lifeless the grass was, compared to our
rain-soaked equivalent on the Island. That was something. It's
also a digression, so apologies once more, though it ought to
be clear by now I don't think digressions are bad, not really.
They have value. Sometimes not getting straight to the point is
the point. Did you ever hear about the character who could sum
themselves up in one hundred and twenty characters? Didn't
think so.

We climbed back into the mountains and stopped once
we'd found somewhere with a good view of rolling (still green)
hills and vast swathes of forest. From there we walked on and
found another building, an old, communist-style fortress of a
place which was, Jana told me, a kind of community hall. It
had been converted into an information centre with a small,
functional restaurant.

—You must send your Mum a postcard, Ronišu.

That was another nickname, which 'til now I had
somehow forgotten. That's subconsciously purposeful, or just
consciously forgetful.

—Hu?

—Yes. You must send your Mum a
postcard. She will like it. And your sister.

—Hu, I said, nodding.

44

I picked two which I liked, one of Konopište the mythical
mountain man, the other the mountains themselves.

—What about your brother, she said?

Though she'd never met him, Jana occasionally asked after
my brother. I liked that. It made it all feel so very possible
and important and real. I told her my brother wasn't one for
postcards, however. That's the way I saw it, though it mightn't
have been true. I'd never asked.
    We bought postcards, and after we bought the postcards,
we wrote them. I wrote another for Jana's parents in my pidgin,
childlike Czech whilst Jana wrote the ones for my mother and
sister. She'd met both of them only once, my mother for several
days while she stayed at our house and my sister at a family
BBQ. They liked her, she them, and that boded well. Life had
other ideas, though. Oh well.
    After we had written the postcards and bought the stamps
and posted them to our various family members we walked
down into the valley, and then the forest, flitting in between
open, stony ground bathed in sunlight and deep, dense forest,
where the floor was often muddy, and where Jana pointed out
various types of mushrooms she had picked as a child, telling
me which ones were poisonous and which ones were fine to eat
so long as you cooked them enough. She told me about a kid
she'd grown up with who cooked shrooms the way American
kids in movies might, occasionally British ones too if they
couldn't get their hands on weed or cheap speed.
    He got addicted, or dependent, or whatever the term is.
That's a debate for another day, and the terms and classifications
are as likely to change with the changes of arbiters as the
seasons from summer to autumn to winter and spring. That's the
thing about change. It swings one way, but very often back the
other.
    She talked about the boy she'd known, and even though
it was dark to talk about, I felt closer to her, because we spoke
about everything, good and bad. That wasn't quite true, as there
were worries within me I didn't speak about, but it was nice to
believe as much for a while.
    Eventually, in the dense forest, we found the small castle
the large key was designed for. There was nothing inside, except
a flight of stairs to a small parapet which looked out onto, well,
more nothing. It was perfect. It was peaceful. It had hardly been
worth the walk, which made it all the more worth it, as there was
no one else there and we had walked to it for no reason other

than to walk, to be outdoors and walking, walking, walking.

*

A while later we were back on the road. Cars passed every now and then. I'd drunk a lot of water (and a couple of beers), and needed a piss, so we found a bus stop. I took a piss behind it, glad when no cars passed.

—I think I would like to go to Ireland sometime, Hontag, I said, as we snaked around the meandering roads, back towards Pec pod Sněžkou.

—Yes?

—Yes, just for a holiday. I miss it.

That was true. Earlier that summer we had discussed Ireland as a place where maybe the both of us could live, me because it was home, of sorts, her because it was green and verdant and beautiful, nothing like London, which she hated.

She reminded me that my memories of Ireland were wrapped in the comforting blanket of childhood, that what I remembered wasn't reality. That was not a truth I wanted to hear, but it was a truth. Still, over the last few months, I'd developed a longing to see Ireland again, and the town where my father was born, a place I'd not been to in over thirteen years. I had thought about my grandmother's house a great deal.

One of the companies where I taught reminded me of it. The hallway doors must have been made from similar wood, because whenever I was there, it smelled like the hallway in my grandmother's home. That was called olfactory memory, and that is a lie, because it's something I just made up. It's also a digression, but for me this time, because I had to double-check the meaning of the word 'olfactory'. But it is accurate, because while I worried olfactory meant something to do with the eye, I was right about my initial convictions. That's why I could never be a leader. I ask questions.

That office hallway got me thinking of Cahersiveen, my father's home town, which made me think about the fact I'd not been back in thirteen years, thirteen years to a place I thought of as home, one way or another.

—That would be nice, said Jana,

walking ahead of me.

We continued to walk along the road, which jarred with the mountains and trees and dense thickness of forest. It was pristine, well kept, not quite in keeping with the place.

—Do you want to come to Ireland with me someday, Hontag? I asked. —You would like it.

—I know, Opičko, said Jana. —I was there, remember?

—Oh yes, of course.

She had spent a summer in Ireland, mostly in West Meath. That was in the midlands. The poor woman.

—Yes, I would like to see where did your father come from.

The thought lifted me. I didn't know what it was I wanted to show her, what piece of me, but I did want to, and later would.

—Hu, I said, skipping ahead, walking with renewed purpose. —Dobry.

Eventually, we reached the outer fringes of the town, and stopped in at a little restaurant for coffee and a bite to eat. I was ravenously hungry, and had a large plate of gulaš, then sweet dumplings covered in sour cream and filled with sugar and blueberries. That was just asking for diabetes later in life. But they were worth it.

We made our way back to the cottage. I watched Match of the Day while Jana rested her eyes. Leicester City had beaten Manchester United 5-3, which was at this time utterly extraordinary. That was 2014. That year they would barely survive, but survive nonetheless.

By summer the following year, they would be champions. That was the only good surprise of 2016, and that's coming from a Spurs fan whose team gave them a run for their money before an impressive act of self-immolation which the general public later imitated at large by way of referendum.

I drank a glass of red wine from a two-litre plastic bottle Jana's father had given us, from a batch he'd brought back from a recent trip to Moravia. Later that evening, we went to the large communist-era hotel, where there was a spa. Thankfully, the Czechs wore towels in spas. I wasn't prepared to sit naked in the midst of strangers.

That was a no-no at my end.

When we arrived, there was just one older man, who soon left. We sat in the sauna for some minutes. I felt very European. This is what they did in brochures and on telly, and sometimes the Euro category of various porn sites too, though with a very different atmosphere.

We walked out and jumped into a freezing cold plunge pool, then repeated the process three times in the space of thirty minutes, after which we went down some stairs to a large swimming pool. We were the only ones there. We went for a swim before returning upstairs, changing, and having a soft drink in the restaurant, which was full of old people who looked like they'd probably been coming here since the days of Brezhnev. That's a history reference, look it up.

Later that evening, we went to the restaurant and bar opposite the information centre. It was the biggest in town and the most popular, probably due to its lack of pretentiousness, its cheap prices and its good beer. That was good.

We ate a meal, had a few beers, and after a while, got to discussing children's names. I had Internet on my phone, which I'd only had for about two months by this point. It amazed me. That seems halcyon now.

—How do you say this one? she asked.

I had brought up a list of Irish names. I can't remember how we got to talking about names or the idea of having kids. That itself had cropped up once or twice. Jana had been advised by her doctor to have children before she was thirty. That was what might be called a ticking time bomb.

Now, though, in the pub, it wasn't a serious conversation. It was fun, but as I spoke about it, the idea seemed tangible, desirable, like a nice plan, even if it came about very much at odds with sensible family planning. Jana pointed to one of the names on my phone screen, and widened her eyes.

—How do you say this one?

—What, Caoimhe?

—Yes. What?

— Kwee-va.

She looked at me, utterly confused.

—Don't worry, I said. —We won't use this one. It is a horrible name. I like this one, I said, scrolling my index finger down the screen. —Niamh. Neev.

She mulled it over a moment.

—Yes, this is a beautiful name.

She took a sip of her beer. On the table behind us a group of German or Austrian tourists in their mid-fifties clinked glasses loudly. It was clear they were friends of many years, though I couldn't tell if the wives had been friends first or the husbands had been friends first or if they had all known each other an equally long time. That wasn't important.

—I like your sister's name, said Jana. —That is Irish, isn't it?

—Yes, I said. —It's Irish for Joanne. Ronan is the best Irish name, though.

—Oh, is it? she asked, a little sarcastically.

The Czechs didn't excel at sarcasm, that much was true. Better than the Americans, for whom everything was either completely absurd, or inviolably serious. That was funny, from time to time. Ha-ha funny, especially when they took things personally, as it were. Jana had got a little bit better with sarcasm since we'd been together. She'd had to, in order to survive.

—Yes, I said. —Ronan is the best name, and you know why.

I put my beer back on the bar mat (I was always careful to do this in the Czech Republic) and began slapping my hands together like a seal. That's what Ronan meant (and means). Baby seal.

—Arf, arf, arf, arf.
—No, Monkey! she said, trying to lower my hands.

I resisted her loose grip, and patted my hands together
ever more loudly. Even the Germans with their loud drinking –
and now voluble smoking – turned to watch. I was an attention
seeker who couldn't stand the attention. That was me. I loved it
when I had an audience, yet hated being on the spot. For once,
however, I wanted people to watch, not because I was acting the
fool (and a different animal to boot), but because they would be
able to see me with her, Jana, see the happiness, the joy that was.

—Arf, arf, arf, arf!

She pulled my arms down more forcefully.

—No! You are Monkey. Not Seal.
Monkey.

I put them down. The Germans smiled, the women wryly,
the men with childlike understanding. The barman poured
drinks, three or four at a time, as he had the entire time we'd
been in the pub. The waitresses flurried around like black and
white swirls, almost invisible yet never out of sight. I picked up
my phone.

—This is a pretty name. Saoirse. Sore-shaw. I
love that name.

—Yes, said Jana. —It sounds nice.
But it is impossible. Look at the spelling.

—I know, I said. —I know.

I sipped on my beer, and looked into her eyes a few
moments.

—Hu! I said, loudly enough to make her laugh. I was
monkey.

Indeed I was. I was monkey and mountain climber. I was at home
and torn for far away, for England, or Ireland, even I wasn't sure.
I was in love but didn't know how to keep it all together.
    Most of all, though, I was Monkey, nothing more, nothing
less. That December, though, I moved back to the UK, where the
name Saoirse was no more likely to be understood, but where I
thought I might be.

SWEDEN

Even though it was July, it felt strange to have such good weather. Sheet rain had permeated the previous weeks, with weekends spent largely indoors, something I pretended to be as upset as Jana about, to my shame. I should have been upset. She hated rain, like most, and still generally worked in Kaaba Saturdays and Sundays. When she was free on weekends, Jana liked us to spend time together, to go outside, to live. I could understand that. But to me rain was an opportunity to read and write, to redraft my book, which I'd forced myself into believing wasn't beyond repair and still held promise.

Weekends indoors. That was a guilty pleasure, with emphasis on the word 'guilty'. I was glad whenever tentative plans for bike rides or walks were rained off. Writing made things good. Writing had a purpose; it was the thing that would keep us together some day, when it finally paid off. That was the plan.

At the back of my mind I feared this wasn't true, but couldn't bring myself to accept it. This was around five or six months before I finally fell to pieces, before I started seeing Fluoxetine again, not behind Jana's back, but not with her approval either.

And it was before that trip to the mountains, before I went home to England too, which happened both suddenly and as a consequence of the thoughts that had built up slowly but were then coursing through my mind in December 2014. By the end of that year I would be back in London, broken and defeated, unable to see the monkey from the man in the mirror. That was bad.

Right now, however, I was on my way to Berlin, and that was good.

Heavy summer showers weren't unusual to Prague. They rarely lasted, though, and the long, uninterrupted downpours had caused floods, detrimental to my salary as a freelance teacher. A number of my lessons were being cancelled, and I was losing a lot of money. I didn't mind, really. It gave me free time. At a time when I didn't care too much about money, that was fine.

Few teachers in Prague were paid a salary. Most of us were freelance, even though many technically worked for just one school, and as such should have received all the benefits therein. It wound me up how we were tricked and treated and manipulated into signing contracts for companies we weren't strictly contracted to. That was pointless. Not the contracts, the winding up of oneself.

It achieved nothing except perhaps the slow formulation of a stomach ulcer, the thought of which doubtless perpetuated the problem and the likelihood of that ulcer coming to fruition. Still, I felt wounded, to the extent that I seriously considered setting up a union for all the English teachers in Prague. I thought about it, that's what I did. And then I figured it was probably futile. And that was the end of that.

It was a hot day, clear, bright and sultry. My T-shirt clung to my underarms as we walked to the station. That was so-so, but while it was unpleasant (though importantly, not humiliating), Jana was used to me that way. I was a sweaty man. She didn't mind. That was good. And not feeling the shame and humiliation, that was even better. Still, it was very hot. Only in leaving the Island had I come to appreciate the mistral winds which keep it cool, even at the height of summer. In my black skinny jeans, I was poorly dressed for the weather, yet refused to wear shorts. I thought them stupid, and while *that* was stupid, I stand by it.

A lot of teachers in my school wore shorts to work. That was absurd. Usually, it was the young American guys just passing through, the boys for whom teaching was a conduit to paying rent and travelling around Europe before heading back to reality, to the world of work, to America. Some of them could barely string a sentence of English together, let alone teach it. That surprised me, but was also another reason not to unionise, or unionize.

As we walked towards Flora to catch our bus, I felt extremely uncomfortable in my jeans. That was to be expected. Perhaps it was me who was absurd, not the innocent young men merely trying to see a bit of the world with limited lexis, a word I spelt wrong the first time trying. Perhaps it was me, Opičko, with his superfluous layers and his proclivity for spelling mishaps.

We reached the station, found our platform and boarded the bus. That was all as straightforward as it sounds, and I was delighted. We were criminally early. I'd insisted on it. It kept the chaos at bay. That was important for my state of mind. Jana understood. She didn't like it, but she understood. That was love with a heavy dose of toleration.

I looked out of the window as we left the depot and made our way out onto the narrow Czech road, equivalent to an A-Road back home, before reaching the motorway. It was still warm. I disliked the British obsession with weather, couldn't understand why we complained about something we'd been born into. But here I was, on my way to Berlin, thinking about weather in typically obsessive British fashion, despite my loyalties. Regardless of where those loyalties lay, however, there was one question that stuck out: Why the hell had I worn black skinny jeans? Ty vole! Fool!

Why hadn't I let Jana pack for me, like she'd offered? She was good at packing, at making plans, of thinking ahead. She'd said we could leave thirty minutes later than we eventually did. That would have been too late, but only for my peace of mind. She was, as usual, right.

As it was, we arrived with over half an hour to spare, were forced to buy terrible coffee and asked for change by four people, three of whom ended up with all the shrapnel I had in my wallet. That was fine by me, Jana too. But she didn't really like the waiting, and that was fair.

No, common sense wasn't my forte. But we were on our way now, sitting together on the back of the bus. I looked over at Jana. She was already asleep, even though the bus had just left the terminal. There was a screen on the seat in front of me. It was dusty, and the sun highlighted that. I started watching a programme and tried to focus, but noticed a man three rows up making lots of noise. I couldn't ignore noise. Once noticed, it was all I could focus on, no matter how minor or insignificant; a dripping tap, a couple chatting quietly, shutters shuttering in the wind. Noise was the enemy of my days. But you have to listen to thunder. I looked over at the man. He was complaining to his girlfriend.

—What's he going on about? I
said, nudging Jana awake.

She yawned, and half opened her eyes with a slightly put out look.

—He is complaining about the shit
on the television, she said, closing them again. —Shit
television, she added, either for effect or in a daze.

I looked at his screen, then back at the man. He had a tattoo down one arm – something Maori – and a large faux-diamond earring. I couldn't tell if the girlfriend agreed with him or was telling him to shut up and watch. Whatever it was, he finally settled on something. It all reminded me of car journeys to Ireland as a kid, me in the back seat with nothing but football magazines or books to enjoy, and endless games of I Spy that must have driven my family to the brink of insanity. And of course, 'Born in the USA', the song, not the album. That's right. As we travelled through southeast England and up into Wales,

I'd insist that my mum play 'Born in the USA' over and over.

That was great, unless you happened to be my siblings, or royalty claimants, for 'Born in the USA' garners no royalties when played in private vehicles.

I'm no legal expert, but I believe that is true.

I looked back at the Maori man. He seemed put out again, and was flicking through the channels. He had more than fifteen films to choose from, yet there he was, unable to settle on something. People were such idiots. What was wrong with us? We couldn't remember what true boredom felt like, and it had killed our imagination. That bothered me. We complained too much. Admittedly, I'm complaining now, albeit about a Czech man with a faux-diamond earring and a Maori tattoo. It was as if complaining was in our nature, like anything else; that we had an ability to adapt, yet only ever to a higher state of need. That's so-so.

Ours, a generation that grew up on Duplo, Rainbow and, in this part of the world, black and white telly, now screamed bloody murder if there wasn't a catalogue of crap to watch on a four-hour journey to Berlin. That was modern man.

What an idiot this guy was. I decided not to read my book and, almost to make a point, check out the films on offer. It turned out there were thirteen to choose from, which was plenty. I would show him.

And that's when I watched *Gangster Squad*.

*

I was dissatisfied with life. That was the problem. But I was also happier than I'd ever been. That was another problem.

It felt important not to let on about it to Jana. I'd no right to be unhappy, not with what we had together. We'd both been lonely before meeting each other, neither of us happy on our own. Now, I was the happiest I'd been in my life, and for that reason, more afraid than ever before. I hid my worries for Jana's sake, but more so for my own. That was unsmart.

No, it wasn't right for me to be dissatisfied. She urged me to be open, but openness led to trouble. I knew that. At work, I had recently been refused a raise I felt I deserved after three years of service; a minor one, but a raise nonetheless. I'd lost better paid work elsewhere while working for them. I'd also been lazy in looking for it. That's called fessing up.

I had convinced myself I was the best teacher in Prague after winning an award from my school, the biggest in the city. That made me the best language teacher in the city, I figured.

It was a Trumpian way of looking at things. Despite this, confidence wasn't big in me – far from it. But the award was a way to make myself feel okay about what I did, a job which went in rotation rather than forward, teaching a way of getting by, a job that ironically meant I learned nothing about the world, less so with each passing day and every lesson repeated to another class. In truth, I was just another teacher. That was fine. But it wasn't fine for me.

I looked over at Jana. I could live with dissatisfaction, I told myself. But there was more to it than that. In spite of all my egotistical misgivings about teaching and my selfish desire for *more*, there was a truth about teaching that stood out like a sore thumb in a finger factory: the money wasn't enough for both of us. That was plain obvious to me.

For me, it was enough, or had been for the last two years or so, once I'd settled and picked up plenty of work. But now, it wasn't enough to get by on, never mind make those all-important plans. For one person, perhaps, for two, no. For three or more, not a chance. This preyed on my mind. There were parts of happiness I could afford to compromise; her, I could not.

I didn't want this to end. I had the woman of my dreams, and she was real for once, whereas for years she'd been a figment of my imagination; an ideal, a fantasy, another part of the scenarios I dreamed up in my mind. She was someone I thought about as a tangible part of me, a woman whose blue eyes I looked into in the night, while making love or after coming home from work, an almost sorrowful look peering up at me from below as she hugged my midriff while I was still standing and yet to remove my coat. A look of pure love.

She was real, flawed, vulnerable, and perfect in every way. She was beautiful and kind. Kindness was something I had never realised to be important for me, but it was. I was far too meek for tumultuous passion. That was obvious now.

I needed quiet love, and I had it.

And yet, there was no denying I'd hit a wall with teaching, personally and financially. The refusal of a raise made it clear to me I would always live pay check to pay check; the manner in which I'd begun to fantasise about doing something, anything else, made it clear I had been doing it too long. My students were no longer interested in improvement (whatever the hell that really meant), and neither was I. Their companies paid for the classes, which for most were more of an excuse to have an hour off work than anything else. That was fair enough. Work was hard. English with Ronan was not. Unless it involved the second conditional.

After three years I was out of methods, tired of rehashing the same subjects over and over, tired too of preparing new classes. There were only so many times you could hear a new student tell you their hobbies were climbing in the mountains or spending weekends in their family cottage and still feign surprise and keen interest. That was a reality. It wasn't a nice one, because I knew that each new student was a person who deserved the same level of interest as my new students two years earlier, but I couldn't help it.

With new students, I was desperate to hear something original; that they liked to dust their balls with speed and listen to minimalist techno on weekends, that they knitted, that they had a secret lover called Gregor who they met in the Moravian city of Zlín whenever time permitted. I would even have been happy had one of them told me how they spent their free time baking bread, that god-awful, stodgy, dry Czech bread. That I could engage with, that I could argue about.

But no, it was hiking in the mountains or DIY in the cottage. It was what Czech adults did, and that was fine. But not after three years. The problem was me. That was clear.

I was no longer stressed about teaching. That worried me. I'd woken up each morning riddled with anxiety over the day ahead for about two years; not so much anxious over teaching but for the *day*, how and if I would get through it, whether my teaching materials would fall flat and my lessons – and therefore my very being – fall apart.

No one ever saw it, not my students or my friends or the admin staff at the language school; I had a calm demeanour and a friendly, if toothy, smile, my left front tooth (or right if you were looking at me) much smaller than the right (or left if you were looking at me) due to my having run into a door at the age of eleven, resulting in a crown which wasn't put in at the same length. I was calm on the outside but a babbling brook of anxiety underneath, a man as incapable of keeping calm as he was of constructing passable metaphors.

And I didn't feel that way anymore.

The loss of that feeling sat uneasily with me. Worry was my natural state, and now I didn't really care. The longer it went on like this, the more depressed I would become. I'd known it on a sunny afternoon in Letná a few weeks earlier when I stood at the bar buying drinks, thinking, 'It's okay, I am not going to live in Prague forever. We'll figure something out.'

I'd known it as I stood outside our flat smoking on a Friday night while she slept upstairs, saying to myself aloud in the cold night, 'I hope she comes with me'.

The desperation in my voice surprised even me. I knew it, but I also knew that changing the situation risked losing everything. That was a quandary.

I turned back to my screen. *Gangster Squad* was still on. It was a terrible film. I expected better of Gosling. That was the danger of believing.

As we drove, the trees grew higher around us and the streets became lined with hookers. Occasional casinos sprung up in seemingly dead-end locations.

That was a clear-cut sign we were near the border.

*

We got off the bus in Berlin. I turned to Jana.

—Let's have a cigarette before we get the train.

The last hour of the journey had been torture, traffic into the city so vast we'd crawled the last five or six miles, the heat near unbearable. Though I'd been in England not that long ago, Berlin came as a shock to me, the throngs of people toing and froing in stark contrast to the comforting though staid calm of Prague. I had expected it to be busy, but the urgent energy with which people moved around contrasted with the image of Germany I'd been fed, in a way that surprised me.

I lit my cigarette and exhaled, Jana likewise. The smoke rose blue from the cherry, drifting up towards the afternoon sun. That was divine.

We sat on a verge beside the bus stop. I was surprised by the amount of litter, but then I had been raised on a diet of German stereotypes passed on to me by Basil Fawlty and a school system that did little to dispel the myth of the austere, conscious, serious German.

That view couldn't have differed more to the one where I lived now. In Prague, the Germans were known for loudness over seriousness, boorish behaviour over quiet efficiency. They came to Prague for cheap booze, much as a British tourist might head to Greece or Spain, and it resulted in the kind of reputation you would expect of fast-boozing, boisterous tourists. That was the beauty of perspective.

As I sat beside the bus stop, realigning my impression of Berlin, I couldn't shake the nagging feeling that I might not be suited to life in Prague. I'd only been in Berlin – off a bus, at least – for five minutes, but there was something in the beeping of horns and constant sound of cars and sight of people rushing

to and fro that felt familiar and comforting to me. I loved
Prague, and always had. I had only cursed it twice, once when
I couldn't communicate with an employee at a state office, the
second time when my heart had been broken, in which case I
could have been any place and I would have cursed it.

Yes, I'd always loved Prague, but with the stakes suddenly
raised over the last few months, I felt uncertain in myself. For
the first time, it felt so small, even though that smallness had
once been what I loved about it. I kept telling myself it would
get better. The job was the problem. Were I to solve that – or
better yet, get published – everything would turn out okay,
the smallness figure itself out, my anxieties abate with my
succession from one lifestyle to another. Something better.

That was the plan.

I looked around me, soaking up Berlin. I liked it. Though we
were still in the station, I sensed it was a place I would like;
dirty, dingy, yet fascinating and lively. Still, I knew Jana wanted
to get out of the station as quickly as possible. She didn't like
cities, and probably didn't like city train stations either. That was
fair.

I was torn between the bustling life of a metropolis and
the quiet beauty of Bohemia, where little happened but all
was calm; torn between staying where I was happy or going
to where I might be comfortable. Who was I kidding? I was
no more decisive than the Maori-tattooed man on the bus, just
– marginally – better dressed. That was undeniable. We finished
our cigarettes and tried to buy tickets, but were pointed in the
direction of the metro station about 100 yards away when we got
to the kiosk.

—I would take something to eat, said Jana, noticing a
small building on the way, part information centre, part food
vendor.

I loved her malapropisms – wrong, yet correct in their
own way, steeped in an earlier form of English. I never corrected
her. They gave me joy. That was good. No, that was great.

—Let's try here, I said.

We walked into a kiosk and bought Currywurst. That summed
up Germany in 2014. Currywurst. Generations of tension
between native and immigrant culminating in a modus vivendi,
a fast food compromise. If only it'd worked in England.

We ate in a blisteringly hot car park as I brooded over my thoughts, unable to simply have and be inside them. Did I really think Berlin would be any better than Prague? It was difficult to make an informed analysis while standing in a car park. That much was true. Who ever made an important decision in a car park? Churchill? I doubt he was ever in one. They probably didn't exist at the time. And look at us now, car parks everywhere, taken for granted and taken as gospel. That, I'll admit, is a digression, but didn't you enjoy the ride?

When we tried to buy tickets at the station we couldn't, but fortunately a group of young teenage boys (an increasingly dangerous threesome of words for any writer to use) helped. This never happened in Prague. They were friendlier than the Czechs, I told myself. That was a plus. It was also me looking for pluses wherever I could.

The young teenage boys (they were tall, athletic and blonde too) directed us towards the station, over a bridge and down a tunnel. When we got inside, we couldn't figure out how to use the machines. A queue began to swell behind us. I felt awkward and embarrassed and became (silently) angry with Jana, who was fiddling with the buttons, Jana, who had the bottle to try and figure out how to get us to Pankow. I knew I was wrong, but couldn't help it.

   —Let's stand to one side, I said, burning with shame as I looked at the growing queue behind us.

She gave the queue behind us a dismissive look as if to say 'piss on you'. That's a poorly translated Czech phrase she sometimes used that always conjured up horrible images but made me laugh all the same in the way it was delivered with such venom and dismissiveness and spite.

Jana followed reluctantly. The queue didn't bother her. We needed tickets, and queuing was a part of that, figuring out the machine a part of *that*. That was just logical. But I didn't work on logic.

Shame was my M.O. It was always there. I hated awkwardness, hated standing out, and yet there was another side to me, a deluded side. That man wanted to stand out, fantasised about it even. He wanted to be *impressive*. It was an illusion, an abstract alternative, worlds apart from what the real me wanted in the queue: to flee from awkwardness, conflict, and generally anyone other than me and Jana.

In truth, what I needed was to blend in, to go unnoticed as much as was humanly possible. That was ideal. I was too shy for

it to be any other way, too self-conscious to boot. We returned to
the queue. I asked a girl for help.

That was one thing I had going for me. I didn't go in for
pig-headed displays of male pride. The smallest, most trifling of
mistakes made me ashamed, but I had no truck with asking for
help, felt no prick to my manhood, which had been punctured by
childhood and deflated by life.

—What time are we meeting him? I asked Jana,
once we had our tickets.

She smiled. She'd made all the arrangements and knew I
was worrying that she'd got something wrong, or that we would
be late. I hated being late, hated it when others were late too,
though I rarely, if ever, betrayed any of that irritation.

It was important for me to be on time. I'd leave an hour
early for a fifteen-minute journey rather than leave sixteen
minutes early and risk being late. That's how I did my bit to
stick to plans.

We were couchsurfing. Our host wouldn't care if we were
a little late. But I couldn't risk it. I'd always been this way,
and didn't know why. My mum had always been relaxed about
timekeeping. She referred to lateness as *Irish Time*, not to be
confused with *The Irish Times*. That's a digression, but only a
minor one.

She was never late herself, but forgave it in others. But
for me, to be late was the height of rudeness, the worst thing
you could do. It sent me into silent, ulcer-inducing rages never
voiced, only resented. That was unhealthy. But time was there
for a reason. That was just plain obvious. When waiting, I was a
ticking time bomb but also a dud, never to go off.

—Don't worry, said Jana, looking at her watch.

I tried to see it her way, people's way, the normal way, acceptant
of the twists and turns that could make a person a minute or two
late here and there: a passport mislaid, a train missed, a stiflingly
hot day like today. But I couldn't. The minutes ticked away.

We were going to be late. That wasn't good at all, and I
felt it within me, a deep, burning shame for the fact that we were
going to keep our host waiting on a stiflingly hot summer's day
in Berlin.

*

Philipp met us at the station. I recognised him straight off, even though I'd never seen him before. He had an air of *waiting* about him.

He was tall, wiry and almost bald, with a round face and narrow eyes, in his early thirties I reckoned, and had on a blue surfing T-shirt, shorts and flip-flops, as if dressed for the beach. I watched him as the train crawled the final few metres.

—Hi, he said, shaking our hands, first mine, then Jana's.

We walked down the station steps and out onto the concourse where advertising posters caught my attention simply because I'd no idea what they meant, save for a couple of brands known throughout Europe. That was nice.

—There is a Lidl near here, said Philipp as we neared his car, an old Sedan of royal blue that was flecked with dirt. — Would you like to go?

—We should get something for breakfast, said Jana.

—Yeah, sure, I said, and turned to Philipp. — That'd be great, thanks.

As he drove, our eyes fell upon the Berlin suburbs. They were unremarkable, or would have been if we'd never seen them before.

Everything was new, from the height of the apartment buildings to the style of the balconies and the position of the trees in the street.

Through sheer difference in town planning, it was another world, everything a sea of novelty.

My eyes widened with delight at the sheerity of difference. But when we arrived in Lidl, the opposite was true. It could have been Prague or London.

We scoured the aisles.

I picked up some beer for us, and a bottle of wine for Philipp, while Jana bought some rolls, some ham and some sliced cheese. That was called bringing your idea of Czech breakfast with you. It was also a woeful overuse of the word 'some', for which I can only apologise, or apologize, if you're reading in America or abroad, where they always print English translations in American English. That's something that irritates me. It's also called hedging your bets that you're going to have an international audience. That's called optimism.

Now that *is* a digression.

The cashier regarded me with amusement, eyeing me for a second before breaking into English. We bought the items and went back to the car, before driving to Philipp's, just a couple of minutes away.

His flat was on the third floor of an old apartment building with musty, narrow stairwells. From the outside it reminded me of the time I'd been in Chicago as a nineteen-year-old. That was odd, because the part of Berlin we were in would have been part of East Germany. But the simple, monolithic structures with their concrete symmetry were redolent of the Windy City. That's how I figured it.

—Careful of the cat, he said, as we entered.

I walked in. A large, fat tabby ran from under my feet and through to the living room. The hallway was a tiny square of a room, shrouded in darkness. Although there were several pairs of slippers on the floor, I could tell Philipp lived alone. I hated the European custom of taking off your shoes in guests' houses. It was the same in Prague. It made sense. It was common in countries where you fought with snow during the winter and risked traipsing dirt into people's homes. That *did* make sense.

But I still hated the idea of removing my shoes, of becoming infantile in a stranger's house. I always took my shoes off in my own home, had done every day after school from four to eighteen.

That was a nice way of casting off the morning and afternoon, of settling into the haven of home. Nowadays, it was a reversion to the comforts of childhood, but in a stranger's house it was too much, too close.

I took my shoes off and declined the offer of slippers, opting instead to walk around in my socks.

We walked past the kitty litter box and into the living room, which had a large L-shaped sofa that took up all of the far wall and most of the one adjoining it. The flat, like the stairwell, was musty, but in a less antiquated, more lived-in way. It was cramped, more so than our flat back home, and there was little natural light due to the flat's position in the block.

It was as warm as it had been all day, but the sun ought to have been setting by now. Philipp left the light off in spite of the darkness, opting instead for the glow of the television. I looked

around as he flicked the channels so quickly that I couldn't make
out a word with my Year 9 German. It was at this point that it
dawned on me that we were going to be sleeping in here.

And that was a disaster for me and Jana.

The only other rooms in the flat were the bathroom,
kitchen and Philipp's bedroom, and there was no way I was
going to be sleeping in the same room as our host. When
planning our little trip to Berlin, I'd wanted to get a hostel. We
were coming to see the Arctic Monkeys, and yes, I lived and
breathed the existence of Opičko, the dishevelled monkey man.
But damn it, I needed my space.

Jana had other plans, however. She was determined
to couchsurf. I didn't understand this fad for sleeping with
strangers. It wasn't that I didn't like the idea. The romantic (and
deluded) me loved the fantasy of hitching south through Europe,
sleeping outdoors and on people's floors. But reality was a
different kettle of cats. That was something I did understand.

Opičko wasn't as laid back as he liked to believe. I needed
my personal space. I was too risk-averse, too mollycoddled, too
precious over my own privacy. I needed to pay someone money
to know that I was safe. That was the reality of the situation.
Besides, I'd woken up in enough strange places in my time –
friends' sofas, parks, a train station in Long Island one time.
Couchsurfing was like organised *roughin' it*: contrived, a pain in
the arse and not worth the stories. As a result, Jana thought me
old-fashioned and conservative. She was probably right.

—Mind if I smoke? I asked Philipp.

He pushed an ashtray towards me and took out his baccy. I
looked in my pack. There were only two snouts left. I would ask
Philipp for a roll-up later. I disliked asking people for stuff, but
it didn't extend to cigarettes or baccy. I couldn't roll, however,
and needed him to do it for me. Again, this didn't bother me. It
was a minor inconvenience. What's more, it was a good way for
someone shy like me to talk to people. After all, you couldn't
expect them to roll in silence for you. You had to ask some
pleasantries, engage in some sort of conversation, and I found
it easier to talk to someone as they looked down at the papers
rather than into my eyes. That was convenient.

—I will put this in the fridge, he
said, picking up the bottle of wine.

I gawped at Jana as he walked out.

—In the fridge? Red wine?

She shrugged.

—Sure, why not?

There were a lot of things I didn't get about Europeans, even after all this time.
That much was obvious.

*

Mr Creosote meowed loudly. Philipp, it transpired, was a big Monty Python fan, while Mr Creosote, it transpired, was a complete bastard, who refused to let me near him, and had hissed at me three times already. Moreover, he was nothing like his namesake. His food bowl was overflowing with unwanted food.

—I will put him outside, said Philipp, picking up the cat and opening the door so that he would walk out onto the balcony.

We had been chatting awkwardly for about thirty minutes, but there was football on. Germany were playing Armenia in a friendly, their last before the World Cup. That helped stymie the awkwardness.
Though we'd been there nearly an hour, me and Jana had learned little about Philipp, other than the fact he was meeting friends later, in a bar, to play ping pong. He invited us, and we agreed out of politeness. Philipp said he had work in the morning, and that we'd have the flat free to ourselves. He worked in IT, but that was as much as he said and as much as I asked, and after a while, he left to use the bathroom.

—You okay? I asked Jana.
—Yes, she said.

She rubbed the index finger of her left hand with the index finger of her right hand. That was bad. It was a sign I was familiar with, which meant she was nervous. I'd been a little pleased about how couchsurfing was going because it was Jana's idea. That was bad of me. But I wasn't pleased now, to see those fingers the way they were.

—He ignores me, she said. —And only talks to
you.

I hadn't noticed. That was typical.

—It's okay, honey, I said. —It'll be fine.

She nodded.

—He is just a little strange, she said. —But he is fine.

I smiled, at her and within. That more or less summed Philipp
up. A little strange, nothing more. I looked around while he was
in the bathroom. There was an antique cabinet with photos of a
much younger Philipp.
He'd been in the army, but was much too young to have
been conscripted, I thought, so it seemed odd. He certainly
didn't have the look of a soldier, and didn't appear physically
strong enough to have joined of his own accord. There was a
photo of him with an older woman who I took to be his mother.
Other than that, I saw no evidence of family. Everything in the
room reeked of antiquity. The furniture, the photos, everything.
He may have worked in modernity, but his home harked back
to a different time, determinedly so. That was something he'd
worked on.
What also stood out were a number of A-Z style maps and
books about Scandinavia, piled up all over the place.
I looked around to see whether his interest extended to
other regions, but no. That was his niche.
There was one specifically on northeastern Norway,
another on Denmark, and four or five on Sweden, either as a
whole or regionally. The maps were pockmarked with green,
white and yellow pins, places he had either visited or intended
to. Philipp was on the phone to someone. The call was short and
he soon returned to the living room.

—So there are two other guys who will be staying, if that
is cool?

Orgy. He was planning an orgy. I was certain of that.

—They are coming for a concert, he said.

He went on to explain that they were visiting Berlin to see
a famous German comedian – they existed, apparently – attempt

a world record for the largest stadium performance by a comic.

—Sure, no problem, I said, cutting Jana off before she had a chance to weigh in, with just the slightest satisfaction (again) at the manner in which couchsurfing was going tits up.

The five of us, shacked up together. How awful. How fantastic. I couldn't help it.

*

I sipped my beer. It wasn't great, but it was cold. Given the quality of German beer, I gathered only penury or poor taste would force a local's hand. It was cheap, nearly tasteless, and a clear mistake on my part. But it was cold. There were only a couple of scenarios when that was good, and this was one of them. The other? That involved processed meats.

We watched the game. Germany won 6-1. After it was over, I asked Philipp about Scandinavia. Jana looked at me nervously, like I was encroaching, but he suddenly became animated, his narrow eyes widening, showing the faintest hints of vigour, life and passion.

      —I am going to Sweden in three weeks, he said.
       He pointed towards one of his maps, reaching, elongating his arm towards a remote part in the northeast.
      —Here.

He'd been to Scandinavia many times, he told us. He had friends there, though on this occasion he would be camping in the countryside, alone. That was funny.

I'd travelled like that a lot in my time. Alone, that is, not camping.

That was an out-and-out no-no for me, though I had done it. That was both love and necessity, at different times. Jana still looked nervous and uncomfortable as I asked him about Sweden, and I knew what she was thinking. He was shy. He didn't like questions. She was wrong.

Philipp was like me.

He loved questions, but wasn't used to them. Men like us craved the very attention we were uncomfortable with, dreamed of it even. When it came, we didn't know how to behave and became tentative, awkward, yet excited at the same time.

—I try to go to Scandinavia four or five times a year, he said. —I go to Denmark and Norway, but Sweden is my favourite.

Why was that, I flirted with asking. But I didn't. I wanted to let my imagination wander, to leave him something others didn't know. I looked up at the pins on the map, and the solitary one he'd pointed towards before. I liked the mystery of it, and this strange, lonely man with his bucolic distractions.

I looked at the lonesome green pin and knew whatever drew him there was rooted here, in Germany, in his soul. He wanted escape, not to but *from*. That wasn't a good idea. I believed him when he said he had friends in Sweden. He would be something of a novelty there, the strange German boy who came up from the city a few times a year, spending his time and money in the dull Swedish countryside, an amusement to bored locals who never left, whose lives revolved around routine and isolation, lives quietly happy or desperately lonely and near-obsolete.

—May I use your bathroom? I asked.

May I? That was odd. In day-to-day life, I spoke in demotic (plain) English, consonants dropped here, malaprops there. But after teaching for three years I'd developed a filter, and paid better attention to the rules my mother tried so painstakingly – and with great frustration – to have me follow.

The bathroom was a tiny, narrow room. The bath was small. The shower, like so many in this part of Europe, wasn't attached to the wall, and needed to be held in one hand. That kind of thing drove me to the brink.I liked how it felt to cover my skin in gel or soap after sport or, more often, a big session. It was part of the ritual of purgation, of casting off the night before, starting afresh in the naïve belief that it would never happen again. But when you had to hold the showerhead with one hand you couldn't clean yourself the same way. The whole enterprise was an ordeal, particularly washing your hair. That was far from ideal.

I was afraid I'd fall over in this particular shower in the morning. For now, I just needed a piss, and so I took a piss, freeing my hosepipe from the dark, cavernous skinny jeans (size an issue contributing to the cavernousness) and pointed it at the porcelain firing range. As I pissed away, I noticed that Philipp had a number of Panini stickers on his mirror. That wasn't cool, but I liked it. He supported Hertha Berlin, which I'd just learned even though we'd watched a game of football. That seemed odd.

Learning that earlier would have helped me string out a lengthy conversation. It would have been good. It would have taken us from slightly awkward to at the very least so-so.

I looked at the stickers. He had the whole team there. One player stood out. His name was John Anthony Brooks. I'd gone to school with a guy called Anthony Brookes. That was a similar name, with an extra 'e' thrown in for good measure.

I wondered where this John Anthony Brooks was from. He had an English name, but I figured maybe he was second generation American, an army kid, but German-born. That was an educated guess. It was funny (ha-ha, if you ask me) how the Germans were now reaping the benefits of being invaded, albeit in a long, roundabout and mostly sports-related way.

Philipp also had posters stuck precariously to the inside wall of the shower. That seemed like a recipe for disaster to me. I looked about the place, hosepipe reeled back in and skinny jeans zipped back up. Philipp's was a bachelor pad through and through, in the legal rather than cultural sense. That's what happened when you remained a bachelor too long. You acclimatised. That was something I hoped would never happened to me. I returned to the living room.

—It is very hard to get jobs. I   would like
something in my area of study but it is not
possible in Czech now.

I was relieved to find Jana and Philipp talking, having worried I'd find them sitting in silence, Jana clamouring to get away with no escape route. She wasn't good with new people. We had that in common. That made us good together.

I was nervous, prone to contretemps, or fuck-ups, as normal people called them.

But I was a teacher, and I'd been a barman, and had some degree of nous when it came to first meetings. Some degree. Jana, on the other hand, became insular and removed herself from groups. That could be frustrating. If we went to a party where she didn't know anyone, she felt out of place and became quiet, to the point of seeming unfriendly. I would watch her with both love and resentment, wanting to sit next to her, and only her, and be with her, but at the same time wishing she would engage with others.

That was called being conflicted in your thoughts, and that too was love.

Not long before this trip we'd visited a party of friends of mine, where she had struggled to talk to anyone and couldn't get her head around the games we played, bullshit conditional ramblings where we asked each other stupid things like "what would you invent if you could go back in time?" or "if you'd been around in Jesus' time, what would you have done?" Nonsense stuff, English stuff.

That kind of thing simply wasn't normal to Czechs, wasn't part of the prism through which they viewed the world. She grew frustrated, went inside, and I found her alone, flicking through a photography book, as content as I'd seen her all evening. My frustration dissipated at that moment.

That was love, a moment, one person utterly in love with someone completely unaware of the other. I loved her very much there, with her vulnerability, and her difference.

Relieved as I was to find them talking, I joined the conversation, worried it wouldn't be long before they ran out of things to say.

—Christ, it's hot, I said, sitting down.

The two of them nodded. This was nothing but a matter of fact. I could see them wonder why I'd stated the obvious. British small talk is like Guinness. It doesn't travel well. Not unlike the British, for that matter.

—I noticed you support Hertha?

        —Yes, said Philipp, lighting a neatly rolled cigarette, which I eyed with envy. I'd
finished   my snouts.
        —I go to every game. We are not so good. But not too bad either. We reached the German cup final this season, though we lost.

I nodded, and he asked me if I had a team in England.

—Yes, Tottenham Hotspur.

We'd had some great Germans over the years. Klinsmann. Freund. We'd had two great Germans over the years. I hadn't realised it at the time, but the fact that Klinsmann had played for us was unbelievable. He was still at the top of his game when he came over, or not far off at least. He had won the World Cup.

Freund was a good player in my mind, though others

said he was terrible for us, too one-dimensional, inclined to pass sideways and safely rather than forwards. And he was famous for never scoring, to the extent that fans affectionately screamed *shoot* whenever he got the ball. That was a nice touch, in its own way.

He was a legend for us, even now. There was also strong evidence to suggest he'd simply been a great player in a time of transition, a central midfielder playing at a time when the central midfield position was changing. That was just bad timing.

Christian Ziege was another good German we'd had, with a left foot like a rifle. Lewis Holtby was on the books, and I liked the look of him, though he never got much game time. Philipp smiled and named Kevin Prince-Boateng, who was German-born but now played for Ghana, unlike his brother, who was German-born but much better, and played for Germany. That did nothing to lessen the commitment and pride of Kevin, and I'd hate for it to come across that way.

He'd played for us, briefly.

We'd bought him from Hertha. Me and Philipp talked about that for a while, about how he could be a great player. I said he *was*, but Philipp reiterated, three times, that he could be better. Why he wasn't was unclear, but I inferred that Philipp had a problem with his attitude, and that was the end of that conversation.

Philipp wasn't happy, even though Germany had won 6-1. They'd lost their talisman, Marco Reus, who was stretchered off, and would clearly miss the World Cup. The injury gave us a little more to talk about, but eventually the well dried up and we fell silent again. That's when my eyes fell upon a chessboard on the table I'd heretofore ignored.

—That board's beautiful, I said.

Philipp looked over, flicked some ash into the tray and smiled.

—Yes, he said. —It was my grandmother's. Would you like to play?

I nodded. He unfolded the box. It was extremely old, with hand-carved pieces. He proceeded to set them up, saying I had to be White as the guest. That was letting your guests go first, but a cynic would say it was letting your guest make the first – and mistaken – move. I agreed.

I didn't care less, and was playing only to ensure silence didn't become a constant of our evening, like the Scandinavian

maps east, west, north and south, or Mr Creosote meowing
on the balcony, or the impending doom of two German boys
joining us soon, making an already crowded apartment yet more
crowded. We began to play.

I moved whatever pieces I thought might be smart to
move, as did Philipp, though he had the advantage of knowing
what he was doing.

—Where did you get
the board, I asked after a while. —It's lovely.

—My grandmother had it in Terezin.

That was a concentration camp north of Prague. He glanced at
Jana as he said it, and there was an awkward – more than usual
– silence that was ha-ha funny as fuck to me but probably not to
either of them two.

A German giving out to a Czech for something that
happened in the war. The real hoot was that he had good reason.
I knew they wouldn't see it as ha-ha or funny funny, though, and
kept quiet, with the result that the awkwardness remained.

I hated awkwardness. I loved it on TV, on shows like *The
Office* or *Nathan Barley*. Sometimes a show was so awkward
I'd squirm, even flick the channel, but it was intangible, unreal,
and I loved it, the reason I found it so funny lying in how far it
pushed me from my comfort zone and everything I considered
acceptable and decent and safe. That might seem like another
digression, but it's not, I promise. Here's why.

In real life, awkward situations were among my biggest fears,
perhaps my biggest. The slightest hint of embarrassment or
conflict drove me to despair – an overly confident child talking
loudly among adults, a demanding customer in a shop, anything.

If I saw a group of loud teenagers on a bus I didn't feel
afraid or irritated, just awkward, and would want the world to
open up and swallow me.

As a child, parents' evening had always been the worst.
I was never afraid of my grades or the thought a teacher might
criticise me in front of my mother. The former were usually
good and the latter unlikely.

The only thing I feared was a classmate saying something
to my mum, maybe referencing an embarrassing nickname of
mine (there were plenty) or, worst of all, mentioning a girl I was
rumoured to like (there were plenty). That was unbearable.

As we approached the school gates, my stomach would

tie itself in knots, and I'd feel no relief 'til our car had safely
crossed the junction between my hometown and the borough
in which my school stood, safely away from the other students.
That was fucked up.

The fact that I was relatively good at making conversation
now, therefore, was something of a minor miracle.That had only
taken a decade.

—How do you call this one? I said, holding up
a pawn after moving it two spaces forward.

—Bauer, said Philipp, explaining that it meant 'peasant',
which wasn't so unlike our 'pawn'.

He went on to name all the pieces in German. Jana eased up as
me and Philipp filled the gaps in conversation. It interested me
how the Germans called the pieces.

Where we said knight they just said horse, where we said
pawn they said peasant. I couldn't decide which one was more
real. In place of our bishop they had the more secular runner.

King was könig, but our queen was their lady, which
might have sounded less patronising to German ears.

—Do you speak any Swedish, I asked, moving a pawn
two spaces forward.

I had decided to make that move about thirty seconds
earlier, but wanted Philipp to think I was discerning, and not
resigned to him trouncing me. That was called gilding the lie.
Everyone does it.

—I have been learning Swedish, said Philipp. —But... it
is a very difficult language.

I waited for him to move, though his small eyes didn't
appear to be considering the pieces. It seemed like he was
waiting for me to say something else. He was enjoying the
conversation about Sweden.

—I can imagine, I said, moving my bishop, answering
him at the same time. —Can't be as hard as Czech, though.

—Yes, Czech is very difficult, he said, without
elaboration.

I glanced at Jana, regretting what I'd said immediately. She
didn't show it, but I could tell it had pricked her. Every mention
of my difficulties with Czech pierced her heart, gave her a sense
of the future, knowing that what was a difficulty to me now
would become something much bigger later.

I'd been in Prague nigh on three years, long enough to
understand what it was like to live there, day in, day out. And I
did. I knew what Czech life was, and yet I knew nothing.

I'd been with Jana about eight months, and had met her
parents. Life outside the city, outside our little goldfish bowl,
that was the real Czech life.

And the reality was that I didn't really live in Prague,
but in a pastiche of the city, an anglicised, accommodating
simulacrum of what it really was, a place where people in bars
and clubs served me without ever expecting me to speak a word
of Czech, where I could do my food shopping without opening
my mouth, or buy a bus ticket or groceries in the potraviny shops.

That was not the real Prague.

I felt like telling Philipp about this, to rid him of his childish
obsession. That was important. Sweden will not be what you
think, I wanted to say. You will have to work. The things you feel
and struggle and carry with you each day will follow you there.
It might be better, but it will not be so different from now. But I
didn't tell him. He needed his naïve dream. *That* was vital.

He took my bishop in one desultory move. I was going
to lose. That was fine. Upon moving to Prague, I'd never
experienced that wonder a person gets when they see a city for
the first time. As soon as I arrived I began studying, and working
not long after, the experience intense, getting to grips not just
with the culture but also a profession I was new to, navigating
through errors and embarrassments in order to pay the rent and
be able to look at myself in the mirror. That was half the battle.

You will make fuck-ups, I wanted to tell him. You will
understand why Swedes complain about life when you go to a
state office, or pay for something you think is expensive, which,
for a German in Sweden, will be everything. If you are shy here,
you will be shy there also. Your nationality will mean nothing.
You will be just another foreigner. A man is a man is a man.
Nationality doesn't change that. That, my friend, is the sad truth.

Another rook was taken.

I had moved to Prague because it held no ties. There was
nothing I loved or hated, no memories or disappointments. It
appeared a beautiful place to exist.

And at times that rang true, on mornings when I sat on the
tram on the way to work, thinking it was better than London,

or anywhere for that matter. But there were also days when the harsh realities of life bit.

Waking up at quarter to six, getting the first train to an industrial estate to teach a group of near pension-age state employees far more used to working at ungodly hours, having lived through Communism, when people started early, finished early and worked less, if at all. That was life in Prague.

Philipp beat me, and then again in a rematch, after which I quit playing, much to his disappointment. Chess was his one area of prowess.

I'd noted this early on, the way he played with enthusiasm, well aware there were few who could beat him, well aware he could *shine*. That was important to him, and I was glad to help.

*

I'd bought the Arctic Monkeys tickets on a whim. I was obsessed with them. In an era where indie had become staid and flaccid, when bands couldn't stand for something or had to stand for *everything*, they were one group that didn't seem contrived. They looked and sounded like a rock band. They brought no message, didn't claim to be experts on any social issues, just had great melodies and ethereal, sometimes nonsensical lyrics, but ones that worked. They were old school and, perversely, that was a breath of fresh air. That's what rock and roll was. The Beatles knew that. It didn't matter if the lyrics were nonsense because they fitted. And of course, they were never nonsense to the men writing them. There was no pretence or artifice. I loved that.

For me, this trip was a way of harking back to my teenage years, in London, when all we seemed to do was watch concerts and listen to music, which, naturally, is horseshit.

In the summer after my second year at university, I was excited to be back in London, having not enjoyed the last couple of terms. Keen to make up for lost time, as it were. My friends had spent the previous summer meeting new, cool people from bands, hanging out with them, partying, partying with cool girls, drinking and doing coke or ecstasy, and sometimes weed.

Meanwhile, I'd worked as a porter in a country club in the USA, then as a gardener and, finally, as a clerk in a student bookshop. It should have been better, but I didn't enjoy myself; the solitude, the currency that all looked the same, the refrigerators that were better than what we had at home, but not, because it was not home. I was determined to make up for it.

The solitude and the missing out, that is. I could live with the refrigerators.

But that following summer no one had any money and we only met once a week at most. It was great when we did, but the summer I'd envisaged, of endless days of rock and roll and three-day weekends without sleep, never came to fruition. That was a lesson in reality, but also in painting yourself a picture that was either utterly untrue or true in only parts.

Even still, there had been great times; this trip seemed a fine way to remember that, to show Jana who I was and where I was from. What spurred me into buying the tickets, however, wasn't avid fandom but jealousy; photos on Facebook of friends at the Arctic Monkeys' gigs in Hyde Park which caused a fit of nostomania to grip me like a vice. I bought the tickets, telling myself it would be a nice trip. And it would, but somewhere underneath, I was compensating for the nascent sense of homesickness welling inside me.

Philipp had gone to his room to take a call from the two German boys. I looked at his maps again. I was afraid. Not because he was odd, but because he was familiar, an amplification of myself, a megaphone version of the man I'd been, maybe still was.

I'd never put pins in maps, but I'd sought my escape nonetheless, in cities, just as now I was seeking refuge from my dissatisfaction in Prague, away from it all – the fear that I could not stay, the pain I felt at the idea of losing Jana, the dead-end job I'd deadheaded myself into.

My line to people was that I'd left London because there was no work, but that's all it was – a line. I'd have found work through patience. I'd no mouths to feed, not even my own, and could have lived under my mother's roof as long as I needed. But it was easier to blame the government and romanticise unemployment than just stick it out. No matter what I told myself, I *had* run from London these last three years.

That was the ugly truth.

Prague was an opportunity to work, but there was always *work* for people like me – qualified, trustworthy, pliant people. Prague was a different world.

The things men would give for a different world.

It didn't turn out to be that different. That was okay, though. I knew that now.

People worked, struggled and got by. That was the same everywhere. But it was different enough and, most importantly, it was where I'd met Jana. Life changed. I wasn't lonely the way

I'd been. I wasn't depressed, or not so much as before.

I even ignored Fluoxetine and Citalopram these days, no matter the looks they sent my way.

I'd not been in therapy since before Prague, and upon my arrival I considered myself fixed. That was naïve. Kind of ha-ha funny if you think about just how naïve that was. Kind of not if you're me. Ha-ha.

I made mistakes after coming to Prague. I carried on partying, which would have been fine if I'd just gone about it in a different way. I hooked up with the short, blonde, pretty Republican girl, who loved me, but who I didn't love back – yet needed for comfort all the same. I should have just pushed her away. Maybe. After she left, I met and fell for a Czech woman who was sweet on me, introduced me to her dad after only a week, then chucked me after three or four more. I figured that was punishment for screwing the American girl around. That was topsy-turvy.

I became lonely again, smoked and drank more, before putting a lid on it. I started exercising and became healthier, yet remained lonely. Then I met Jana, and the loneliness evaporated.

That was dangerous.

We became dependent on one another. It was wonderful. I was in love, but lived in fear. What about the future? How could I provide? I wanted to have a family, I knew that. It was one thing to work twenty-five hours a week for yourself, to hold dreams of writing or travel. It was quite another to *provide*.

Could I do another job? There weren't many for people who didn't speak Czech, and mine was poor, very poor still after three years. I beat myself up over it. I should have been better. I didn't know what to do.

Berlin was more than a concert. It was a litmus test. Maybe, just maybe, if we both loved it, we'd find a middle ground for the two of us. Maybe. Perhaps I wasn't homesick, just sick of Prague, or not Prague, but the life I had there, the job, the seemingly insurmountable difficulties with the language. I just needed to be somewhere else – over *there*.

I was in danger of repeating the mistakes of my early twenties, but, well, mistakes are there to be made. That much is true. I wanted Jana. That was all that mattered.

*

The German boys arrived. Me and Jana said hello, then went to get some food. We ended up choosing a kebab takeaway.

78

We were too hungry to wait, and, after all, kebabs were now as
German as bratwurst or sauerkraut.

—Would you like a cigarette, I asked, as we
made our way back to Philipp's.
—No, I don't want to smoke anymore.

I couldn't tell if she meant over the weekend, or just
tonight. Either way, it was true we'd both smoked plenty, far too
much after months of relative abstinence.

—Me neither, I said, though I did. I really wanted another
one.

I put the pack back in my pocket. We returned to the flat.
The Germans were, as you might expect, speaking
German. That was more than fair enough. They said hello when
they saw us, and tried to be inclusive, but naturally slipped
back into German, which we didn't mind. Neither of us felt like
talking. I wanted to be alone with my thoughts, to go to bed
and hold Jana, and fear for us. I wanted to think even though it
would hurt, to lie awake thinking. It was normal for me. I can
spend a whole day ignoring the great worries of my life, only
for them to attack me as I try to sleep. That's called the tortoise
catching up with the hare.
However, for a change, I knew I would be with my
thoughts that night, and wanted to be.

—I am tired, said Jana.
—Me too.

—I
don't really want to go out again. Is that
okay?

She looked at me as if I'd be disappointed. I'd told Philipp
we would join them, hoping the whole time we wouldn't. Jana
thought of me as the social one. But I wanted to be alone with
her, to sleep, to rest.

—Yes, I said. —Yes, of course.

It was gone midnight already and I was tired after the heat and
the journey and the nagging thought inside me that it might
not be Prague that was wrong, or Berlin, but something within

myself, something that caused me to run in every time of crisis.

Despite this, I drifted off quickly that evening, which was odd, but woke several times in the night, as the inflatable airbed kept removing one half of its description.

Eventually, we gave up, accepting it couldn't be blown up to full. Pathetically, I enjoyed this supplementary prick to the grandiose world of couchsurfing. I thought of the hotel or hostel that Jana had insisted we not go to, thought of the comfortable – or at least flat – bedding, and the lack of two German boys at the foot of our bed. I slept peacefully after that.

*

The concert itself went well. The extreme temperatures caused a power failure midway through 'Arabella', and the band walked offstage. For a brief period it seemed like that was it. Only three songs. What a joke.

That was not funny in any sense of the word.

But they returned, and took up where they had left off. This wasn't something I usually liked. If I was walking somewhere while listening to music and had to stop, I couldn't restart the song afterwards; the incompleteness jarred too readily with me and I had to skip to the next track, or pick another altogether.

But here, it seemed fitting that they pick up where they left off, that they move forward rather than go back to the start, as I sometimes did with songs interrupted too.

Maybe it was the fact that they had been interrupted by the elements, or the theatre of it, the four of them returning to the stage, crashing into electric guitars and drums from the very note when the heat had stymied them. Somehow, it worked.

Jana swayed from side to side, holding my hands over her shoulders. She didn't recognise the songs but enjoyed herself nonetheless, enjoyed the way I stared at the group in adoration. That was a nice moment then and that's a nice memory now.

When the concert was over we shuffled towards the exit of the venue, an ancient citadel which had been converted into a beautiful space for music and other events. I liked that. You didn't get that in London. The beer was more expensive than elsewhere in Berlin but not extortionate. You didn't get that in London either. Or Sweden, for that matter.

*

In Philipp's communist-era flat that summer, I would never have

80

predicted that a year later I'd be in western Ireland, under such different circumstances. But that's where I was. That's where we were, holidaying. I had lived in Prague for three and a half years. It would have been four and a half now, if I hadn't moved back to Britain in December 2014. But that's where we were.

It'd rained off and on all day, but now, at four-thirty, it was bright and sunny in my father's hometown. Out in the open, it was warm, but as we walked down Main Street I felt a chill, with the buildings hiding the sun from us. It was thirteen years since I'd been home. I scanned the town for things both familiar and unfamiliar – shops, restaurants, pubs. There were more restaurants than before. I couldn't remember eating in one here as a child, but they were ubiquitous now.

The town's coastal location made it a tourist hotspot, but it was a destination for big travel groups passing through to either Cork or further north to Killarney. The town was quieter than I remembered. We walked down the street, hand in hand. Yes, I'd moved home just months after Berlin, but still, we'd made it this far. I'd found a job, moved into a flat, but we were still making it. There was hope.

I'd wanted to make this trip ever since going home, to show her where my father was from. It had been too many years, and now Jana was with me. That was good. But of course, it wasn't the same town I'd enjoyed as a child. It was smaller than I remembered. Then again, I was bigger, so in a very minute sense, it was literally smaller than before. Still, incremental human growth aside, it was possible to walk from one end to the other in about fifteen minutes. The far end of town had been forbidden to me as a child, the limits of my freedom demarcated to Peggy's sweet shop, which I now realised was less than two minutes' walk from my grandmother's house.

The fact that I hadn't been allowed to go further made the town seem vast, the petrol station and bank and church at the top of town a mystery. Now, however, they were just part of the same tiny Irish town.

Many of the buildings were rundown, with paint peeling off the window ledges and walls, dust in the windows and For Sale signs, which were doubtlessly ignored and had been for some time. From my count, around a third of the houses were unoccupied, particularly those near my grandmother's place.

We had sold the house not long after her death in 1998, but here it was, falling apart. The Gaelic pitch was still opposite the house my father had grown up in, but an estate had been built next to it. It was rough, we were told. The Garda were always called down to deal with trouble.

We were told that too.

I tried to open the door to the house. It was in such a poor state I figured the owners might have left it open. But it was locked. We crossed the street and turned left.

—Let's have a look in here, I said, pointing towards a pottery shop.

It was Anton's. It'd always been there. Perhaps he'd remember me. We went in and looked around a few moments before he emerged from his backroom.

—Hello, can I help you?

—No, I said. —We're just looking.

I nodded towards my grandmother's house.
—My grandmother used to live in that house.

He said nothing for a moment, and appeared uninterested. But his features shifted suddenly.

—Who?
—Brede Sullivan, I said.

That brought a flicker of recognition. He had known her well. A sign for his shop was still attached to the side of her house. That was called free advertising. But as the look of recognition came upon his face, I realised he probably hadn't thought of her much in the years since she'd died.

I realised there were people I had hoped would have thought of me over the years who hadn't, much like there may have been people who had hoped I'd have thought of them, but I also hadn't.

He asked me how long it had been and I told him it was nearly twenty years, rounding up slightly. He said that sounded about right.

—It's very different here now, I said.

He shook his head.
—It is empty. All the young people are moving away. There is no work, he said, extending his hands for

emphasis.
—No one wants to be a farmer
anymore. All the young people are going to Dublin or
Cork. Or abroad.

He looked down the street, as if looking for those errant
young people.

—It's very quiet here now, he said. —I get a few
good months in the summer, when the tourists come in.
But between September and May, it is a dull place.

His accent, still distinctly German, was occasionally
pockmarked with a strange Irish inflection. He'd been here for
more than thirty years. I introduced Jana. She told him she was
Czech.

—Do you live in London? he asked her.
—No, she said with a sad coyness.
—We're just on holiday, I said, hoping he'd put a sock in
it.

He ignored me and went on.

—It is not easy to live in another
country.

I let it hang in the air. The sock knew no putting.

—When I was with my wife it was okay, he
said. —But now, I am just a foreigner. The Irish are
strange like that. You can get to know them, but they
are never friends. You are always an outsider.

He picked up a piece of hardened clay, turning it in his
hands.

—Do you ever think of returning to Germany? I asked.

He looked up.

—Sure, he said, again with a slightly Irish
inflection. —What would I do?
He gave a desultory laugh.
—There's nothing for me

there.

He nodded towards the quiet town, which we were on the fringes of now.

—No, I'm here now. I get by.

I looked over at Jana, thinking thinking thinking of something to say.

—If we are going to go on this bike ride, we should go.

—You are riding bikes? asked Anton.

Glad to discuss something other than international relations, I looked back. The football pitch sat behind his work desk, a constant reminder of the local game, the local way, the insurmountable difference.

—Yes, we're thinking of riding out to Valentia, I said.

—I'd like to show Jana the island.

Anton pointed down the street, in the other direction.

—Go to Carroll's. He'll rent you bikes. It's about fifteen, sixteen euros, not too bad.

—Okay, I said. —Thank you. Good to see you.

He talked to us a few more moments, perhaps clinging to our company, which he'd initially seemed disinclined to put up with. We walked towards Carroll's to get our bikes.

—Anton's crazy, I said.

Jana had been quiet for too long. That was not good. She nodded thoughtfully. It was, after all, no kind of explanation on my part. The sooner we got the bikes, the better.

I walked into Carroll's shop and paid him the thirty-two euros, electing not to take helmets. That was maverick of me, but also a reflection of the fact that I had a rather large head.

We began to cycle out of the town, towards the island. I

cycled ahead of Jana, despite her being a far more competent cyclist. I looked out towards the bay, where we would be in about twenty minutes, my hopes that we would both fall in love with the southwest dashed. Deep down, I'd always known, but still. That's funny. Hope was hope. Hope for compromise, hope for a place we *could*, even if we couldn't.

It was a calm day, but there was always a light wind in South Kerry, that and the perpetual threat of rain, somewhere along the line. We cycled up over the hill and down towards the port. The ferry was close to arriving, just a few more minutes, I reckoned.

Jana kept telling me how beautiful it all was, and took pictures of the scenery, balancing her phone on the handlebars of her bike. I watched her, then looked over towards the island, hoping to enjoy our trip, as I had enjoyed trips here as a child.

—It is so beautiful, Opičko, she said, struggling to keep her phone safe on the handlebars.

I was looking forward to showing her the scenery and the semi-tropical gardens and the beach, to watching the Gaelic football in a pub and maybe dropping in on my cousin too. I was looking forward to walking through the verdant farmland for an afternoon.

—Yes, it is.

The waves roiled louder and louder as the ferry approached.

—Come on, Jana, we're getting on. It's even more beautiful on the island. Let's get going.

She smiled. The boat wouldn't be here for another thirty seconds or so. That she knew.

—One more, she said, turning the camera towards the mountains in the far distance.

I looked over to where I figured she had the camera pointed, somewhere in the direction of Cappawee, towards the green drumlins and the cottages and, behind them, the mountains that poked up into the sky with their brown, rocky hilltops.

—All right, I said. —One more.

RAINBOWS AND BOTTLETOPS

I was surprised by the buzzer. That was no surprise.

It was a short, shrill sound that made me jump whenever someone came to the door. I was in the kitchen preparing breakfast. I walked to the door, opened it and saw an outstretched hand. The postman gave me a package, turned and walked out of the gate without saying a word. The package was tiny, though too big to fit through the letterbox.

Back inside, I finished preparing breakfast.

I'd gone back and forth in my mind over whether to make something special – the previous week I'd had black pudding and potato patties with eggs – or settle for something dull and efficient. I went for the latter, as I'd much work to do. It was Saturday, a whole day free to write. I never wrote for hours on end, though I'd made my peace with that. It seemed like the writers I loved wrote 'til their fingers bled. I was never going to be a writer, not now. I was too old, and incapable of sitting still for long periods of time, or concentrating on one thing for hours. I had a full-time job, and aside from weekends could only write in the evenings. I was no night owl. That was a shame. By ten o'clock I was always tired, a habit that began not long after I left university and started work. Instead of focusing on the merits and weaknesses of my writing, I had homed in on this, blaming it for my lack of output.

One book in nearly four years, one unpublished, unpublishable book. That was poor going.

But I didn't think that way anymore.

There were writers who did what I did, writing in short bursts, letting it all out without forcing the issue.

Forcing the issue was a mistake I'd made before, when I wasn't always fit to write, yet felt compelled to.

Not writing didn't make me feel guilty these days, unless it was due to drink. If work stressed me out, I rested. That was important. Jana had taught me that. That was a lifetime ago, even if it was technically just a month ago, and even then, only *technically*, and from afar.

It was mid-October now, only a couple of months following what ultimately became *Sweden*. I lived in South London now, not temporarily, or with designs and dreams of it being temporary, but as a state of being and fact. Prague was off the table. Prague was gone, except in my every waking thought. Jana and I had broken up in mid-September, nearly a year after I'd left in the winter of 2014. It was she who ended it, knowing I couldn't. That was that.

I tried not to think about it too much.

That didn't last, but it seemed to work for a while. On

this particular weekend, at least, I wanted to write as much as I could, to throw myself into writing. I had a dull breakfast of eggs (boiled) and supermarket bread. Up in my room, I opened the package, ordered off eBay a week before, a Dosette tray with seven coloured boxes, one for each day of the week.

There were four compartments to each: Breakfast, Lunch, Dinner and Bedtime. I only needed one. I'd been having trouble remembering whether or not I'd taken my pills. I was getting forgetful and hoped the Dosette trays might help. That was organised. The question as to whether they did anything, good or bad, remained a question.

I walked over to my dresser and picked up one of the packets that lay there, unorganised and chaotic. It sat beside a flyer for a two-for-one on cocktails at The Brown Derby which I'd picked up but never used, even though I'd often thought about visiting that pub, near Oval Station, ever since moving into the area. It hadn't felt right to visit a cocktail bar while me and Jana were together, though I wasn't sure why. Beside the flyer was a prescription I'd not picked up, and a letter from Santander Bank that I'd opened but not read, with the now corrugated and unevenly torn envelope beside it. It was very still in the room, but everything about it was an untidy vignette of the man renting it. Dormant chaos.

The room was a shoebox, a metre and a half wide and not much more long, the shelves above the bed full of items in no particular order: books, files, medicaments, old plugs, wristbands and cards, some flat, others standing. The dresser was untidy. The clothes inside were folded, except for some socks strewn hither and thither. The dresser top was a mix of cables from various appliances, a bottle of sake (unopened) and a stuffed toy I'd picked up on my travels.

The floor was evidence of both my vices and ambitions.

Below my feet lay the yoga mat I'd bought a month or two earlier. I'd taken up yoga to improve back problems that had plagued me since my early twenties. That's what I told myself, at least. In all honesty, I just needed something on a Monday night that wasn't hitting the pub first thing after work, something to put me in good stead for the coming week, a healthy distraction. My plan had been to do yoga at home two or three times a week, in addition to the class I was attending.

That was me there, a maker of far-flung, overly ambitious plans that spoke volumes of my manic tendencies, tendencies I'd got some hold over now but which had consumed me for years.

I was forever in a rush, always regretting the doing or not

doing of something, be it due to the night before or just plain
inertia. My mind fretted over action and inaction. No, I wasn't
calm these days, but I was calmer about time. Sometimes, at
least. I didn't worry about goals or self-imposed deadlines as
I had when I'd been a teacher, unhappy in my work, stuck in
a hamster wheel, desperate for someone to put a metal pole
through the spokes, for better or worse.

Beside the yoga mat were two empty beer bottles I'd
drained the previous night, which would have been fine had they
not been supplemented earlier by four beers with a friend, after
which more felt a necessity.

That was foolish. It'd screwed up my sleep pattern,
and now I felt regret, which was a problem, for regret always
stopped me making hay with my plans. I had no off switch. That
was my biggest problem.

When I drank, I always had my eyes focused on the
next beer, even when I had a full one in my hand, the desire
for oblivion greater than the awareness of all that it entailed.
Alcohol was beautiful, and beautifully destructive, in that way.

Things were simple when I was drinking, electric even.

Everything was better under its spell: depression, solitude,
company, weddings, funerals, Monday nights, Saturday
evenings, lazy afternoons and airport mornings. Hell, even
watching a film alone with sadness and defeat was better than
doing it with only the sadness and defeat for company.

And, of course, there was the drunken writer thing.
Though I knew the best drank spirits on ice, and had probably
been writing several hours before they started pouring out
measures, I still embraced it, despite sticking to beer.

Booze cast a pall over everything, but at the time it felt
like a blanket.

I looked out the window. There was a local madman
shouting at a shopping trolley, the kind of sight Londoners from
the home counties created listicles to celebrate the city's diverse
madness. To me, it just appeared sad.

In my own manic fashion, I suddenly realised I'd
forgotten to put wax in my hair. I put the pills and trays to one
side and went to the bathroom. My cheeks were puffy, the two-
day stubble blonde in its shortness. My eyes were a little red,
though I'd slept a long time. I felt my hair. It was getting longer,
wiry in a way I never liked. I hadn't let it dry completely, so
the wax was easier to put in, though I knew that in four or five
hours, it would be unkempt again. That was hair.

Back in my room, I started putting the pills into trays, from

Sunday to Saturday. It amused me, the way the week ran in a
Christian fashion. To me, that was ha-ha funny.

After finishing I took a pill from the pack rather than a
tray. The Christian calendar thing would start from tomorrow.
I swallowed it with some water, then put my laptop in my
bag, along with my phone charger, a book, my diary and some
materials for writing an article I needed to get done within the
next few weeks; a write-up of a trip I'd taken to the Middle East
just after things had ended between me and Jana. That was good
timing.

*

I'd written a draft of the article and now it was just a case of
cutting it down. I always wrote too much. It was the only way
I knew how to write, in frenzied, discordant streams, words
flowing freely, though often without beauty, cohesion or sense.
They might be good or bad, but they would be whatever came
from me at the time. It was often shit, but it was never contrived
or forced, and that in itself felt good, much better than before.
There was no feeling as bad as trying to write and being
incapable. When that happened, I felt like a fool who'd kidded
himself. That was unpleasant.
There was a lot to read over. Going through swathes
of text meant a lot of rereading of pieces which often left me
appalled, not for the quality that was there, but for the quality
I'd assigned it first time around. But that was okay. It was all
part of the process.
I saw that now.
I'd never written a travel feature before, and knew I would
overwrite. There were around five hundred words to cut, yet
more to improve. I didn't know how I was able to put so much
information – five days of Emirati goodness, in this case – on
the page, to write so quickly, while at the same time being the
complete opposite in day-to-day life: a tight-lipped man of few
words, stymied, unable to voice his thoughts. In my mind, I
always had something to say. Whether it was a joke, a come-
on or a putdown, I had the words, or so I thought. They rarely
left my mouth, though sometimes they came out through the
keyboard.
It was all so much simpler on the page.

*

The first café I went to was on the Camberwell Road. It was nine months since I'd left Prague, where I'd been that teacher, that naïve writer who sat in cafés wringing himself dry, trying to force out words that just weren't there, words that weren't even thoughts yet and would never be of use.

It was true, I missed the city, missed writing in the cafés, though when I thought about it with clarity I'd spent most of my time in the same one, over and over, a bustling little boho place at the bottom of my street, with faux-antique furniture and pretty barmaids — Kaaba, naturally.

The beer was fantastic. That's not quite right. The beer was okay, it was just different from the beer served elsewhere. They had Žatec and they had Hoegaarden. The spirits, for what it's worth, were also said to be good, though I never drank spirits.

The coffee wasn't bad.

Kaaba was my writing haunt, and *we'd* met there, but I remember it best in a rose-tinted, nostalgic way for being the place I drank with Brad. We'd sit there hours, drinking beers quickly (the only thing at which we were equals), talking about everything or nothing with the same level of fervour. Sometimes he'd talk about American politics (he didn't know much of ours), mostly the impending revolution. He was vague about what that would constitute or how it would happen, but he was certain we were approaching boiling point.

It turned out he was right, but not the way he wanted, and fundamentally, not how either of us could have wanted or dreamed for. That's often the way with revolutions.

Other times we talked about women. I'd recount my coy, drawn-out, piss-poor attempts to talk to receptionists in the companies where I taught, which amused him highly. He would discuss his sexual exploits – in depth – whether they were with girlfriends or the women he needed so as not to be alone after relationships crashed and so readily burned. I would protest that I didn't want to hear his stories, though I did. For one reason or another, the dynamic worked, and I was always glad when he walked into the café to distract me from writing, or thinking.

He was always short on money, and so I would usually pick up the tab. It frustrated me at the time, but now, a lifetime away, I missed it, his endless monologues about philosophy or sex interspersed with me occasionally trying to explain an English comedy and why it was so funny, something that never worked. I missed the lonely winter nights writing in Kaaba when Brad wasn't around, just as I missed the cheap, clean, plentiful beer. Thinking back on it hard, I know this wasn't the sum of my time there; that these pockets of hours in the evenings or the night were just a part of what Prague was to me, mere moments compared to the hours I spent trudging around the city between monochrome office business rooms, talking to disinterested students and waiting in office lobbies, or wandering the city aimlessly at weekends when my friends weren't around and I'd exhausted my interest in television box sets or video games or refreshing Facebook in hope of news from home. I know that Kaaba and all it entailed wasn't *Prague*.

But the mind holds on to what is fondest, forgetting that which is dull or breaks the heart.
Still, those nights with Brad, so sadly gone now.

Here, in London, there were endless cafés to choose from, but none quite like Kaaba.
None had Jana. None had Brad. None were Prague, where I'd lived young, and felt it. A moveable feast.
Nowadays I think anywhere is a moveable feast if you're there young enough. Except maybe Buckinghamshire.

*

After walking around Camberwell for roughly thirty minutes, I found a café to write in: an old, converted tailors with a tiny bar and just two tables.
There were more outside, but although it was mild, it wasn't warm, so I sat indoors, taking a seat at the window and watching a young family outside with a baby in a pram.
I ordered tea – rare for me – and set to work cutting the article. Should I remove the allegory about my teenage years, where I made fun of my non-existent romantic life? It showed character, an ability on the part of the writer to display weakness, bridging the gap between the unseen writer and merciless reader.
But I was unsure. Maybe it didn't fit. There were other parts of the story I felt could be cut, like the paragraph I'd written about the cultural centre, to which I'd been indifferent. Our hosts had pressed us to include it in the copy, but it had been boring, a preview of an art museum that was set to open in two years, an exhibition of exhibitions to come, if you will. That didn't seem worthy of inclusion. I didn't know what to do, but figured I would figure it out. That seemed the best course of action.
I sipped my tea.

It was a good morning, sitting in a Camberwell café, trying to decide between two strands of the same tale, doing the thing I loved and so often failed to do: writing.

There was a semblance of calm in me.

I decided to leave both parts in for now, wrote on for forty-five minutes, then decided to leave, the smallness of the café getting to me, just like the slamming of the door with every customer who came or went.

I left, turned right, and in the meantime looked up another café online. I walked down an unfamiliar street and got lost, but it was okay. I'd no plan as such. That was good.

Eventually, I reached the Peckham Road and found the café. It was busy, but there was extra seating in the back beside a gallery, which belonged to the café. That was convenient. I took a seat, and was wondering whether my cheeks still looked puffy or if my T-shirt, Zippy from Rainbow, made me looked childish, something which didn't bother me day to day, but did now that I was alone, conspicuously so. After a couple of minutes, a waitress asked me to move so she could make space for a group of four.

I took up a seat in the middle of the room, surrounded by others, most of them small groups rather than the solitary, and began to write after ordering a latte. The story was finding shape.

I was down to just over fifteen hundred words now, and the latte tasted good. It was at least two and a half, maybe three hours since my last coffee, and I felt better with the taste of caffeine and milk in my mouth, though I hoped I wouldn't get a moustache of froth on my upper lip, for fear that I would look truly childish. After a while, the people around me became more noticeable, the groups of friends, the families with prams and young children. I began to feel anxious, and questioned whether I had taken my pill in the morning, before remembering that after looking at the madman in the street, I had.

Nevertheless, I became angry with the noise, and the people, all around. I didn't like this about myself, that indignant, righteous feeling I got when people were simply making noise, enjoying their mornings and the company of others. Cafés were for work, I would think to myself in such moments. Even unvoiced, it sounded vapid and self-righteous. I told myself not to mind the people around me, but it was no good. I did.

I couldn't concentrate, even with the headphones on and the music relatively loud, though not so loud that others would hear it and I would feel selfish and concerned that perhaps it was me who was the distraction. After a short while, and some more editing, I paid and left, walking towards another café. It'd started to rain. When I got to the café, just off the Camberwell Road (but further down than the first place) I noticed, to my disappointment, that it was completely packed.

While walking back up the street in search of another cafe, I realised I was hungry, and instead went home. It was grey and morbid inside the flat when I arrived, so I turned the light on. There was an unpleasant stillness and quiet in the room, and although I'd not been upstairs yet, it was clear the house was empty.

There was a thick pile of unopened letters belonging to housemates past and present – it was a transient apartment – which gave me pause for thought. Perhaps I was no more chaotic than the rest of them, I thought. There was also a stack of takeaway menus; reams and reams of glossy fast food, the contents destined to go unread and at best thrown into the recycling bin. I looked at the tree in the back garden, its pendulous branches overhanging the now thick tussocks of grass which our landlord had said he was going to come around and cut, but probably wouldn't now – or shouldn't – until the weather was better.

I started making lunch – pasta, with tuna. As the pasta boiled and the tomato sauce bubbled, I turned the telly on. The Rugby World Cup final was on. I didn't like rugby, but it was a cultural event of sorts and silence-filling noise. If I turned the sound off, I wondered, maybe I'd hear cheering in the adjacent apartments when tries were scored and points kicked. But I doubted it. Though many Kiwis and Australians lived in the area, they were now huddled together in bars in town, screaming and shouting, though mostly at the screen. It was a shame and a farce that we thought ourselves more reserved and mild-mannered, when we could never do the same with class, panache or pleasure.

There was a shop just ten yards from my flat, and it occurred to me that I could get a beer, relax, watch the rugby and attempt to figure out the rules of the game, which had baffled but not overly interested me for life. I decided against it, firstly because I did not care about the rules of rugby and it was more interesting to watch it without understanding (like *Game of Thrones*), secondly because that kind of drinking was a slippery slope to the kind of drinking that stopped me getting up, assembling my rainbow-coloured Dosette trays and walking to cafés to do work. It was drinking less for pleasure, more as a vain and futile attack on loneliness.

There'd been a time in Prague when I kept a lid on that kind of drinking, but in doing so had needed to shut myself

away, under lock and key. I wrote more than ever with relentless
routine, a routine that near-destroyed me, and my sanity, as
much as any liquid brutality could.

I went months without seeing friends, except maybe on a
Sunday afternoon, when I'd watch Tottenham with my friend Dan.

Yes, I wrote a lot, but at what cost? Only the routine of
the week kept me sane: scrambling around the city to ensure I
arrived to each lesson on time with all the materials I needed,
chasing gaps in the working hours in which I could write or
reading my books on the trams and trains of Prague. It seemed
better now, not to be so harsh on myself, to choose my routines
wisely too.

Cooking lunch took longer than expected, and afterwards
I couldn't decide between the café near my house or somewhere
further afield. I opted for the latter. If I went somewhere near
the apartment I would doubtless buy and drink a coffee quickly,
then maybe another, and then that would be enough for one day.
If I wanted to stay and work, I'd buy a beer. I never bought juice
in cafés. That was string at silk prices.

So I made my way to Shoreditch, walking to the station
and jumping on a train to Old Street. The rain was really
heavy now. It was only a fifteen-minute journey, easy. I read
Knausgaard, whose work I was enjoying a great deal at the time
and had since around January, when I'd first come across his
handsome Nordic features in a feature in *The Observer*. I'd read
two of his books since, and was halfway through the third in the
My Struggle series. They read like my own life, even though
they were not similar at all. He had a way with words. And he
was honest, matter-of-fact. Not purposefully witty, but open and
characterised by candour; unafraid to look the fool if it meant
being truthful, not afraid to appear selfish if it was the way it had
been. Human.

When I got to Old Street, it didn't take me long to get lost, that
big, awful roundabout taking advantage of my piss-poor sense of
direction as it had for the last decade. No matter how many times
I looked up where to go, I took the wrong exit, bringing me back
to square – or perhaps circle – one. That was Old Street.

After walking past a hipster café and a cocktail bar and an
Asian restaurant, I turned back on myself and eventually found
my way out. I walked to a café with bikes in the windows and
a bike shop in the back. It was nearly four in the afternoon and
I'd not written as much as intended. I certainly hadn't finished
the article, but it was getting there. I ordered a coffee and got
to work. It was muggy in the café. Although it was October, it

was still quite warm and the combination of the heat and the unremitting rain made the windows fog up. I began to sweat.

If writing came to me hard, sweating was easy. I could do it in any environment: rain, shine, snow. No matter the weather, I always found a way. It caused me all sorts of problems, as it meant turning up to both social and work situations with beads (at least) of sweat dotted on my forehead and patches under my arms, making me look physically unpleasant or mentally ill at ease.

That's an unfortunate turn of phrase.

My body betrayed me at every turn, but then again, it was fair to say that over the years, I'd betrayed it too. That's only fair to concede.

I worked for another hour, sitting on an uncomfortable stool 'til I could take it no longer.

I had haemorrhoids. That was unfortunate.

A doctor in Prague had given me cream and a pamphlet, neither of which did much use. I used the cream but not the pamphlet, which had recommended the abstinence of coffee and alcohol and hot baths. I never took hot baths and didn't start. That was something. We didn't have one. That helped. I didn't cut out alcohol and coffee. That would have been too big a lifestyle change.

Anyway, after an hour or so I got up, paid and left the bicycle baristas to their coffees and their bikes. By the time I got back to Oval it was nearly quarter to six, so I went to my favourite café, where I had two small bottles of beer and wrote about fifteen hundred words of fiction.

I knew writing and drinking didn't mix, always had. That was so-so, verging on that's a pity. Alcohol never made the words better, no matter what people thought. But when they talked about drinking and writing, they meant heavy stuff, session drinking, Orwell in a stupor, Fleming with his gin, Hemingway mainlining Listerine because he'd run out of whatever he'd had to hand to begin with -that kind of drinking.

A couple of beers weren't going to cloud my thoughts any more than the average day. I wrote, and the words came freely, until they didn't come freely, at which point I decided to stop working.

On my way home the two-drink itch hit me. I'd done well this day to stay calm, not given in 'til the evening, and then that was just relaxing, normal. I hadn't thought too much about the now insuperable gap between myself and Jana, and myself and Prague, that could no longer be bridged. Although it had been that way for some time, our still being together (if apart, also) had given me hope, but also a delusion, like all my others, which

I so desperately needed to get by.

For a day at least, I'd not thought too much about that, nor had I given in to reckless abandon. But while it was possible to write well on a couple of beers, there was always a danger of the switch, which ignored the creeping doubt, the voice contradicting that other, often more powerful voice that said, one more won't do any harm. It was often right, but it didn't understand accumulation either, how two more tonight built into two more tomorrow and then gradually, one Saturday, to the flicking of the switch earlier and earlier, 'til I drank as if in fine company, for the very reason that I *wasn't*.

That was sad.

I resisted, went home, cooked dinner, watched a film and went to bed. In the morning, I took out the pink tray from the Dosette box, Sunday's tray, took the tablet and went about my day with a plan to write as much as possible before going to the cinema. *Skyfall* was out. It was all the rage. That was exciting.

My plans to write often meant good films passed me by, which was no good, no good at all.

I went to my favourite café for coffee and cake, wrote a little, went home and exercised a little there. That was productive. Around lunchtime, I left the house and went to the cinema in Peckham to watch the film. I enjoyed it. The old, chewing-gum and perhaps bodily fluid covered seats in the Peckham Plex prodded into my backside, and the rustling of popcorn and sweets and slurping of coke were ever present. But so were the sounds of explosions and the shouting of psychotic British spies and foreign villains occasionally interspersed with the disjointing equanimity of Dame Judy Dench. I enjoyed the film.

On the way home I stopped in at a bar in Camberwell and wrote fifteen hundred words, before heading to another pub, where I wrote another five hundred. I stopped in for one more on the way home.

It was Sunday. That wasn't a ruination of the plan.

After starting to write I gave up quickly, knowing that the combination of a light lunch and a few drinks wasn't a combination conducive to good writing. That was a slight alteration of the plan, so I read instead, and that was fine.

I was about a hundred pages from finishing the third book in Knausgaard's *My Struggle* series, which I'd been reading for some time. I went home, cooked a simple dinner of pasta with vegetables, watched television and went to bed.

In the morning I took out the green tray, Monday's tray. I took

the tablet and went to work, fresh. It went well. In the evening,
I went to yoga. It still seemed ridiculous to me, and I think I
seemed ridiculous to the lithe, flexible group of men and women
who followed the instructor in stretch and cantillation and
positivity in a way I struggled to emulate.

The rest of that week was okay, though I went out
Tuesday, Wednesday and Thursday. On Tuesday and Wednesday,
I met friends for drinks. We had only two or three, so it wasn't
so bad, but on Thursday, I had a stressful day at work. On my
way home, I bought an eight-pound bottle of wine and had it
with homemade risotto. It was justified because of work, and
because the wine was good and the risotto was good.

On Friday I woke up feeling fine and went to the gym.
I went to work afterwards and covertly took out Friday's tray
(blue), which I'd put into my bag. That was smart. I didn't want
anyone to know about my depression, although of course I did,
really. I wanted the world to know, to give sense and meaning
to it all, whatever that meant. If someone found out I was a
depressive, I would want to have the earth open up and swallow
me, but I would also be glad another person had seen into the
window of my soul, whatever that meant.

Hell, I just wanted to be interesting, really, or understood.

I never gave off the slightest hint of mental torment. I
wanted people to know, I wanted no one to know. That's the way
it was.

During the morning, I drank lots of water and coffee, and
the day passed and was less stressful than Thursday. At five-
thirty, my colleagues said they were going for drinks. I joined,
drinking faster than the others but not so fast, and remained
there for four or five pints, leaving in a good mood because it
was Friday night, I wasn't going out, and knew the weekend
wasn't going to be ruined.

On the way home I stopped in at a wine shop. I'd decided to
have fish and chips. I wanted red wine. The guy behind the counter
recommended white with fish, but I wanted red, as that had been the
plan, albeit one recently formed. Red was good of an evening.

Back home, I decided against the fish and chips after all
and instead ate cold, leftover risotto. I began watching a film and
had two glasses, before slowly drinking the rest of the bottle. It
was good wine, which had cost me around ten pounds.

In the morning I woke up dry-mouthed. But it was nine
in the morning. It wasn't like I'd ruined my weekend, and some
water sorted me out. I took Saturday's tray (red) and the pill and
made a breakfast before realising that I *was* a little groggy after
all. A couple of hours later, I texted a friend and asked what he

was up to. He said nothing, asked if I wanted a pint. I said yes. We met in London and chatted all day and drank 'til around six o'clock, at which point it was me who suggested we put an end to it because we ran the risk of getting blackout drunk.

The next day I felt all right. I exercised, wrote around a thousand words and went to watch football in a pub, where I drank two beers, before a friend joined and we had four more. He invited me round for dinner.

—How was your weekend? his wife asked, as we sat down to a dinner of lamb with roasted vegetables and big glasses of red wine.

—It was good, I said.
That was true at the time of speaking.
—Pretty quiet. I got some writing done.

—Good, she said, topping up my glass.

—Thank you.

On Monday, I woke at six-thirty and took the pill from Monday's tray before picking up the bottle of beer I'd had after getting back from dinner. I went to the gym, a bit groggy but overall not so bad.

Leaving the gym, I felt refreshed, but on the way to work felt myself starting to sweat the way I did after a big weekend: clammy, my brow and fringe regularly soaked, the weather or my activity of no influence at all.

At work I drank coffee and lots of water and went back and forth in my mind all day as to whether or not to attend yoga in the evening. I was, after all, feeling kind of tired and didn't want to be the guy in class who couldn't keep up. That was undesirable.

At five-thirty, I walked home in the dark autumn night, the Overground train rattling above my head on the Wandsworth Road Bridge. I took the park so as to get home more quickly, but when I was close to my flat I decided not to go to the class. I went into my flat, said hello to my housemate, who was cooking chicken with vegetables, and climbed the stairs. I went into my room, changed into some jogging bottoms and lay down. That was when it occurred to me that my weekend plans hadn't gone to plan after all.

Red Indians and Irish

I'd come to accept that my room was a mess and always would be. I considered myself a tidy person, but with its small size and the number of bulky items I owned, there was next to no way of keeping the room in order for a prolonged period of time.

That's the way it was.

Clothes were on the floor near the door and my gym bag too, and there were diaries and notepads and books and a tube of unopened Absolut Vodka, there only because I'd got it for Christmas from my aunt and had yet to find a home for it, permanent or otherwise. I looked at the pink bag where I stored dirty clothes. Laundry. That was something I'd do with the day.

My head was sore. I'd only been out 'til eleven, but we'd put away a fair few drinks in that time. Usually, I would have felt bad about this, but it had been my last day in a job I'd just lost to the whims of circumstance, and I was all too happy to find a willing drinking buddy, or buddess, as ultimately proved to be the case.

I'd been going out less of late, not drinking too much, save for that episode in November that resulted in *Rainbows And Bottletops*, when I'd drunk heavily while eating fish and chips and – something I failed to mention – watched the final instalment of *The Hobbit*. That was a long final instalment.

I'd also been on a few dates with a Lithuanian woman I'd met in The Dog & Pony, a bar where I watched football on Sundays to take my mind off Sundays. It was a bad idea. Though their countries were barely alike, something about her reminded me of Jana, who was still within me. I never cried when thinking about her. That wasn't my nature, though it wasn't stoicism either.

When she did cross my mind, I made a guttural groan, a tiny, near inaudible noise, my body forcing me to feel what the mind could not. It was fair to say that I was a little numb.

I walked the earth with despondency over what had happened, a tiredness. But I was resilient too (or so I thought), burying myself in work, comforting myself in the knowledge I'd done all I could to keep *us* going, that I'd fought for a place and a time and a parallel universe where we could be together.

Yes, I was bitter, but I was proud that I'd tried.

That was about all I could be.

I'd high hopes for the New Year of 2016. I was now editor of the website where I worked, by pure dint of my predecessor having left and the substantial difference in age between me and my closest colleague. Still, I was editor. However, in the first week of the New Year, it became apparent that many people in the company were being led to the couches in the office where

I worked for prolonged talks. That, I knew, was about to be the end of that. The end didn't come as a shock, not immediately at least. The shocks never did. I had a plan. I'd find a new job soon enough. That was naïve, the kind one often needs to survive.

*

The morning after my final day at work, I walked downstairs to get water, hoping to hydrate the burgeoning hangover away, filling up a two-litre Evian bottle which contributed to the squalid atmosphere of my small room.

Light pouring through the window advertised the saliva marks on its plastic rim. That was unsightly. In the small room there was a wooden Ikea storage rack where I kept my shirts and jackets, and at the foot of the bed was a wooden rack, on top of which was the yoga mat I'd bought in a fit of healthy mindedness months earlier.

There was also a holdall case I'd taken to the UAE in October. I was going to return it to my mother, not because she needed it, but to garner more space in the room. Its presence meant I needed to keep my gym bag on the floor, and as the gym bag was beside the pink laundry bag, there was very little space with the bed taken into account.

On the floor, there were two empty glasses, and two empty cups I'd used for coffee, the bottoms sticky with a dark layer of dried caffeine residue. There were also two small notebooks I used occasionally to practice mnemonics, but I hadn't done this for months. The shelves above my bed were chaos. Three folders lined in a row created a façade of order. Inside, there was no order, or only the kind of order I had crafted – half-arsed, papers from various institutions or banks lumped in together free of reason or rhyme. Jana would have laughed, sighed or, most likely, done both.

The papers from the HSBC were separated from the ones from UniCredit and the ones from Santander were separated from the ones from Smile. The papers in each section weren't assembled in chronological order and were often upside down, but at least everything was hidden away in the pink and green folders. Amidst all the chaos of disordered officialdom, one thought stood out. How in the name of God could a man have so many banks, yet so little money? That was mindboggling.

There were wires and cables for various devices on the shelf, and about forty Euros. The only thing that stood with dignity was the Hemingway collage Jana had collated in a frame for my birthday, forever ago. Even the books were not stacked

106

well, and I saw that one of them was on the floor: *The Second Half* by Roy Keane, which was actually ghostwritten. That was what you did when you weren't famous enough to be a famed writer. It was what you got someone to do when you weren't good enough to write your own book. It paid well for the non-writer, okay for the ghostwriter. I could get on board with that, and I wanted in, some point down the line. And besides, Roddy Doyle was no slouch, rendering that whole philosophy (and digression) more or less redundant.

That's no surprise.

I'd bought the book in an Irish charity shop back in August, on an afternoon when the future preyed upon our minds and we tried in vain to rid it by wandering the town where my father was born. I'd hoped she might fall in love with the place. And she did, but only in the way a tourist does, enamoured, charmed, yet secretly yearning for home after a while. For my part, the small Irish village I'd adored as a child had grown yet smaller. I didn't know anyone. I couldn't work there. It was as likely to be home for us as London or Prague. It was neither ha-ha nor isn't-that-funny funny to find yourself a victim of geography.

Now, months and months later, I'd yet to finish the Roy Keane book. That was ridiculous. It wasn't exactly Proust, and the less said about how far I'd got with him the better. I'd read Keano's sophomore effort in bits and pieces, never quite able to commit to it over other works. I was the fanatical sort when it came to books. I stuck them out 'til the bitter end. I felt anxious if I left a book behind. It felt like a failing of sorts on my part.

But if I did give up on a book, it was final, or at least I wouldn't return to it for years. That's what I'd done with *The Devils*, after a five-year gap. I'd got about two hundred pages in the first time; but with a book like *The Devils* that was like saying you'd climbed Everest when all you'd done was dick about at the bottom for a bit, chatting with the Sherpas, asking for war stories you could approximate as your own. That was crafty.

Anyway, I didn't like reading books in a fair-weather manner, but here I was, with Roy Keane on my floor, unread and unloved. That was a pity for Roy.

My head was sore, and I'd accepted it would be for some time. I lay in bed for a while reading articles about football, just about all I could do.

They were well-written and it created a veneer of activity in my day, but still, I knew I was only reading about football, my most anodyne of past times, something I could lose hours in just because it allowed me to think about nothing other than the ping ping ping of the ball to and fro, and not the need to find a new job or to mourn lost love or curse the way I felt then compared to the way I felt now about that city of castles and goulash and cobbled streets and trams and snow and Vietnamese corner shops and stodgy, heretic bread.

I read the headlines. Alan Rickman was dead. Bowie had gone to find life on Mars days earlier. As both he and Rickman had died at sixty-nine, a number of half-baked conspiracy theories were doing the rounds of a sudden. Some even started calling it the 69 Club. I was fairly certain that was an entirely different kind of club.

Eventually, I left the news behind and went back to football articles about players and the season and how Spurs were not *Spursy* anymore, a pithy epithet that hadn't been meant as a compliment over the years. That was ha-ha funny, so long as you were a Spurs fan with a sense of perspective, of which there were few. I felt pleased about the fact that I was, and the fact that they were doing well. That was called setting yourself up for disappointment, and I should have known better.

I finished the article and put a couple of Berocca tablets in the two-litre bottle of water and waited for them to effervesce. Then I drank about a third of a pint's worth, then a little more. My throat hurt, though I'd not smoked any cigarettes during my drinking session with the buddess, a clean-living blonde I'd seen with a cigarette in her mouth just once, used only as a photo prop at the staff Christmas party.

After another ten or so minutes of sipping orange water and reading more football articles, I took my tablet from Wednesday's tray. It was Fluoxetine I was on these days. I'd been with both her and Citalopram. Fluoxetine wore a green and white skirt. That was classy. Citalopram usually had on a red and yellow number. That was flirty. Both were fine.

I swallowed the pill and got in the shower, standing under the hot water for ten minutes, a long time for me. I usually only showered for one or two. I had waterproof skin, and it was easy to clean. That was convenient.

The shower was an act of purgation, the first step in finding renewed purpose and resolve. The job was gone. Life had thrown up lemons, as it were. It was vital I react well, to not let it get to me. To make the most lemony of lemonades. As it were. It was important not to fall into routines of self-pity and abasement. My plans for the year had fallen into disarray. Now my main plan centred on the most pertinent of needs, to not become a routine piss-artist by day (and preferably night too).

With a small pay-off awaiting me, it was highly tempting. But I knew how I'd feel if I didn't find work soon; the shame, the feeling of worthlessness I'd felt the previous year when I'd returned to England without a job or any direction, and missed Jana by the day, by the hour and the second even if I'd betrayed her by boarding a flight home and leaving it all behind, for the simple reason that life had become borderline untenable. That was unideal.

I had felt the guilt in Prague, perhaps more than ever before in my life. I'd hit a dead end with teaching. I'd a job that paid poorly and went nowhere, but I had Jana too, and that went everywhere: love, children, a life. But the two couldn't be made to meet. I hated myself for not being able to marry them, so as to allow myself to marry her. That's the way it was.

No, it wouldn't do to become a piss-artist, no matter the appeal. That wasn't a smart plan or an isn't-that-funny kind of plan. It was no plan at all.

Back in my room, I stared at the unopened and half opened letters from Santander and elsewhere, while towelling myself off. It occurred to me just how much I missed Brad. If he were here now, I'd happily listen to his obloquies on the meaning of life, or the philosophy of Slavoj Žižek, or even how hard it was for him to have as much sex as he did, how it left him exhausted and created awkward problems. I'd despaired of him at the time, but it was a distraction, and I'd no distractions from my thoughts now.

I brushed my teeth, flossed, got dressed and put my dirty clothes in the pink laundry bag before going downstairs. Even though I was completely dehydrated, I needed coffee.

Mine was a life of routine, and over the years I'd developed a healthy coffee habit. I drank it in plastic-lined paper cups and I bought it in supermarkets to make at home in my Moka pot or French press. I drank it all the time, planning my consumption, planning to buy it at certain cafés at certain times of day. I rarely delineated from this plan. That was good.

Coffee, and the ritual of making, buying and drinking it, was the final vestige of Catholicism left in me (aside from the perpetual feeling that I was doing something wrong, and the shame and childish glee with which I approached all matters sexual). Coffee resembled the structure of Mass more closely than any other part of my life. I wasn't interested in jargon or nomenclature, whether Peruvian small batch or Bolivian Peak

was the best bean. No, I loved the process of *making* the coffee;
spooning opulent amounts into the Moka Pot filter, watching,
waiting for it to cook, or waiting as a barista prepared what was
for all intents and purposes high street sludge, just so I could
have it, another coffee in my day, another one of my coffees.
Even now, as I think about it, six minutes shy of 7:30, I know
it's not long before I will be drinking coffee, perhaps even two
in a row. And after showering and getting dressed, it is only an
hour or so before I will have another between the ten-thirty and
eleven mark, as planned. Then one more, after lunch. What a
beautiful routine.

Coffee.

Yes, it could be argued that a man with an anxiety
disorder, a broken heart and a hangover which was soon to be
punishing shouldn't have been drinking caffeine, but fuck it, I
loved the stuff. I was going to have my coffee.

*

It was foggy out. The pendulous tree branches hung over the
still-long grass, but whereas it'd been frosty in recent days, there
was now a dew-like condensation on the windows. I watched
the morning news. Knowing I wasn't going to get anything
overly productive done any time soon, I decided to make a fry
up. Nothing in the news had led to the decision. There were no
stories of deflation on eggs or price reductions in ground coffee;
I just watched the news, then decided to have a fry up. It was
non-planned. That was good.

Out of the house I went, and over the road to buy my
things. I didn't buy ground coffee for the Moka pot and can't
explain why, only to say that as I'd just been made redundant
I'd lost one of my most important routines, that of getting up
and going to work. The domino effect was akin to that feared by
the Americans before Vietnam – only more justified – and I can
only assume my reasoning had been affected.

I set to work, cooking three sausages, two eggs and beans,
but not bacon, which I'd read caused cancer. So did sausages, but
it was bacon I'd seen in the picture, and so I didn't cook bacon.
That was the danger of reading online news.I was going to start
baking again soon, I'd decided. It was something I'd taken up
not long after returning to the UK. I liked the measuring out
– planning, if you will – of ingredients, the process of kneading,
which – loosely – resembled physical labour. I liked how it didn't
require attuned senses of smell and taste, both of which had been
done few favours by my fondness of the little brown but mostly

white sticks.

Baking had taken my mind off not being able to find work after I'd first returned to the UK, and it had given me reason to believe me and Jana would survive. I made cake and bread and sent it to her in tightly sealed, bubble-wrapped envelopes. It gave me hope. That too was good.

After getting my job, I didn't bake so much, though I occasionally took a cake to work, which ingratiated me with my colleagues. Given that I was shy, that was smart. A good plan too. Still, I didn't do much baking after I got my job, and when I lost it, well, I did no baking at all. That was a pity.

When I first returned to England, me and Jana didn't talk much either. She was angry. That was understandable. Life was up in the air, and the plans we'd made were on the mountain also. That's how it was. I was angry with myself for feeling depressed. I was in a fugue, scared the wall I'd hit might be insuperable. Baking helped a little in those days, except the time I picked a hot pan out of the oven without gloves. That was dumb.

I couldn't bake after that for three or four weeks, and couldn't go to the gym either, something I'd tried to do most days so as not to think so much on it all.

It was fair to say I'd time on my side now, to think and find work and miss Jana, but also to bake if I wasn't to spend my days tugging on the end of my watering can, knocking back beers and mulling on what the hell had happened in life. That idea was attractive in theory, less so in practice.I lit two stovetops – one for the eggs, one for the beans. I put the sausages under the grill. The beans warmed and the eggs fried gently for a few minutes. I took care not to overdo either. But my mind drifted away, perhaps to Jana or the job or just too far onto the beans and eggs, and I forgot all about the sausages.

As I was sitting down to eat the former, the latter made themselves heard, then smelt. A sizzling sound commenced, and by the time I realised what the sizzling sound was there was smoke rising from beneath the grill like an Irish waterfall, filling the room.

—Shit! Shit!

The alarm was going to go off, I knew that. I prayed to the gods of coffee and Catholicism and everyone in between that none of my housemates were at home. I opened the downstairs windows and the back and front doors and hoped for the best. Thirty seconds passed without incident. I sat down again.

The alarm went off with a sound both clanging and thudding. That was physiologically unwelcome.

My head hurt a great deal more than I'd realised. I worried about the neighbours and Miranda, my Australian housemate, who might be home. She was a nurse, and often worked nights.

I pressed the green button on the alarm, to no avail, and tried the red one beside it, also to no avail, so I tried to take off the casing but it wouldn't come free. The sound grew ever louder and more piercing. The only thing left to try was holding down the green button, so I did that, and eventually the sound did stop.

Unfortunately, there was another alarm on the second floor, outside Miranda's room. That was health and safety gone mad 2016-style, or just the landlord covering his ass, which was more than fair enough. I ran up, repeating the methods of before. Miranda came out of her room wearing pyjamas and much sleep in her eyes.

That was unfortunate. What if she was working later? What I'd done might make her sleep deprived. Someone in the geriatric ward where she worked could die because of her tiredness and subsequent lapses in attention. That wouldn't be good.

—You need to wave something at it, she said.

She walked back into her room, returned with a tea towel, and waved it under the alarm 'til the sound stopped, only for it to transpire that there was a third alarm on the third floor. I copied her method, and the house was soon silent, oddly so. Miranda had already gone back to bed when I walked down. Vapours of smoke remained in the kitchen, but they soon disappeared and I closed the front and back doors once it got cold. After all the drama, the novelty of a fry up had fizzled, and I ate the food in front of the TV with an intense self-loathing.

My plans had quite literally gone up in smoke.

Why had I focused all my attention on the eggs and beans? Sure, you had to be careful not to boil beans for reasons of taste, but that wasn't rocket science. They wouldn't set the house alight either, something in which I had some (near) experience.

I'd once come close to setting my flat on fire in Prague. Jana was away. It was before we lived together, and I'd gone out with friends to Café Neustadt, a trendy bar near Karlovo náměstí.

They sold good beer and had DJs and decent seating and it wasn't so loud as to stop you from hearing each other. After that we decided against stumbling through Karlovo náměstí, with its collection of harmless homeless people who didn't seem harmless in the midst of night, and went instead to a place called U Sudu, a cavernous, smoky underground bar.

The smoke stung my eyes but I stayed and drank for hours.

I was very happy at this time in my life, yet that feeling of getting blackout drunk still held a strange appeal, even though I knew what it did to me in the mornings, how it controlled my mind, made me worry over the things I might have done and said and the things I certainly *had* done to my body.

That night, I returned home and tried to cook sausages, only to fall asleep during a short visit to my bedroom.

Fortunately for me, my housemate returned from her own evening out shortly afterwards, woke me up, slapped me in the face and asked me what was wrong with me. I had nearly burned the flat down, she said.

We argued. My arguments were not strong.

We fell out, and I moved in with Jana shortly afterwards. In hindsight, I shouldn't have cooked sausages late at night, while drunk. I also shouldn't have picked an argument with the woman who saved my life. That wasn't a very grateful way to behave. Oh well.

*

I made another cup of coffee. Routine was routine. I checked my email. I'd bought a guitar before New Year, and it still hadn't arrived. They'd tried to deliver it once when I was out and today was the second date of delivery. I rang the company to see when it was coming.

—Hi, I'm expecting a package. I was just wondering if you could tell me when it's going to arrive?

The woman at the end of the line sounded both bored and tired. I imagined her there, cupping her hands together, blowing into them for warmth, of which there would be little in the cold of January and the half-exposed warehouse.

—Okay, what's the consignment number?
—1095494.

She clicked a few keys on her keyboard and sighed.

—They tried to deliver it this
morning at 8:32.

—Really? I never got a delivery card.

—Well, they should definitely have left a card, but they did try and deliver it. I'm afraid you'll have to come collect it now.

—Okay.

That was irritating, but there was nothing for it. I'd have to go to Bermondsey tomorrow.

A moment's indignant rage passed into further self-loathing. I should have got up earlier, and shouldn't have drunk so much the night before with the budding blonde buddess. That was unwise.

It'd been ha-ha funny, though. Free from the shackles of employment (admittedly a lot freer than I'd have liked) I was able to make jokes about the people we worked with (I still wasn't quite able to talk in the past tense) without fear of retribution.

Still, I now had to go to Bermondsey with a headache, and Bermondsey was difficult to get to at the best of times. In the pantheon of my errors, it was relatively minor. Yes, I'd known the guitar was coming, but I hadn't known when exactly. I'd also just been made redundant. But it was for that reason I felt foolish. I wanted to get right back into work, to show I was trying my best to do so.

There was something almost Protestant in my work ethic, or at least my ethic to work towards the finding of work.

I knew how the world looked upon people who were out of work. I wanted to be back in gainful employment as soon as possible, so as not to be judged by society, much as I spent a great deal of my time judging that society. That was conflicted.

—I'll come tomorrow, I said.

I heard her shuffling papers in the background and clasping together what I knew to be the inimitable sound of a stapler.

—You can come any time from five today, if you

like, she said. —It'll be back in by then.

—No, I'll have to come tomorrow. Thanks.

The phone rang off. I'd made plans to meet a friend in the afternoon for a drink, though in the current climate the notion of more alcohol troubled my stomach. I decided to go to the gym in the hope it would rid me of the blues – which threatened to go from a simmer to a boil – and the toxins lying dormant but maliciously in my system. Putting a bottle of water, a pen and paper and my skipping rope into a backpack, I changed into my gym gear, went to the gym and started listening to music on my wireless headphones.

I'd only recently discovered wireless headphones, and how much easier they made life.

But they also made me feel spoilt. I owned headphones that could speak to my phone, for goodness' sake. That was insane.

Who was I to feel self-pity, when my headphones could quite literally communicate with my mobile phone? When I owned both a mobile phone and a set of headphones? Wireless headphones!

Taking out the phone, I began using an app which taught you how to jump rope. That seemed odd. The instructions were in the name.

I liked having a programme to follow, though, the rhythmic motion of jump, jump, jump, over and over, coupled with progress I could measure on a screen. That was lovely.

I completed the first set of seven minutes, with ten seconds skipping and twenty seconds rest. It was far too easy, but I was determined to stick to the plan and go through the sessions in order.

Running before I could walk, as it were, was evidence of manic behaviour, and I was all too familiar with manic behaviour, with my tendencies to take on new hobbies or turn ever more leaves, only to crunch them through my inability to make and stick to realistic goals.

On the next session, the time increased to eight minutes. After that, I stretched briefly and did some pull-ups and core exercises. I lay on a mat, out of breath, and decided to go home. I felt much better. My skin felt dry and exhausted, but all in all I was better off than in the morning. The plan had gone well.

I went home, showered and thought about what to do next. The

CV was my priority, but despite the exercise it was still hard to focus on anything but the most mundane and easy of tasks.

I got up, and inspected myself in the thin mirror which ran up the wall beside my bed. I still looked like shit. Granted, not as shitty as before, but shit all the same. That was self-evident.

I began to shave, having tried and failed earlier, only for the trimmer to run out of juice. But it was charged now. I didn't want to get rid of the beard, just wanted it shorter.

With rare diligence and patience I succeeded, and then looked in the mirror once more. It wasn't good. I still looked like shit.

However, I understood the root cause now. My hair.

It had grown thick and wiry and I hated it long. I wanted it short. Then I'd be fine. That was the plan.

Walking downstairs, I left the flat, crossed the street and took some cash out before heading towards Brixton. There was a barber's around the corner I'd seen but not been to. I made my way to the door, where I spotted an elderly man in a chair, his head resting in his hands. He was sleeping. That was endearing.

Still, endearing didn't bode well for a good cut, so I moved to change direction and walk away. But just then he opened his eyes, smiled and motioned for me to come in. I had no choice.

    —There's nobody here, he said, as I walked in. He had a thick Greek accent. — That's why I fell asleep. Everyone came for haircuts before Christmas.

—Are you open?

    —Yes, he said, beckoning me to a chair. —Sit down.

I took off my lumberjack coat. I'd got it free at work, from a company peddling what was called the 'lumber sexual' style.

I wasn't sure what that meant – and was certain I wanted no part in it – but agreed to advertise it on the website on condition they gave me one. That was opportunistic. The warmth it gave me in the pissing and freezing January winter, though, that was most welcome.I hung it up and sat down.

    —What can I do for you?

I pointed to my temple.

>—I like it short at the back and the sides,
> I said, taking the thick shock of my fringe by
> the hand. —I'd like about two-thirds off up top.
> My hair gets very thick and wiry.

He nodded and took the longer parts of my hair in his hands, as
if to see for himself whether it required much cutting.
He then began to shear away the back and sides. After
about thirty seconds he stopped, put a mint in his mouth,
swallowed it and coughed the heavy cough of a lifelong smoker.

>—My son was in earlier, he said after the
> coughing had ended. —He works here sometimes. I told
> him to go home, it's so quiet.

He trailed off, allowing the buzz of the clippers to fill the
gaps. After a while, he stopped again, and popped another mint
into his mouth.
He reminded me of my grandfather, who'd also had a
fondness for mints in his old age, albeit of a different variety, his
the kind purchased at supermarket tills, while the Greek was on
the Fisherman's Friend. That was a pricier mint.
He looked kind, in his knitted grey jumper. He had watery
old eyes, a large nose and ears growing out towards death.
His clipped moustache looked professional, and I
reckoned he'd kept it the same (except for colour) most of his
life. That too was endearing.

The barbershop was extremely old, with no mod cons
whatsoever, save for a digital radio in the corner blaring daytime
radio – *Magic*, I think.
The chairs were the sort that fetched into the thousands
these days due to their chic value, but it was clear they'd been
bought years ago for the sole purpose of barbering.
He shaved half of the back of my head. The clippers
hummed gently.

>—You have work today?
> —No, not today.
> —What do you do?

I hesitated before telling him I was a journalist.

He continued.

The silence was filled by the clippers and a woman on the radio, around thirty-odd, telling the presenter how she'd met her husband. The conversation was anguished, and I gathered the programme was about finances.

The presenter listened patiently, asking only the occasional question here and there to validate the woman's point and the purpose of the show overall.

The clippers, meanwhile, hummed away, until they didn't.

—I will have to replace them, he said, putting them to one side with an air of disappointment.
            —People. They throw away everything nowadays.
    I don't like to do it.

He stopped, coughed again, recomposed himself and continued.

—Me and my wife go to Cyprus twice a year, to the village where I was born. We walk in, and everything is the same. There are three chairs.

He counted them out in the air, his thick, elderly fingers leading the way.

            —One for me,
                        one for my sister,
                                one for my
                        brother. With our
                        names on, just like
                        when we was kids. But
                        now–

He trailed off, and continued a while with new clippers.

I was no good at talking to hairdressers, or the general populace for that matter.

That was unfortunate for a man whose professions to date read, in chronological order: gadget salesman, barman (x3), teacher, journalist. I'd made certain choices that might not have been good.

I agreed with the old man about waste. I tried not to throw things out, to be responsible, yet I often failed. When I went out for coffee I often got those plastic-lined paper cups with plastic lids, though I'd try to keep the empty cups to recycle later. But, of course, coffee would spill in my bag, all over my pens and paper and laptop, rendering the do-gooder appeal of recycling unattractive.

I also tried to keep plastic bags on me at all times. But they overcrowded my backpack, or I would forget, adding to the endless sea of blue and red ironically stored in the huge Bag for Life in our kitchen. I liked to think I lived a simple enough life, but to look around my room you'd think it was a sci-fi movie, with cables and wires protruding from all the *things* I owned, like the insides of a Borg cube. I take no pleasure in making references to *Star Trek*.

That point can't be overstated. I could digress to explain why, but I won't. That's kind of me, if I say so myself.

My life was not materially simple, and if ever it seemed as such, it was only by comparison to those with more things than me. That was the human condition. And it made me nervous.

There were good habits I tried to keep, like trying to fix clothes instead of replacing them at the first tear or rip. This had much to do with me not wanting to spend money on things I didn't like, such as rent or food, and spend it on things I did, like coffee and alcohol, Haribo and cake, and luxurious loaves of freshly baked bread in the Morrison's near my apartment, which I kidded myself into believing were far superior to the stodgy Czech equivalents of yore.

In my periphery, I noticed a woman with a pram passing by the barbershop, and the cognisance of something external made me notice that the conversation on the radio had changed. The old hairdresser noticed it too, and began to talk about the new subject, which happened to be Gary Lineker's latest divorce. I did my best to engage in small talk, but it wasn't my forte. I was worse than the Czechs, and by God, the Czechs were bad at small talk. I had tried so many times.

What did you do on the weekend?
Nothing.

What was the weather like?
You saw it, sunny.

Did you hear what the president said?
We don't like the president.
I know; did you hear what he said?
Yes, but we don't want to talk about him.

It was like herding cats in a brewery, and in relative terms, the Czechs made me seem as if I'd the jovial charm of Dara Ó Briain and the chattiness of Alan Carr.

But now I was home, and the reality of my limitations
was laid out in all its naked disglory. Yes, I did my best, but my
best wasn't all that good. That was a smack-back-down-to-earth
moment.

I was stilted and awkward, and felt shame whenever
I couldn't speak, as I had in earlier years. It reminded me of
standing with friends in nightclubs in utter silence, the sound of
late '00s dance or indie serving only to highlight the void in my
social skills. Friends! I couldn't even speak with people I knew.
I stared at my sea-blue eyes in the mirror and urged myself not
to be that young man, full of self-loathing and fear and constant
doubt. That was a weighty expectation.

Having shaved the back and sides of my head, the old man
sprayed some water on my hair.

—You have very good hair, he said.
—Irish, I answered, by way of explaining its
thickness and density.

He nodded.
—It's important to look after hair.

The thinners tugged slightly as he worked the top,
cutting strands, pulling them out the way I'd pulled cattails in
muddy swamps in Illinois eight summers, two world cups, an
election, two Olympics, zero Spurs league titles and numerous
earthquakes, BGT winners and dead celebrities ago.

—You know what the worst two things you can do with
hair are?
I shook my head.
—Colouring and perming, he said.

I was glad to say I'd never permed my hair, and had only ever
dyed it once after a drunken night out at university, spending the
next three months in America – as planned – looking the spitting
image of an albino hedgehog.
That wasn't so planned.

—There is a shop over there, he said, pointing
down the street.
—Run by a Pakistani family. They've
been here as long as me. The boy, he must be
thirty-five now, he used to come to me for his
cuts. Still does. One day in the '90s, he comes

in. There was a trend at that time. All the young
men wanted permed hair.

Although I would have only been six or seven, I
remembered it clearly. It was the age of Ryan Giggs, with his
shaggy locks and silky skills. Thinking back to the '90s with
Giggs and Girl Power and Saturday Night da ba da dumb dee
dee da da, I was suddenly heartened that my formative years had
not been in the '90s, but rather the staid blandness of the early
millennium, when Travis and Coldplay ruled the waves, and the
fashion choices of footballers had become vanilla to the point of
being uninfluential.

—To perm hair, you must test it first, to see if it's
suitable. Hair is like anything. Sometimes it's strong,
sometimes weak. It *must* be the right kind of hair.
—So this boy comes in saying he wants it
permed. I test it. I tell him, you *cannot* perm this
hair. It is too thin. It will damage it forever.

The old hairdresser looked me in the eye as he held a lock
of my hair, like it was the young Pakistani boy's. He shrugged.

—Did he listen? No. He went somewhere
else. They put the lotion in. What happened?
After ten seconds he jumps up from the chair -
his head, it's like it's on fire.

He smiled slightly, drawing an invisible ring around his
scalp.

—Now he has a big bald patch here. Today it's
okay; he's in his thirties. But when he was a teenager,
it embarrassed him. He came back to me and he said,
'Michael, I should have listened to you'.
—I still cut his hair.

He smiled again.
—But of course, there isn't so much of it
now.

The hairdresser looked towards the window and pointed at
the sign etched into it.

—I have been here since 1967. I arrived in

England when I was fifteen. I studied my trade in Coventry. I've been here since.

Feeling the flicker of enthusiasm a taciturn man has at the chance to speak about a subject with which he is familiar, I perked up.

        —I know Coventry, I said. —I studied in Warwick.

The old man arched his eyebrows.
        —Very nice university, he said. —Very nice place.

It was then that I noticed for the first time who he reminded me of, and who he reminded me of was Super Mario.
        That is, he reminded me of Super Mario if the 8-bit plumber were ever allowed to age, to grow old, to leave behind toadstools and princesses and Bowser, and settle into a life of Fisherman's Friend and remembering the times good and bad, the heady days of '64, the lows of *Super Smash Bros.*
        That was what he reminded me of.

        —It's very green there, I said.

He nodded in agreement, and after some time, caught my eye in the mirror again.

        —You said you were Irish?
        —Yes.
        —I have a friend from Ireland. Where is he from, now? Coke, no, Cork?
        —Cork, yes.
        —Yes, yes. He told me something very interesting recently. And you will not believe it when I tell you.
        —What is it?
        —During the Famine, many people died.

I gathered this wasn't the surprise, and waited for him to go on.
        —Do you know who helped the Irish? he asked me.

I had no idea. That was the god's honest truth. Help and pity weren't words I much associated with the Famine. I shook my head.

—The Red Indians, he said. —From America.

He combed my forelock, snipping away three to four millimetres. I half expected him to cough again or eat one of his mints.

—They knew what it was like to lose everything. He smiled again. —Crazy. The Red Indians.

He continued to snip away, and I sat there wondering if it was true. It sounded too beautifully apocryphal, the sort of thing told to kids to make them grow up knowing right from wrong, only to forget the difference anyway.

—They sent a ship to Ireland during the Famine, with food. No one else. No one. Amazing, isn't it?
—Yes, I said. —That's so strange.
—You said you were a journalist?
—Yes.
—You could write a story about that, he said. —It's interesting.

And with that, he continued to thin my hair, and was finished within moments. He took a mirror out and showed me the back and sides. I said I was pleased. He brushed the loose hair off my shoulders and onto the floor. Then he took a sharp razor and shaved my neck and after that stopped and asked if I wanted some cream. I said yes, and so he put some thick white cream in his hands, melded it together and styled my hair.

—Just pull it over this way, he said, pulling it to the left.

The style was redolent of the '60s, though given the times it didn't look unsimilar to styles that were popular now.I wasn't sure I'd recreate it later myself. I looked like Harry Kane.
He was a talented man, but also a man who bore the look of someone who has just been confronted with, confused and appalled by an updated menu at Nandos.
Still, it was nice there, in the microcosm of the place.I thought about the old man's Red Indians as I got up and put my heavy lumberjack coat on once again, and heard the sound of *Magic* in the background as I looked for my wallet.

—How much is that? I asked.
—Eight pounds, please.

I took out a tenner and handed it to him. I considered
tipping him the extra two, but then thought he was most likely
the proud sort.

—I'll do some research, I said. —It sounds like an
interesting story.

—Yes, do some research, he
said. —Very interesting.

And with that, his manner changed completely.

—Bye now, he said.

It wasn't unfriendly. We were simply done. He waited for me to
leave so he could sweep the hair off the floor and return to his
chair beside the heater.
I left so he could do so. I had to be getting home anyway.
I felt better sheared, and I'd my CV to look at and needed
to eat, before meeting my friend to discuss my options and
where to go from here. That was the plan for the evening.

Woodlice and Sundown

There was a reasty, disconcerting smell in the kitchen, the source of which I couldn't find. I decided to ignore it, as I'd much to be getting on with. That was the plan of action. Unemployment was funny like that. There was both so much and so little to do. Time stretched itself out agonisingly, yet ran fast, faster than you could keep up with. That's a point I made earlier. But people are wont to reiterate their points. That's an unnecessarily big word for repeat, or the answer to the question, 'come again'?

I looked around the kitchen once more. The floor was dirty. There were garlic casings and coffee granules scattered around the small compost bin, both my doing. I'd a habit of not bending down to empty the Moka pot's funnel. That was bad of me. Instead, I hoped for the best, but that was like pissing with the bowl down. You'd get it right one in ten and feel great, but wrong nine times and feel the fool and a slob to boot.

The tray of the washing machine had come out. It often did that during washes, and the work surfaces were littered with crumbs from various housemates' breakfasts, and egg residue from my own. The room was dark, the blind held down by the chopping boards, which my housemate John had placed on the radiator to dry.

I left the blinds down because I was going upstairs to work anyway, and I left the smell behind too. It was 9:33.

I'd woken at 6:15, got up, donned my heavy lumberjack coat, and made my way to the gym like some kind of Midwestern Rocky Balboa. It was all part of a new routine of living healthily, eating well and exercising often. That was the new plan. The resolve and stoicism of the first two weeks since being made redundant had evaporated, and I'd decided to instigate healthy routines to keep me on the straight and narrow. I got up each day, exercised, ate and then set about finding a job. That was good.

Early that morning, I walked out the door, gym bag slung over my shoulder as usual. The lights in Morrison's were on, as usual, workers stacking shelves and mopping floors, readying the place for its seven a.m. opening, as usual.

Walking past an old woman with a stick and a Sholeco trolley, I saw a man roughly my age. His face was hidden beneath the dark of his hoody, though I could make out the smouldering cherry of a cigarette. I was wary of him. Calm people didn't smoke so early in the morning.

When I got to the lights near Tesco, I passed a Mediterranean man with mutton chop sideburns, the panglossian cheer of a full-time drunk, and a black bag in hand containing at least four cans. Tennent's, I reckoned. Possibly K.

At the gym I punched in my code and passed through the cylindrical tubes which passed for an entrance, went to the changing rooms, found a locker big enough for my bag and changed into two-year-old Nike trainers, Nike trackies that were older by maybe a year and a replica Ireland football jersey, most likely sweatshop-made. It was my first ethical failure of the day, and I'd not yet been fully naked.

That was fine.

Walking down the large metal staircase of the Oval branch of Pure Gym, I enjoyed the ferric sound of my feet thudding against each metal step. When I was at the bottom, I saw a number of familiar faces. It was as if they never left, but then the thought occurred that I only saw them here as often as I came, so perhaps they didn't go to the gym any more than me. That was possible.

Then again, my routine had been erratic until recently. Sometimes I exercised Mondays and Tuesdays, sometimes Tuesdays and Wednesdays, sometimes three days a week and sometimes none at all. However, after thinking it through for a minute or so while limbering up, I concluded that it was likely these people came to the gym daily. That was called overthinking.

After warming up by skipping for twenty minutes, I lifted whichever weights I could get my hands on. The fives and tens were mostly in use, and though I could lift fifteens and, at a stretch, twenties, I dared not risk looking the fool. I had the rest of the day to do that.

I used various machines and mats and whatever else was free, and exercised for around forty-five minutes, checking the clock every now and then, keen to be out by eight. My new regime – in truth, it was the fourth new leaf turned (the others scrunched) in as many weeks – meant cramming an awful lot into a day and, like I said, the days had a habit of running away from me, perhaps due to all the cramming.

Time was always in deficit, and I never achieved what I set out to. This inability to conquer time tormented me, though it had been worse in earlier years. I was, or believed myself to be, more patient these days. Recent events, of course, were testing that patience.

Impatience aided some – mainly the shouting classes, who *got things done* – but for me it was a millstone.

I demanded much of myself, yet achieved so very little. That was the human condition, or perhaps it was just me. Time couldn't be defeated, but I was still surprised by the limits of

what could be done in twenty-four hours. There was a lot to do
with the day: jobs to apply for, pitches to make, and writing, if
possible.

Today, I also had to sign on. Needs musted. I'd resisted
for a long time, knowing full well that signing on made me feel
like a worthless piece of shit, but, well, needs musted, turd or no
turd.

After exercising, I stretched and went to the changing
rooms. I took off the sweaty green replica shirt and then my
socks and the trackie bottoms, which I put into my bag, along
with everything else. I took off my boxers in the changing room
rather than the shower and immediately regretted exposing
my shrivelled Celtic Tiger to those around me, which in all
honesty had never really graduated past cubhood. That was
embarrassing.

I walked home, made a breakfast of eggs, avocado and coffee,
then cleaned the plates and emptied the Moka pot's funnel. And
that's where I was at 9:33.

I emptied the compost bin in the hope it would rid the
room of the reasty smell and went upstairs to work, content in
the knowledge that I'd done all this (the exercise, cooking and
eating breakfast) before nine, before most had reached the office
or had their morning coffee. That was fabulous.

Before signing on, I had to scour the web for jobs, but
also write two freelance articles for American clients. The first
was about high-end toilets for a home and furniture website. It
wasn't quite clear what high-end toilets were, given the means
and ends for which they were designed. The second was an
article on fitness, which I wrote with ease. Neither paid well, but
I lived in the hope they would lead to more, better paid work in
the future. That was somewhat naïve.

The article on toilets wasn't so much unpleasant as dull,
but I quickly discovered the usefulness of the words 'aesthetic'
and 'value'. When unsure of a subject and in need of adjectives,
the words 'aesthetic' and 'value' are a great help. That's called
sneaky, but sneaky's nothing if not smart.

Scrambling towards my 5000-word count – all for a
measly $40 – I had no choice but to fluff my lines here and
there with a needless, flowery adjective or adverb. It meant
breaking all the conventions of good writing I so cherished,
but this wasn't writing, this was feeding oneself. Those were,
unfortunately, two completely different things.

I was working for American dollars at sweatshop hours,
but I was also being paid to talk shite about the receptacle

of shits. That wasn't to be sniffed at, if you'll excuse the expression. There are worse ways to earn a dollar.

As I wrote, I did my best not to be distracted by emails (of which there were few) and Facebook (on which there was nothing) and porn (of which there was a surfeit); but try as I might, distraction found its way towards me through the comforts of home.

In an odd way, I felt like an intruder. The things I owned sat there day in, day out, ignored more often than not: the Xbox, the guitar, the books on the shelves. Only in pockets of my existence did we experience each other in tandem. I felt like an unfaithful lover crawling back on his hands and knees in the hour of need.

I worked on for another hour and a half, finished the articles, looked for jobs, and told myself that so long as I was looking there was no reason to feel bad, even though I couldn't help but feel a deep sense of shame for the position I'd found myself in. That was my curse.

I'd passed it off for years as something to do with being Catholic, but when I thought on it hard, I knew it had nothing to do with Catholicism, which only ever made me smile or laugh. It filled me with warm memories of childhood: twee hymns at school, stultifying but harmless boredom on Sundays, my grandmother handing me Fox's Glacier Mints in the aisles to keep me mollified and quiet during Communion whilst she shuffled up to the altar, her bag still dangling on her arm.

That was childhood. It was beautiful. Even 'Gloria, in excelsis Deo'. Clap, clap, clap.

No, the shame came from elsewhere. My father's death perhaps. Chemical imbalance? Maybe. Being too grumpy or too nice or not nice enough all had strong claims, though overall overthinking (and repetition) seemed the worst offender.

It was a mind boggler.

Shame was everywhere, silent but within me, though there were a few occasions which had stood out, rare occasions when I had let it come to the surface.

I'd signed on twice in my life, crying rivers the first time, too defeated to cry the second. Those had been occasions when I'd let shame show, and though I didn't feel so ashamed now for signing on (it was my right), the tears were only a setback or insult or news headline away.

I sat in my room and played 'Factory' by Bruce Springsteen, as I always did when at a low ebb. It provided a necessary sense of perspective. I wasn't a factory worker; no kids to feed, no machinery destroying my hearing, no lathe to operate just to survive. I was fortunate. That was the truth of it.

It'd been a month since I'd lost my job, nothing more. I was down on my luck, but I was also in a position where I could go for a coffee, write and read, or revert to pornography for elevenses. A brighter day was just round the corner.

That wasn't the plan. It was a dogma, and I sorely needed its reassuring warmth, even if it might prove to be a delusion. Sure, there were moments, usually about mid-afternoon, when the sameness of things grew stark and the days became elongated and characterised by nothingness.

But redundancy was just a thing, and things were just things that happened and were. Loss, depression, Moka pots, Prague, Shileco trolleys, they were just things, just as I was a thing, nothing more nor less. All I could do was strive, not for ambition or reward or ideology or fulfilment, but just because. I was in the world of no accord and so it was vital to move forward, even when the sound of silence rang in my mind like a tocsin all the livelong day. That was a strong plan of action. Perhaps.

I looked for a few more jobs, saved some to look at later, then prepared a bag and left to go to the Job Centre. My appointment wasn't for a while, and I knew I'd be early, as always. It was a bitterly cold February day. I walked from the flat onto the Brixton Road. The industrial fryers of the chicken shop (the first of many) burned bright and yellow, a gleaming beacon among the other shops, all of which were either closed or had their shutters down. I walked past the Reformed Church and the small park where there were always at least two hobos sitting on metal, perforated benches drinking Kronenburg, Holsten, Special Brew or Stella.

As I neared Brixton, the noise grew; cars and buses, people shouting to or greeting each other. The Job Centre was beside a secondhand video game and DVD store. I thought about browsing a while, but then thought someone from the Job Centre might catch me looking at DVDs and video games when I was asking for benefit. That was funny, strange funny. It was paranoia.

I walked into the Job Centre and found a security guard, a Caribbean man in his early to mid-fifties, with sunken eyes, slumped shoulders and an air of weary dejection.

—I have a meeting at twelve, I said.

He took out a list to find my name, but the two of us were
distracted by an argument between a claimant and a Job Centre
employee.

—Your appointment was this morning, said
the employee, a woman in her mid-forties with a red
cardigan. She looked up from her computer.

The claimant was a gangly man with a shaven head and
angry eyes. He stood over her, jabbing a finger into a piece of
paper, the faded parchment that beigey-yellow you find only on
vague, stilted correspondence from the State.

—Yeah, he said. —But I need to re-ar-ange for *now*. I
want my money today.

The woman sighed, and tried to explain that it wasn't
possible. That was futile. I pitied her, working here with its
rivers of misery, frustration and destitution, genuine need and
feigned plight side by side with indistinct fear and anger.

—You can't. You'll have to rearrange.

Slamming the paper on the desk, he told her she was the
devil, which was an interesting plan of action. He proceeded
to tell her what he was going to do. That boded bad and,
unsurprisingly, he was soon cut off before he had a chance to
finish. That was ha-ha funny, or would have been were it not so
sad.

The woman told him she wasn't going to do anything,
now that he'd spoken to her the way he had. That was bold. She
turned her back to him. He began to shout wildly (this wasn't in
line with his stated plan).
The guards threatened to call the police. That also erred, I
believe, from his plan.
He became quiet then, and tried a new plan: reason.
Reason failed, and when reason failed, he became
splenetic with rage, and it was this, I gathered, which made up
his weekly *plan*. It was what he'd expected to do all along; a
kind of maniacal certainty in him that each week need involve a
drama with the folk at the Job Centre, the man subconsciously
aware that his claims and demands and pleas would fall on deaf
ears, the drama to be played out the same way each time, simply
for the sake of it.

The situation continued to unfold, and I wondered whether to intervene. I was scared, but I wasn't a coward. At the same time, it wasn't my responsibility to do something. Perhaps it was *because* of that lack of responsibility that I wanted to intervene, being as I was, by some distance, the youngest and fittest person in the room. While I was thinking about it, the guards tried and failed to calm him down. It seemed a lazy excuse to claim lack of responsibility, yet I still stood there not doing anything.

Did I really want to do the right thing? Or was it just the cumulative effect of redundancy, of solitude, of not being able to empty a Moka pot correctly, and of losing her, which had made me feel insignificant once more? The consequence of that was an innate desire for hero status. That was dangerous.

I had always been a fantasist, a trait borne of a childhood spent amid the last great Cowboy and Indian generation of young boys, when it wasn't just okay but also expected to have a toy gun or bow and arrow, and to make inappropriate clarion cries with hand and mouth, in lieu of headdress or war paint. It made mock gods of us, or at least mock men.

I wanted to believe that if anything happened I'd do the right thing, step in and say something, do *something*. Being unemployed and redundant – professionally and otherwise – made it easier to believe I could be a different self: conspicuous, impressive, a man who allowed himself to be ruled by his id rather than his superego. That I had to look up those terms to be certain of their meaning suggests the superego continues to rule the roost, acting impulsively likely to remain but an idea.

About a year before meeting Jana, I'd briefly dated a secretary from the language school where I taught. I got head over heels. That was dumb. I began making big plans. That was dumber still.

It fizzled and faded and disappeared as these things do, but it did result in *The Whiskey Dreams*, a short story I wrote that winter, about that winter, when I went half mad trying to find her in my dreams because she had become unobtainable in the conscious world, when I stalked her around street corners and followed her to places unknown because I would never have been so bold as to do so in the waking hours.

And yet, in the long run, it wasn't she who occupied my mind. It was her friend, who also worked at the school. She was short, blonde and pretty. That had become 'my type', much as I hated the idea; men without women couldn't afford such a luxury. She treated me with indifference at best and unfriendliness at worst, and I wanted her to like me all the more for it. I thought constantly not only about how unfriendly she was, but also about why she disliked me – as I saw it – and what I could do to alter her perception. She often wore red lipstick.

That probably aided my fascination.

My relationship with her friend hadn't ended badly per se but had done so in essence. We'd started seeing each other after a staff party, where we kissed. After a month or so we were inseparable, after another month we were separate. That was fine, but it wasn't fine at the time, as is the way with these things.

She left me via text, which was unclassy, though I'd forced her hand, telling her one cold Friday to just get it over and done with because I saw it coming. That was context.Still, it left me unsure of how I'd gone from suitable to not so suitable and, given my innate paranoia, fed the perception I held that I was a weirdo and that others probably knew it.

And so I became convinced that the girl I'd seen told her friend all about me; that I was a fool, that I was weird, that, worst of all, I'd been awful in bed. I had farted once close to the moment of climax. That was unfortunate.

I soon began fantasising about what I could do to convince the girl that her friend had misinformed her, to do something which might elevate me in her eyes and those of everyone in the company, a place I visited four or five times a week to print materials, a place where I felt anonymous amidst the silence and the diligence of everyday life.

Life was humdrum, and I fantasised about all sorts of things.

When I jogged through Riegrovy Sady I didn't focus on my breathing or the pleasant surroundings of dog walkers and mothers with young children strolling through the park, but imagined winning the marathon at the Olympics in Rio. The Olympics in Rio is the past now. That's unforgiveable.

When listening to music, I saw myself on stage. I didn't have the capacity to just enjoy music, or anything else I considered to be of value, for that matter. I was incapable of removing myself from the theatre of glory. It distracted me from the realities of everyday life, and in that sense it had its merits. But my main fantasy, which centred on the short, blonde and pretty friend of the former near-girlfriend was something of pure cinematic theatre.

*

She is walking to work. I'm not far behind, on my way to the school to print materials for class. She nears the passageway of the old Kotva Department Store, a drab, communist-era department store where dreams generally went to be neutered not nurtured.

As she walks, a pickpocket grabs the bag from her shoulder and runs off. She turns with the shock and horror of someone who knows they have been categorically wronged, but in such a short space of time that the brain has yet to fully catch up. Fortunately, I'm ahead of the game (this is fantasy, and my brain works much faster than usual). That's a plot hole.

The street is full of people. The department store is in the heart of Prague, an area busy with office workers and tourists. Pickpockets are canny. They usually operate in groups, working the trams, stealing bags and purses and wallets before passing them to accomplices, or 'runners'. Yes, I made that term up, as it sounds fitting, but I imagine they do have their own Czech equivalent of a not dissimilar meaning.

The runners jump off at the nearest stop, usually before the victim has even realised they've been robbed. Of course, this jars with my fantasy. If it happened on the tram it's likely I wouldn't notice in time. If it happened on the tram it's likely she wouldn't be there, because if she were on the tram at that time of day, I wouldn't be bumping into her by happenstance. Prague is a small city.

You get to know the faces on your morning commute like the back of your hand.

And so I'm forced to ignore pickpocket custom, conveniently, forced to ignore the fact that no pickpocket is dumb enough to mug a woman in the centre of Prague at nine a.m. without the protective shell of contiguous bodies. I said they were canny. I never said they were either brave or stupid.

The pickpocket is a short, slender gypsy in a large puffer jacket, which he wears to compensate for his stature. He snatches her bag from her shoulder and begins to run off. Naturally, I chase him down the street, maybe a hundred, two hundred metres, surprisingly fast in my winklepicker shoes with their flat, slippery soles. I tackle him, gashing my knees and tearing my jeans in the process. I punch him once in the face before he's had a chance to get up, twice more to ensure he doesn't try any funny business. In the process, I'm either stabbed or slashed across the chest and so, naturally, I punch him again, obtain the knife and either take it with me or, if feeling particularly primal, plant it squarely in his foot.

I walk back to her, hand over the bag and calmly take the

lift up to the language school where we work. I'm not trying
to show off my bravery – even in fantasy, I'm delusional – but
I'll need a Czech speaker to ring an ambulance so I can sort out
my wound, a shallow but nonetheless bloody and impressive
wound. Walking into the school, I go straight to the teachers'
room, where there are many computers and a small kitchen. The
room is full of people preparing lessons. That's good.

They are photocopying. They are drinking coffee. That's
good too. Or green tea. That's not. There was always a lot of
green tea floating around the place in those days. It had become
fashionable.

That's a shame.

In the kitchen, I take a bottle of whiskey from a cupboard.
That's not far-fetched. There always was a half-drunk bottle of
Jack there for reasons I never understood, probably the result of
parties gone past.

A swig helps me dull the pain. Naturally, a group forms
around me. People ask what happened, but my reaction is one of
near total indifference, aside from asking one of the (beautiful)
women in my language school if they could do me a favour and
phone an ambulance.

Of course, I'm waiting for the short, blonde, pretty girl to
arrive. That's both the whole point and the plan. And then she
does. That's convenient. It never occurred to me to make sure
she wasn't shaken. That's dumb, but single-mindedly sexy too, I
imagine. I'm no expert in that field.

And she arrives. She looks at me with a measure of awe
and fear. She composes herself, explaining what I did to the
gathered, impressed masses. Our eyes meet. I hold her gaze,
impervious to the crowd whose attention I've been basking in
the last few moments. Now it's my turn to be indifferent. That's
sublime. But inside I'm glowing, of course, glowing and alive.
I'm looking forward to us getting to know each other. That's
going to be nice. The fact I'm drinking whiskey at nine in the
morning isn't a problem. That's what bloodied heroes do, is it
not?

Now that's a fantasy.

Of all the deluded, absurd scenarios I'd played out in my mind's
eye over the years, it was the most extreme, and it sustained me
through the cold winter months of 2013, as well as the long,
dragged-out summer of solitude, when I had too much time to
think about everything and not enough gumption to just sit down
and write, write it all.

The fantasies weren't so bad or vivid after I met Jana,

though they didn't go away. I still dreamt of winning awards as a writer, still pictured myself winning the marathon when I ran, or playing to crowds with a microphone or guitar in my hand, the usual stuff. But I didn't rely on fantasy.

Reality had finally taken over. That was good.

When I met Jana, she said she had thought me and Brad fools who drank too much beer, but that she'd found me attractive also, and that when I finally started talking to her, I didn't seem anywhere near as brash and bold as she'd thought. That was accurate.

I got to know her. I revealed myself. She didn't go away.

I played the fool, pulling my jeans down in public to make her laugh with embarrassment, and it was good. I made impressions of apes because it was fun to do and put a smile on her face and that was good. I wrote better because I was happy, and sometimes worse because I was happy and that was good. I taught better, I even flirted better with students because it was sexless and didn't mean a damn thing and it was good. I didn't think only of *I*. That was great. I was happy.

In short, I lived a fantasy.

*

A Thursday in February at the Job Centre in Brixton was a far cry from all that. That wasn't in the plan.

The claimant had lost his temper again. The plan had gone to pot, or was going swimmingly, depending on his derangement. I wasn't sure. The guards threatened to call the police. He left after that. I doubted that had been the plan. He left, dignity in tatters, melting into the Brixton High Street. That was so-so. I was glad to see the back of him, but pitied him too.

I didn't like Brixton, didn't like the crowds or the shouting or the constant beeping of cars and revving of motorcycles. It was vibrant, but it was lost on me. That was bad. When I'd left Prague, in a fug of depression and sadness at leaving her there, I'd planned to enjoy the vibrancy of London if nothing else.

There was nothing wrong with the things. The crowds were a part of the area as much as the Bowie mural with its dying flowers, or the Job Centre, or the ever-gentrifying market protected by white immigrants because it was now lovely; the Poundlands and chuggers, the screeching school kids and the nutjobs, the steel drum players and preachers of love and hate, the middle-aged, unemployed drinkers and the retired barflies who stared out from Wetherspoons each afternoon, or the Christian book store with its amusing board games and literature and ever friendly volunteers. It was all Brixton and I couldn't give a damn for it. That's the god's honest truth. I missed and grieved for Prague, the city I'd left so suddenly after three and a half years. I'd promised her I would get myself straight and then maybe come back. That was naïve.

I missed Prague with its ghost-like quality on weekends, when the masses went to their hometowns or cottages and you could walk for long periods without seeing a soul but for the occasional cyclist or driver or hobo. The silence had driven me mad, and now I yearned for it. That was men for you.

I missed the silence that drove me mad in the end, and that drove me mad too because it seemed like I complained when it was loud and complained when it was quiet and never found a moment's peace within me. That was unflattering.

I watched the Brixton crowds and tried to remember what it felt like towards the end, in Prague, when I hit a wall in my work and in my life, when I reached a point where I couldn't get out of bed in the morning, couldn't understand what my students were saying because the thought was reverberating in my mind: I can't do this anymore. I can't do this.

Depression. That was a cunt.

My thoughts were interrupted by a woman across the room, beckoning me to her desk. I walked over, handed her a piece of paper and sat down.

—I was told to bring my tenancy agreement.
She took the sheets.
—Did you bring your letter of appointment?
—No, I said. —I didn't get a letter.
—Really?I nodded. She typed for a few moments, pursing her lips with a surprised expression.
—Odd.

She said she would ask me a few questions that someone, somewhere else in the vast, unseen nexus of the Job Centre was asking her to ask me. I nodded, said that was fine, and sat down.

Behind me, I heard the chatter of security guards, and the automatic doors wushing open and then shut again.

—So, when exactly did you first enter the UK?

I'd known this would come up. It'd been a mandatory question, so I had done the only thing I thought logical and entered my date of birth. That was logical, in my opinion.

Technically, it was accurate, unless you were Catholic,

which I technically was, but I didn't want to investigate the finer details of what that meant.

I explained that I'd lived abroad for some years. She nodded, typing everything I said and more.

—Where did you live?
—In the Czech Republic. I came back last December.
—And this is a new claim?
—Yes, I said and, realising she had the impression I'd been out of work all this time, added —I had work between March to January of this year. I was made redundant.

I'd left by choice. That was the reality of the fact of the situation. I had left Prague by choice.

—They would like to know what you did when you were in the Czech Republic.

I had left by choice. I answered her questions as fully as possible, though my thoughts were elsewhere. There had been a time when I defined myself by what I did, a writer with a teaching problem, but a teaching problem that was just fine for the now. I took pride in teaching in a way that surprised me, striving for perfection with an almost Protestant fervour that was worrying.

It distracted me from my writing, but it was important to me to be good at my job. And I was always anxious if I felt I was doing it badly or was not well prepared.
That made everything worse.
Good writers, to my mind, were useless at everyday life, while I, at least on face value, got on just fine with it. I worked hard. I didn't let responsibilities drift just for the sake of my writing. I had to eat, after all. A thought preyed on my mind, that I was too normal, too everyday. In part, it was work ethic, but it was also damage limitation, a way to handle my anxiety. I was too frantic a human to leave anything to chance.
It was strange, how this diligence had defined me for so long. Now it was nothing but a moment in time boiled down to a few keystrokes on a Qwerty keyboard from a bored-looking woman in Brixton. That's plans for you.
But it *had* been more than that. It'd been the place where I left the house each morning at six, six-thirty, taking the same

buses and trams and Metro trains to my classes to teach the same faces week in and week out.

A place where I'd read short passages of novels as I floated around the city or listened to English podcasts with laughter, and American singers with empathy, as I walked into town for lessons close to home, or on my way to watch football with my friends.

Yes, if I thought about the daily humdrum activities of life, I remembered a great deal, but on the surface, there was little. I had lived there, and so the lucid memories were few and far between.

That was fine.

The rest, well, it had just been. It was where I ate eggs in the morning, where I packed my bags with folders and teaching materials, where I cracked under the pressures of life and wandered down to the potraviny to buy cigarettes but also, later on and in better times, Haribo for myself and Jana. That was a good time.

People back home had a vague idea of what Prague was but they didn't really know it, just as I could never know Copenhagen or Berlin or Lyon from mere dalliances. No one ever asked me about Prague now. It bothered me, because it cast a light upon the reality that it had simply been where I'd been living my life while they had been living theirs. Just as they hadn't asked about Prague, I had not asked about their lives in Brixton and Camden and the outer fringes of London where many of my childhood friends had moved: Northwood, Boreham Wood, Luton.

Admittedly, the views and museums in Luton aren't much to write home about, but it didn't mean I couldn't ask.

The disinterest I was met with when I spoke of Prague bothered me because I wanted to attach some meaning to it, to a place I'd loved and left so suddenly. The meaning, of course, was in the gaps. It was the everyday that had meant something, the bits I remembered only with effort, the *living* of it. That was Prague. The eggs and the coffee and the morning tram rides, heavy boot steps on timeworn cobbled streets in snow and fingers on elevator buttons, shirt collars wafting in the hot summer sun and classes taught and quickly forgotten.

To most, it was just another place in Eastern Europe. That was a tag that bothered me. It was a stag party locale, a dot on an interactive Ryanair map, a cobbled fairy tale, with a castle ideal for Instagramming in the nighttime. To most it was just a word. To me, it'd been everything, and yet here I was. That was that.

> —I was a teacher for three and a half
> years, I said.

The woman typed it all in and asked if I'd owned property in the Czech Republic. I laughed, and shook my head.

> —No.
> —Any other assets?
> —Like what?
> —Bank account, that kind of thing.
> —I had a bank account, yes. When I left I had about eight hundred pounds which I transferred over last year.
> —Is the account still open?
> —No.
> —Sorry about all the questions.
> —It's okay.
> —They want to know if you were forcibly deported from the Czech Republic.

> —No, I said, with a smile.

And therein lay my guilt. No one had twisted my arm. I had simply left her and everything behind, homesick and mind sick, as deluded about London as I had been about marathons or music or girls mugged on streets and not trams. I'd wanted a better life for us, me and her, and *them*, should it ever come to it. But Prague didn't quite allow for that. Impossible dreams, those.

When I think of Prague now, I think of it at its best, even if most of my time was spent on trams and in the cramped, whitewashed offices of multinational companies, on industrial estates far out from the centre and buzzing in and out of offices with my electronic key card. Now, I picture the Romanesque beauty of Vinohrady, the reasty – yes, reasty – squalor of Žižkov, with its endless graffiti and bohemian charm, and Jiřího z Poděbrad, with its sea of pink and yellow and blue apartment blocks of various mild hues: a storybook fantasy, an architect's dream, a piss-artist's nirvana.

Prague is a city where a man can find beauty simply by looking up. In the end, I could look no higher than my shoes. If a man can't crane his neck in Prague and at least teeter on the brink of a smile, the world in him has become a spoiled and rotten place.

The woman continued to ask dull, Kafkafian questions.

I answered them best I could, thinking all the while that I'd do anything to have it back, to look up and ahead, in mirrors and in life. The Job Centre was very quiet now without the lunatic, with only the wushing open and wushing shut of the automatic door, and the occasional clicking of mice, or mouses, here and there.

*

In the morning I went to the gym, then home, and cooked a breakfast of avocado and eggs. I felt good for having started the day in a healthy manner. I had a job application to finish and wanted to write too, as I'd never got round to it the day before. There were many things to fit in my plan for the day. That was good, but also ran the risk of becoming overwhelming.

I started to walk towards a café I liked, where I tended to work better than in my room with all its distractions and comforts of home: the oft-neglected guitar, the books, the console and television, the acceptability of watching porn in private that was not the case in public, and the opportunity to be languorous and gaze out the window.

I walked up the Vassall Road towards a Tesco that I tended to avoid if possible, and turned right onto the Brixton Road, towards the café. When I'd been in work, I would often walk via the Brixton Road, taking in the hub of activity of a city of people toing and froing towards the centre of town, to buses and trains; the click clacking of heels, the swing swing swing of briefcases. There was none of that now. The working day had begun.

Everyone who was a *someone* was in work. Everyone else just blended into the background. Here we were now, a ragtag bunch of the elderly and unemployed, and that nebulous group of men who are vague in their existence, for whom it is impossible to say with any degree of certainty whether they are homeless, whether they are high or merely working towards it, drunk or drinking towards that too.

The street was one of contrasts. On one side there was the Van Gogh café next to the church, followed by several shops and small businesses: an Eritrean restaurant, an Afro-Caribbean barber's, the grocers owned by a Chelsea supporting couple who never charged me for chillies or rosemary or sage or any other culinary embellishment which reminded me that, no matter how long and fruitless the days were, I was not of that forgotten class of people whose days are filled with boredom and purposelessness and paper-thin black plastic bags with an

142

indistinct number of 568ml cans of something strong. That was good.

On the other side of the street was a row of beautiful Georgian houses that struck me every time I passed. Although on the main road, they were slightly elevated and stood behind a small grass verge, away from the traffic.

They were unique to the Brixton Road, which consisted of largely '60s tenements, once tenebrous but now highly sought-after by pure dint of proximity to Oval and Stockwell stations. Yet when I looked at the Georgian houses, I realised they were not the three or four-storey palaces of grandeur and space they appeared to be.

On the inner recess of each porch was a large, grey metallic box with silver buttons and names written on laminated paper. Like woodlice, they climbed up the walls, evidence of a city growing smaller with each passing year, its people packed in like sardines. It was a kind of funny, though I'm not sure which.

Why did it sadden me? Why did I care what had happened to these once grand houses? After all, the nameless and faceless had always passed them by.

It was only the innards of them that differed now.

I continued on towards the café, past the grocer's and then a corner shop which wasn't on a corner, and a chemist's where an orderly queue had formed, two mothers with prams and a man with long, straggly white hair, who stood behind them. He wore a faded camouflage jacket and had his hands behind his back, which were stained with a treacle brown layer of dirt. He shuffled his fingers as he waited patiently for his morning Methadone. I walked into the café, bought a coffee, and sat down and checked emails before writing.

The next morning I did more or less the same thing, changing my route slightly. Instead of turning up the Vassall Road I only walked on it as much as necessary before going down Foxley Road. That was a detour for the sake of variety.

I walked past the Ambulance Depot and the mechanic's, where I caught a glance of a guy who looked a lot like a Greek kid I'd been to school with. But it couldn't have been him, as I was next to certain he still lived in North London.

I passed the mechanic's and walked up the A202, past the gym and towards Oval. The pavements were chalked with warning signs. *Wet Paint*. Although I could smell it, I couldn't figure out where it came from, before finally realising it was the lampposts, which had a layer of fresh black paint that smelt of ethanol and childhood and the Airfix model shop I visited with my cousin when I was fourteen every Saturday, in that short period between innocent childhood and years of teenage curiosity, which I resisted with every fibre of my being, and he embraced with horny, adolescent fervour. That was funny.

As he left behind toy planes for chasing girls and going out, I sought nothing but the refuge of my video games and the company of my friends, yet was attracted by the glamour of pubs and the notion of drinking beer in all its bounteous variety, more than the thought of meeting girls. My thoughts ran back to the glue on our fingertips and paint on copies of the *Mirror* our aunt laid out for her sanity as much as our benefit. That was my childhood.

I walked over the road to the café, and ordered an Americano with milk. The woman behind the counter took my order and another my money. I spent many moments trying to figure out who she reminded me of but couldn't put my finger on it. It was something in the eyes, someone I'd known, definitely not someone famous. But who?

Later that day, I realised it was a secretary from the language school back in Prague, which was odd, as she'd had long blonde hair, while the woman in the café was black, with black hair. If I remembered rightly, the secretary had had a baby girl in the intervening years. That was funny too.

CARRION AND CORNFLOUR:
THE WHISKEY DREAMS
REVISITED

It'd been a long time since I'd read or even thought of that story. I looked at the website I'd set up four years earlier; paying for a domain with the intention of making a real stab at getting to grips with the world of the Internet, promoting my writing that way. It was the done thing these days. But like many things, I'd used it less than planned. Like many of my plans, it didn't quite go to plan.

Things were going to be different now, though. I'd designs again, serious ones this time. Time, of course, was something I'd wasted a great deal of, and it was important to make up for that. I was going to write daily, going to publish and promote my stories, all with the sight of hind; working patiently, diligently and sparingly with the adverb.

Having worked as a journalist, I now knew how to use Twitter and the like. Sure, I made spelling mistakes, and sometimes sent ill-advised messages to the world at large whilst drunk, but in theory, at least, I knew what I was doing. I wasn't going to get published via the traditional route any time soon, not with my kind of writing.

That was self-aware of me.

It's not that my writing was *out there*, far from it. It was just, well, detailed. Long. You know this.

There weren't any explosions or murders, and there was a hideous dearth of sex involving men and women or men and men or women and women or even more than one person at a time at all. That was a price of writing in a semi-autobiographical fashion.

People didn't like my kind of writing. It demanded time, and if I was a man short on time the world at large took it to another level. My last job had been a reflection of that, a year spent writing lists; Ten Acts to See At this festival, Five Bands Who Should Headline Glastonbury, Six Singers Who Blew Tommy Lee. With advertising concerns, the last one did not pass the censors – my boss – but with so many digi-lines to fill and so little time, it was easy to fall back on lewd ideas. If it couldn't be summed up in a few words with a couple of photographs, it was no good.

My most read article? A news story about the lead singer of The Fall pissing himself onstage. That was fine. On a weekend where Kanye West proclaimed himself the greatest rock star in the world and the Dalai Lama, forever work-shy, took a weekend off to visit a farm in Dorset and hold hands with Patti Smith, that *was* news.

I'd always written longly, or at least had done so ever since deciding to be a writer, six weeks short of graduating from university without a clue of what to do with my life. Fear of the real world made me put pen to paper (in reality, it was digit to keyboard, as debilitating dyspraxia prevents me from reading my own handwriting), but it stopped me at times too.

Sometimes, I was afraid of writing. Nothing had ever happened to me. That was the truth. Of course, many things had. My father's death. Catholicism. The time I pissed myself in PE when I was four and had to wear a pair of frilly girls' knickers because it was all the receptionist had in the cupboard for kids who piss themselves.

But my university career left me thinking I didn't come from a suitably interesting background, neither too poor nor too rich, too troubled nor too carefree, too debauched nor monastic. Somewhere in the middle. And having not studied English literature was another barrier to writing, I believed, something that now seems absurd. English literature students often make bad writers. That's an inconvenient (and increasingly expensive) truth, but a truth nonetheless.

Most of all, I was just afraid of it all, afraid that if I tried to translate the thoughts in my head into feelings splayed on a page, the world would laugh. I'd spent my life fantasising about being creative, but I wasn't, or at least dared not be.

In the end, however, I did it, was all right at it too. Naturally, I was terrible to start with, experimenting with every style and idea big and small. Some things worked, others failed miserably. I spent several years not afraid to write but flitting between a deep-seated fear that everything I did was mediocre or the purest gold. Now, though, having finally been paid to write (even if it generally meant dick jokes and short, tweet-length posts), I believed in my writing, and for the first time, myself; knew how I was meant to write, felt comfortable with the likelihood no one would ever read it. If you wrote something that could sell it would sell, if you didn't, you stuck to it anyway, not out of some pig-headed sense of idealism but just because. The truth shone a glistening turd-brown if you didn't.

That was good to know.

Besides, I was far from finished. I'd written four hundred pages of a novel, much of which would be discarded, and had a host of short stories in the works. One in particular, *Woodlice & Sundown*, had been in the works for some time, to the point that I was unsure where to go with it. My eyes needed respite, and so I looked back over *The Whiskey Dreams*, a story I'd written years earlier, during that second – and longest – winter in Prague. That was quite the winter.

I'd moved into a new apartment not long before. I use the

American word purposely, because it was advertised that way by the Czech realtor (again, purposely) and the American woman who would eventually become my housemate. She was from Seattle. That was irrelevant. She was anally retentive. That was not.

The apartment was on Mánesova, a beautiful, tree-lined street ten minutes' walk from Wenceslas Square but a world away at the same time. In the winter, it was a haven in a busy part of the city, even from Vinohradska, a street that ran parallel, with busy trams shooting up and down the city in each direction. My apartment was right in the middle. If I walked out of the large wooden door, turned right, and hung a left, Riegrovy Sady was in front of me. At the top of the street was Jiřího z Poděbrad, the large square surrounded by pretty, multi-coloured apartment blocks. Near the bottom was Kaaba, which I discovered shortly after moving to the street, and in between there were a smattering of restaurants I couldn't afford and cafés I could. In summer, it was nice to walk from one end to the other with the street bathed in shade due to the height of the apartment blocks, without it being moodily dark, rays of light poking through the side streets or the sun shining up at me at the bottom.

Mánesova was an improvement on my previous road, Hálkova, where I'd lived for a year, close to two busy streets that ran in and out of the city. It was leafy and I was immediately happier there. I took a picture on my camera, uploaded it to my computer and posted it on social media for the world to see. It garnered five likes. That was gratifying in an inexplicable way.

As the buildings on the street were six floors high, I didn't get to enjoy the sunset, but did get to enjoy the orange glow of a late evening. That was better than so-so, it was all right, maybe a little good even.

The apartment itself had a small, beautiful kitchen, with ornate 70s-style furniture. I didn't spend much time with my housemates but was happy. After a month or so, I met Barbara, and was happier still. She was a girl from my language school. Maybe I got too happy. Or maybe she just got to know me better – the 'me' beneath whatever veneer I presented to the world – and didn't like what she saw. That wasn't fine at the time, but it's fine now with hindsight. That's time for you. Makes fools of some and sages of others. That's also an herb, which is why sayings and epithets and tidbits or titbits of advice should always be taken with a pinch of salt, which is in and of itself a seasoning.

We hooked up. It didn't fizzle out as I said. She just

went cold on me after a time. And then after she went cold on me she went off me and then she went away, and we only saw each other at the language school, where I would be as friendly as possible for the sake of my pride. That was a romance summarised in one hundred and sixty-two words. That's funny, ha-ha funny, because it'd meant the world to me at the time.

When winter truly settled in around November, it was bitter, and I was bitter too, and out of that came *The Whiskey Dreams*, the only thing I wrote in those years that ever garnered any praise.

—I liked it, my friend John told me, one evening that Christmas, over beers, when I was back in England. —Shows promise.

That made me laugh. I believed myself to be beyond promise, thought myself the real deal by now, at the age of twenty-five. But deep down, it meant a great deal to hear him say it.

Now, years later, I'd hit a wall with my writing. I no longer thought of myself as the real deal, or any deal for that matter, no longer missed Barbara, no longer tried to put things into as few words as possible, for money or otherwise, no longer saw writing as the answer.

I saved *Woodlice & Sundown*. It was going nowhere in its current form.

At the very least, I was failing it by looking at the words for too long on the screen, running the risk of destroying all my work, good, bad and so-so. I closed Word, found that old story and began reading *The Whiskey Dreams*. Even though it was about a woman, I'd read it to Jana one time on the bed of a room that briefly became mine when I moved in a few months later, before we moved into another bedroom in the small three-bedroom flat on Kubelíkova which we shared with three to four others at a time – depending on who was with whom and whom with who. That's a linguistic thing I've never understood, whom. Only ever gone with what feels right.

That's smart.

We lay on the bed. It was a February evening. She'd asked me to read to her after we'd spent several minutes putting bits of folded paper underneath the casters of her bed, which moved a little without encouragement, and a great deal with it. I read slowly and clear, for effect, and so she'd comprehend. For unknown reasons, I read in an American accent.

That's not quite true, the reasons, that is. I'd always
spoken to myself in accents other than my own. When I walked
the streets I spoke to myself in an American accent, sometimes
Irish or Northern English too, but mostly American. If someone
bumped into me in the street, I was inclined to shout *Jesus
Christ* aloud, in a strange kind of southern drawl.

It was insane, but it was also a way of getting out of a
person I didn't much like. That probably wasn't smart, but it was
too late to change it now.

More important to this particular occasion was the
fact that *The Whiskey Dreams* had always been meant as an
American tale. The idea itself had come from Brad and another
friend. I'd simply stolen it. They had wanted to create a series
of short stories, or a film, or some kind of book entitled *The
Whiskey Dreams*, but they never got beyond the names, and
it was me that did something with it. That was intellectual
property stolen, but at least I put the intellect into it.I read aloud
in my poor southern drawl, a manqué odist. Jana listened, her
eyes intense in my periphery.

We'd only met in November, but I was already
comfortable enough to read to her, or to prance around her room
naked, pumping my chest and pursing my lips with primatial
joy.

I read in the American voice because the story suited it,
but for once, I was comfortable in my skin, happy after all these
years.

I could never have imagined Jana would in turn become
part of the whiskey dreams. At that time, all I saw was the then,
and I called it now, the notion of future seeming absurd, the kind
of thing only a fool would consider. I was right about that. It is a
gift to live *then* and know it only as *now*.

*

Now, two years later, sitting in my South London bedroom
on my Jones as a soughing wind crept through the gap in my
window, I looked out onto the street, and back to my computer
screen. That was a poor attempt at exposition via the elements.

I no longer went out in the evenings like I'd done in
Prague. That's what I'm getting at.

Going out was expensive here. Beer no longer cost less
than a bottle of water, and several times more. Pubs and cafés
teemed with people. There was nowhere you could really
describe as cosy. That was probably good for business, to be fair.

I'd started to see Prague through rose-tinted glasses, and

knew my memories betrayed me, Kaaba now a haven in my mind, a quiet retreat from the city, a place which played great music of every hue. That was nonsense.

Kaaba played some very good music: The National, classic Stones, Nick Drake. But they also played Sting, lots of it, and Jazz, lots of that too, both of which got under my skin so insidiously as to stop me working at all.

It was impossible to write a novel with 'Fields of Gold' in your ears. And that was one of his better ones.

I missed and yearned for Prague, allowing that longing to cloud my memory. When I thought about Kaaba it was of the times when things went well; writing passages of the novel I really believed would take me somewhere, when it flowed freely and I felt happy and fulfilled and full of optimism.

That was beautiful.

And then, of course, Kaaba was inextricably linked to Jana, chasing her with the cowardice of a eunuch naïf, but chasing her nonetheless. That too was beautiful, even if it reflected on me badly.

Kaaba was where it all began, but there were days when the words wouldn't come and all that could be heard were the sounds of babies crying and coffee cups rattling and, of course, 'Fields of Gold'.

There were days before I got her, when I'd go home in a silent rage, fists balled together in anger, not at her or the world but at myself, a craven fool who was falling in love with a stranger yet completely incapable of just asking: *would you like to go for a beer?*

Sadly, that was the that of the that of the that. That was me. I guess it was beautiful too, in its way.

No, Kaaba wasn't just joy, it was sadness too. That was important.

I looked down onto my South London street again, and missed it, forcing myself to recognise with clarity both the joy and pain of that sometimes cosy sometimes noisy café at the bottom of my street. The England I'd returned to was different from that of 2011.

Flocks of birds dotted the skyline, but they were mostly cranes. Prices had risen. That's what prices do.

People had left, others had come in their place. Some had died, others had gotten themselves born. There'd been an Olympics, there hadn't been any more riots. There was a thing called Byron Burger. That was a thing, and I'd never heard of it before.

London seemed a harsher city than before, even though

I'd left in part to find work through lack of patience or nous to simply wait it out. I wrote *The Whiskey Dreams* in the winter of 2012. The summer had been long and difficult. My short, blonde Republican girlfriend had left and gone home. Although I had never called her my girlfriend and did not treat her with the affection and gratitude she deserved, I missed her, or at the very least, I missed the proximity of her body in the evenings, not so much for sexual gratification, but just, well, the proximity of another.

In the autumn I met Barbara. I won an award for teaching, which I felt vindicated the year I had spent struggling to get used to it, and the stress it entailed. It felt as if things were coming together. There are fewer feelings sweeter than the notion that things are coming together, none more sour than them falling apart.

Autumn was followed by winter. That's tradition.

I had no short, blonde Republican girlfriend who I didn't call girlfriend, no blonde (she wasn't short, which may have been the problem) Czech girlfriend either, for that matter. But time, yes, I'd plenty of that.

And so I wrote *The Whiskey Dreams*, drifting between café and home nightly writing, a fuzz of incomprehension carrying me to and fro to the extent I nearly forgot where and what I was. That was fantastic. Sometimes, I miss the nebulousness of it all.

Looking back, it should have been clear to me. I should have recognised the whiskey dreams for what they were, because it was only in my dreams – the classroom aside – that I heard English.

Otherwise, my days were spent talking basic Czech to waiters and waitresses in cafés, staff in shops, or the kindly woman who ran the potraviny at the end of my street. Brad had found yet another new girlfriend and rarely called me for drinks. That was fine. That was just the way men in constant need of female company were.

Yes, I should have seen the whiskey dreams for what they were, but then part of their allure lay in the sparseness of words, the aimless walking, the sounds as I looked for Barbara: a fountain in the centre of town, my footsteps, the thud of a suitcase in the central station, where I once found her leaving the city for a weekend, going away from me again.

When the whiskey dreams returned to my life, it was different from the last time, when I'd sought them out with alacrity, floating through my working hours towards the end of the day, not for want of finishing, but so I could try and find her in my dreams, aware she was beyond me now in the real world.

This time, however, it was different. I didn't seek them, didn't plan on finding anything or anyone. I didn't make plans at all, anymore, not after everything I'd lost through the making of plans.

I kind of, well, fell into them. That was good, I believe.

*

It started one night with a wee dram on ice. That's conjecture. I've no idea how big or small a dram is and I poured without thought for measurements while streaming an American serial I'd not paid for. I felt bad about that, but had yet to find a new job, and decided I couldn't afford to be too moral about the whole endeavour. I certainly wasn't poor, but poor enough – or under threat of it – to justify the theft of leisure.

It was two months since my redundancy. The lamp I'd bought in November to cosy up the room reached halfway up the wall, encased in a thin white paper that made the light glow a nice dim way throughout the room. It was cold and sodden outside, and when I woke each morning there was a layer of water on the windowsill I had to wipe with an absorbent sports towel. My bedroom was small, but not as small as the one I'd had after moving in at the tail-end of July. When one of my flatmates left, I migrated across the hall. The room was larger, but the increase in size had grown relative by now, cramped, with little room for manoeuvre. Still, with a dram or two, a good lamp, and a streamed American serial about zombies, it was cosy and warm.

I don't believe losing my job is to blame for the return of the whiskey dreams in my life, nor for her sudden appearance in them. She'd actually been a figure in my dreams a while - Jana, that is.

Barbara was long gone. I thought about her with a nothingness which sometimes allowed her room in my sexual fantasies. Admittedly, that is a club about as elite as a Wetherspoons.

There had been a time when she meant everything, the way they always did with me, a time when I was haunted by memories of her listening to 'Raglan Road' on a tinny mobile phone as we walked home hand in hand, walking through Riegrovy Sady as autumn nestled into winter. But then she was gone, and years later, meant little to me. She was nothing but a girl I'd known who'd hurt me when we were both young and hurtable and likely to hurt. That was fine.

154

I thought fondly of her. It's crass to remain bitter at the beautiful.

I didn't dream about Jana while we were together. In fact, I never dreamt about anyone close to me. In sleep, as in life, I kept people at arm's length.

The first whiskey dream with Jana was nothing like those of years gone by. For one thing, I knew my surroundings were those of Prague; the city and the streets around the school where I'd worked, the red and white trams that could be heard coming from far off, electricity shooting through them by way of warning; the central station with its assortment of commuters from the satellite towns and bums with their Albert wine, and backpackers coming and going between Prague and other European cities. More than anything, though, it was clear I was there by choice.

That didn't make much sense to me.

I had left it all behind: Jana, the city, the streets and the cafés, the whistling of steamers in coffee shops, the tram inspectors with their sausage roll fingers and thousand-yard stares.

I'd left in the winter of 2014, when I could no longer get out of bed; left and returned to England to get help, still with a return ticket booked for a New Year's Eve we'd intended to spend together, me knowing as I departed I would not be back for that night because I was too sick. That was mental illness for you. Wizz Air online booking too, for that matter.

Yes, I'd left it all behind, yet here I was. Something was amiss, though, and I couldn't tell if I was dreaming of a time before or after I'd met Jana despite her presence.

Nothing made sense. We spoke. It was unpleasant. There was an argument of sorts. That was familiar, though only from the recent past. The year we'd spent together from afar had involved numerous phone calls and Internet chats, confusion heaped upon confusion, me unable to understand my decision to leave, her questioning –wrongly – if it had been due to her. That was absurd, I hoped she knew, but I'd absurdly given her good reason to think that also.

*

When I woke up in the morning, my memory was hazy, though I knew I wanted to return to my dreams as soon as possible, to right whatever wrong I'd done to her.

I looked at the bottle of whiskey beside my window. I'd only had a couple of measures, nowhere near enough to open up the whiskey dreams. But last night's had resembled them so closely. That was good.

I got up, showered, dressed, and walked down the Camberwell Road, towards a shop where I bought celery, onions, three russet potatoes and some carrots, determined as always to follow recipes to the letter of the law.

The slightest delineation led to mistakes, mistakes to chaos, chaos to a lassitude towards cooking, which led to unhealthy diets and habits and further chaos down the line. That was undesirable, bad and not what I planned in terms of lifestyle over the coming months.

I didn't like celery. It was just rhubarb with a good PR team. But that wasn't the point. I had to do as instructed.

On the way back up the Camberwell Road, thinking about how the day was running away from me, I saw her, maybe two, three hundred yards ahead. She was walking on the other side of the street, her ponytail swaying from side to side the way it did back in the days when I would watch as she left for work. I followed, determined to account for whatever I'd said, unable to remember what I'd done wrong in the whiskey dream but certain it had to be fixed, righted and apologised for. What was I thinking? It wasn't Jana. With my mind running wild, I was in danger of following a stranger. I walked home.

That night, I read for half an hour and wrote for forty-five minutes and thought I'd done a good job of not thinking about it. But the folly was in the music. I listened to songs from the early days when we met, when night and day meant nothing, not because I didn't know one from the other, or sought light from dark for escape or vice versa, but because I had in me a deep well of joy, the waters of which washed away any need to recognise the day from the nights and the sun from the stars or the moon from the sun.

The songs reminded me that Jana was a *time* gone and irredeemable, one I longed for in more than memory and song alone. Listening on, it was clear what my job was now. Above finding work, above staying fit and healthy, above everything, I had to find her.

So that night I drank the whiskey like it was medicine, dosing out twenty-millilitre measures carefully. It was as far a cry as you could get from reckless alcoholism, the amounts just enough to keep me lucid and aid me in drifting off, but not so much that I would experience a black, dreamless sleep, better as that might have been.

And I got it right.

*

She was there when I arrived. It was clearly Prague even if it didn't look like the city. I didn't recognise the streets, couldn't see any of the Vietnamese-run potraviny shops, but it was undoubtedly Prague and a whiskey dream.

My plan had worked.

I looked for her: around a corner, up streets, everywhere. She'd been there when I arrived, then as quickly gone.

Why?

Eventually, I bumped into a woman and asked her for directions. She spoke back to me in plain, Canadian-accented English, but was unable to help. And that was it. I didn't find Jana again that night.

In the morning, I wondered whether it had been worth it, that brief sighting, nothing more than a glimmer, Jana more or less as elusive in sleep as she now was in life. I'd rolled back time, rediscovered the whiskey dreams, and achieved nothing. For that reason, it seemed vital to go back in. I got up, showered and dressed, but chose not to exercise the way I had over the last two months by going to the gym before breakfast. My routine had been interrupted and that was bad, but because the whiskey dreams held at least the possibility of finding her, it was worth it.

I made a breakfast of two-day-old bread I'd baked, with butter and damson jam given to me by an old colleague. The bread wasn't fresh but not stale either, and the jam was fine. I chewed carefully, thinking back to every moment of the night before, though all I could recall was getting nowhere by talking to the Canadian woman. I finished my breakfast and began to look for work again but struggled to concentrate, excited for the night, when I could try all over again.

*

Yesterday, I woke up to discover that the Czech Republic is to change its name to Czechia. Several explanations were given, but the official reason was that it would make the country more easily marketable worldwide, its sports teams more widely known, labels easier to print on products and clothing. It was maddening. I didn't know why. That was normal.

I lived in that country three and a half years, three and a half years longer than I have ever lived in Ireland, the nation written on my passport in a language incomprehensible to me. That's the allure of Ireland for you.

157

How sad it is, to see this old country of mine, the Czech Republic, give in to the fear of insignificance, of being forgotten by the world around it. It's normal for countries to fear insignificance. They are, after all, run largely by men.

Czechia. I read it back to myself several times as if in a dream, but it didn't resemble the beer dreams of old with their black emptiness, or the vivid confusion of the whiskey dreams. It was reality, an absurd, conscious reality of a country defiled by its own.

This, a nation kicked about like a football between the Germans' flirtation with evil and the Russians' deluded benevolence. A nation ignored by the Americans and English, now clamouring to be recognised through the medium of a label.

Czechia, a nation wedged between *50% cotton* and *Do not tumble dry.*

*

It quickly became clear that finding the whiskey dreams had been easier in Prague, when my days were filled with activity: travelling between classes, jumping between train and tram to various offices around the city.

Back then, I thought about them constantly, but they were a presence rather than a constant, a part of my working day, a fixture of my thinking rather than my thinking itself.

Sometimes I met Brad – he'd begun arguing with the girlfriend and so leaned on me for emotional support – and put them off a night in order to enjoy his company. And it worked. On those occasions, I had beer dreams. They were rarely vivid, and when they were, it was a nonsensical and absurd vividness. They meant more or less nothing. That was good.

I never woke up worried or frustrated about not making something tangible of them. That was a relief.

Back in London, I'd no Brad to distract me, though I still had dreams. Occasionally, I had a recurring dream I'd often had in Prague. I was back at school, at my current age, studying for more A-levels, despite passing them the first time around.

There was never any explanation. It was always Economics or Geography, and I was either unprepared for an exam or had forgotten to do an essay. Generally, I came to the conclusion things were so fucked it'd be better to sacrifice success in one in order to pass the other, usually favouring Economics over Geography. That's strange, as I'm terrible with money.

Still, it was a nonsense dream, and it didn't much bother

158

me in the mornings. Given the frequency, I figured there was
some deeper meaning, but didn't want to get too Freudian.
Freud was smart, but he was also an addict who had thirty-eight
operations to remove mouth cancer because he just couldn't put
down the funsticks. That was human, and good to know.

There was only one recurring dream that ever bothered
me. It had involved the pretty girl whose handbag I fantasised
about 'reclaiming' from the pickpocketing thief. Much like
the whiskey dreams, I dreamt about finding her, but unlike the
whiskey dreams, I was always successful in my aim. Sometimes
we had sex, and even in the midst of the dream, I'd know I was
asleep, that what was happening was the consequence of that.

This dream may have started when I was still with
Barbara, or shortly afterwards, and it bothered me.

I didn't want to accept that a romance I'd longed for and
mourned for could be fleeting and vague, mistimed or poorly
thought out, like renaming a country to make its cigarette packs
easier to read, or drinking in the morning under the illusion that
you would not continue to do so throughout the day and night,
or searching for home in towns that were not your own.

*

I sat in my room, thinking about all the dreams: the absurd ones,
the meaningless ones, the ones that haunted me. And then I
thought of Jana, of winter nights indoors with fairy lights above
our bed and the warmth of embrace.

In reality, we'd never slept arm in arm all night, me
being too sweaty a man to inflict it on her. We would embrace,
separate, seek out each other's hands, hold them a few moments,
then return to our opposing sides like weary men of the trenches
on Christmas Day, all the while wishing for the contiguity of
recent moments.

But I was an *extremely* sweaty man.

That was genetics for you.

I thought about our bedroom, with its fairy lights,
Jana's unique origami figurines of monkeys made for me, and
the antique cupboard we'd bought which would never open
properly. For once the memories were vivid and almost pleasant,
the whiskey dreams unattractive to me that night, a past without
warmth and closeness, the need and desire to fulfil need. No, I
didn't want whiskey dreams. I wanted beer dreams. And so beer
dreams I went and got. Going out, I met friends, drank several
drinks, and came home, sober enough to think I'd have a black,
dreamless sleep.

How wrong.

I dreamt vivid, dreamt about arguing with family, something that rarely happened in dream or in life. The beer dreams had failed me. The whiskey dreams were back in my life, and I'd little choice but to embrace them. I didn't have to read the story again to remember how they went.

Sometimes I dream vivid.
Sometimes I dream clean.

Did I really want to go back to that, after the failure of the beer dreams? After they entered my nights uninvited, I did my best to avoid Jana and the dreams for a while, much as part of me wanted both.

I went to the cinema one night, the wind howling and rain lashing so heavily it nearly put me off. At the bus stop there were about twenty school children waiting to go home and again I considered turning back, put off by the noise and the pushing and shoving.

But I stayed, and got the bus to Peckham to see the new *Star Wars* film. On the bus, I checked my phone, put it back in my pocket, and repeated that several times in case a friend had messaged me to grab a beer, in which case I'd turn back, not so much for the beer but for the company.

It wouldn't be like it had been with Brad. The best I could hope for was a swift one or two, inane chatter about football or their work, nothing of any real depth or difficulty, no real talk of how things were, or were not, going for either of us. That was London for you. People had jobs and lives of their own; they didn't like to talk about those of others.

At the cinema, I queued for my ticket and checked my phone once more before buying it. I paid five pounds, switched off the phone and went to Screen One.

I'd not seen a film in months.

The Peckhamplex was the only cinema in the city where tickets were cheap, like they had been in Prague.

I knew I needed to stop thinking of the city, but it was under my skin, much as London had got under my skin when it seemed I might never live there again. It was important to leave Prague behind. After all, it was the woman left behind I really missed, and she was gone, irredeemably so.

But Prague itself played a role in my longings. Prague clung to the soul, small vignettes of its horizons and apartment blocks and tramlines a constant, semi-visible kaleidoscope on the retina; the castle poking up into the upper eyelids, the opera house taking up space in the left eye, the apartments with their red roofs dotted around my consciousness like lentils.

A city lived in is not just its immediacy but a tapestry of moments woven in both neat and ragged threads which tug at you from time to time; a stoating of the memory.

*

The film proved a healthy distraction. That was the beauty of *Star Wars*. They did things right, just as they should have the last time they had strung out the franchise. A little of the damage done by *Episodes I-III* was undone. That was a relief to anyone who cared about either childhood or film.

Near the end of the movie I recognised a green and rocky landmass out to sea, a clutch of rocks in Ireland called the Skelligs, where some scenes had been shot in 2015, creating an excited buzz in otherwise sleepy and quiet southwest Kerry. That was exciting, but it was also money, and money was of vital importance when your economy had hitherto been based on fishing and irregular tourism.

The filming had taken place close to my father's hometown. My mother was excited to see the film. I tried to tell her it wouldn't be recognisable. That's what films were like. They chose places based on their aesthetic and then did everything they could to make that aesthetic unrecognisable from reality.That was the bizarre world of Hollywood.

But I was wrong. Low and behold, the island I saw there on that silver screen was Skellig Michael, unmistakably so. They'd tried to create a falsity, a scene, another world, yet I saw it for what it was, and forgot about Jana and the job and Prague and the whiskey dreams for a few minutes. That was good.

It was a brief, wonderful moment of unfettered distraction, from Jana, from Fluoxetine in her green and white skirt, and application forms and beer and days elongated and often wasted.

But then the credits rolled and the John Williams soundtrack came on and while the nostalgia kick was enjoyable, I knew I'd come back to reality, different from what I'd been enjoying moments earlier; the world of the day and the night that was the same, and the search for something unknown that lay ahead in the whiskey dreams, and of course Jana, gone Jana.

On the bus home, I overheard a Czech couple talking. That was pure serendipity, or bad luck maybe. It was normal to hear Polish in London and I sometimes mistook them for Czechs, out

161

of hope more than anything.

But as the bus travelled along the Camberwell Road, I knew for sure these people were Czech, with their inimitable, slow, sardonic back and forth, the cynicism and black humour of a landlocked country clear as day.

I clung to the nonchalance of every word, each one evoking a memory of Prague, of the ins and outs of life there. It wasn't the whiskey dreams I remembered now as I sat sandwiched between two yellow poles, staring at a couple carrying home an ironing board, a clotheshorse and what looked like a cheap guitar, or at least a battered, old and used one.

Remembering the whiskey dreams would have been just fine. I could've laughed, thinking about how I'd descended over a picayune romance I should never have let get to me the way it did. That would have been nice. But instead, I listened to the couple. The girl held the clotheshorse. The way she talked suggested they were discussing something dull: cleaning, tomorrow's plans, things that needed to be done over the weekend.

I thought of the room I'd shared with Jana: the soft mattress of our bed and the cold of the tiles in the bathroom against my feet as I sat to take a piss after sex, the copy of *Maxim* our housemate left on the floor which had inspired me on at least two occasions, the smell of paprika in the kitchen, the clanking noise of the old extractor fan, everything. I thought about it all.

The bus passed the Co-Op on the Camberwell Road; I could taste the beetroot borsch I never liked and now all I wanted was to be eating borsch. I could feel the tiles in our tiny kitchen shared with three and sometimes four others, and could see the recipes Jana pinned to the notice board: a salad with goat cheese and walnuts, a carrot and coriander soup.

I saw the laminated labels on each relevant appliance or cupboard or pot or pan, which Jana's best friend had written in Czech to aid the learning of her Austrian boyfriend. I looked over at the couple.

Jste cech?

It would be so simple for me to say it, to introduce myself, to strike up a conversation. Sure, they would be shocked. There weren't many Czechs in London, fewer Czech-speaking Englishmen still.

That was nonsense. They wouldn't be shocked. Nothing shocked the Czechs. The Czechs lived in a perpetual state of unimpressedness. They were disinterested, resigned, yet often happy about it and wonderfully cynical. It had driven me nuts towards the end, and now that I missed it, it drove me nuts now; that shoulder-shrugging disinclination to anything that wasn't family or friends, the mountains or beer, svíčková, hockey or snow.

I thought about speaking to the couple one more time, but couldn't. Was I still so cripplingly shy after all these years? Yes. So afraid of awkwardness? That too. With the passing of time, I'd learned sweet fuck all.

That was a fact.

I sat down and thought of Jana. She had never judged me for my inability to learn from my mistakes, never criticised my shyness or curiosities, never poured scorn on the odd things I did, whether they were things that amused her – monkey-oriented, generally – or confused her: my passive aggression, the ease with which I became embarrassed to the point of mortification, my lack of self-control when out drinking with my friends. She never judged me for any of it. That was treasurable.

When I got home it was late, but I couldn't sleep, and so I thought about it all, for a while, until I did sleep.

*

On Saturday, I felt restive. I checked my phone roughly every three and a half minutes, as I'd done at the cinema. No one called. There was nothing wrong with this. It was rare for people to contact me every three and a half minutes, but in checking so often, I felt insignificant and ignored to a pathetic extent.

I left the house and made my way to northeast London for my drum lesson. I'd taken up the drums just before Christmas, figuring it was A) a good way to physically drum out my anger, B) I was never going to be good at guitar, I'd been planning on that for the best part of twenty years without success, C) it was something to do on Saturday afternoons.

That was what's known as a highly mature, well-reasoned and considered plan, and for that very reason it was doomed to fail.

I would stop playing the drums a couple of weeks later when they became too expensive in light of recent events, but also when I began working in a pub in Oval. I'd never planned to be a barman again after finding my first writing job. Budding writers currently reading beware; that was, and will remain, naïve. When writing failed – which it does with a remarkably high success rate – the bar was a loyal and willing master.

But that wouldn't be for a few weeks. For now, I lived in hope of finding a new job without reverting to the bar, believing it would be possible to continue with my drum lessons, which I enjoyed more week after week.

After the lesson, I read my book in The Cock Tavern – a name I found funny in spite of my age – before heading home for a quiet night in. Hitting the pillow, I was unprepared for what would come next.

*

I was in an unknown place, a large, green field which couldn't be described as verdant. It was a wet, unbecoming green, and near a group of large oak trees the mud was a reddish-brown, like the mud you see in films set in Africa. It was a mish-mash of ecologies, I knew it even then.

What I didn't understand were the sheep all around me. Some were alive, most not. Strewn lifeless and supine throughout the field, their wool moulted when I touched it, their blue tongues lolled out like those of drunkards.

Not long later, I was in the air, floating above it all, and saw ravens picking at the poor, bloody, dead beasts. I realised it was a farm now. Why were they all dying? I felt sick to my stomach and wanted out, but the body took me elsewhere.

I left the carrion and the bloodied mud and the corpses, and she was there now, unsmiling; her mouth fixed in a moribund grimace, the kind familiar from our final days together, when guilt crushed me because I was leaving, leaving her behind and everything we'd built together and cherished, and I couldn't understand why or how.

Waking up in the morning, I lay there thinking on it all.

Yes, it'd been a dream, but that grimace was not rooted in fantasy or beer or whiskey, it was rooted in memories I couldn't forgive myself for. I spent the day in bed, unable to read or work or bring myself to leave the house even though stewing in the dark and mulling over what I'd seen tormented me. That wasn't a smart choice, but it was the only choice. I prayed for the night, for sleep, though not for dreams, whiskey, beer or otherwise, just sleep, rest, recovery. The following morning, I was refreshed. That was good.

I left the house and went to the gym, but couldn't rid myself of the things I'd seen: the carrion and death and decay and, worst of all, the grimace and sadness on her lips and in her eyes. I didn't understand the carrion, but understood the lips and the eyes and the sadness.

That was the worst of it all.

*

After a day and a night I slept again and woke again and swung my legs out of bed in the morning, taking *Thursday* from my Dosette tray, before heading to the bathroom, where I pulled some toilet paper from the roll and pretended to blow my nose.

I returned to bed, thought of someone for about a minute and a half and then got up, showered, brushed my teeth and dressed, noticing as I did the green diary on my floor. Me and a therapist saw each other roughly once every two months. He'd told me I should write my dreams down, said it might give me a window into their meaning.

That seemed a smart idea.

But I always forgot, or would remember for maybe four or five days in a row, only to forget again for weeks, rendering the whole exercise more or less redundant.

I picked up the diary and wrote about the carrion and the sheep and the crimson mud, and about the night before, when my dreams had been nothing exceptional. I'd dreamt about two old friends from Prague, Paul and John, two Englishmen I still kept in touch with. In the dream, we were meeting after a long time without seeing one another. That was logical. John lived in Japan now, as many teachers from Prague tended to, while Paul lived in Bristol, which for all intents and purposes may as well have been Japan, as I didn't travel much these days.

For reasons unclear we were on a ferry between South Korea and Japan, which, within the confines of that world, was a distance no bigger than the Channel. If the dream meant anything, it could only be that I missed them, having not seen either for a long time despite the three of us making plans to. That was a pity, and one, two or preferably all three of us should have pulled our thumbs out.

After doing that, I left the house and bought ingredients for breakfast, only to realise that the key ingredient – eggs, for scrambled eggs with avocado – was missing.

That was a disaster. I went back and bought the eggs.

Both times I did it all without speaking to another person, paying and interacting only with machines. That wasn't great for me or people, but seemed a relief at the time.

Back in the flat, I cooked breakfast. The avocado was soft and supple, the eggs I did just right. I was pleased with myself, and

165

ate thinking about the strange dream about my friends John and Paul, whose names I'd never said together in a sentence that way. I laughed. That was great.

I thought about how it meant nothing, us there, in the ferry terminal, trying to hurry through so we could get a drink before disembarking. I thought about how the ship sailed past several Korean houses built into the water and how dangerous that was, how it could possibly be a safe place to live. I thought about the bit when our ship submerged and travelled through a myriad system of underground tunnels, towards Japan. It was nonsense, such wonderful nonsense.

But it was undeniable. I still wanted the whiskey dreams, despite all that they were and the harm they'd done. I tried not to think about it for a while, working for a few hours, updating my website, drafting cover letter after cover letter to potential employers. When I got tired, I went back downstairs and looked out of the window, where a local cat was sitting on the ledge, meowing in search of food.

—Go away, Henry, I said. —Not today.

He reminded me of my neighbour's cat. Hence Henry.

I'd no idea of his real name, or if he even had one. Unfortunately, I also had a new flatmate called Henry who was often at home during the day, and I'd twice been caught with the two beings in the presence of each other. That was unfortunate.

I looked past Henry (feline) to the garden table. There were dozens of apples on the table, countless more on the floor. Henry (human) had suggested we use them for something, and I'd decided to make an apple pie. That was a plan.

I'd forgotten to buy cornflour, but began to prepare the other ingredients in the interim. I took out the butter. I'd read it was wise to leave it out for at least half an hour before baking. I'd also learned it was important to measure everything out before starting, as I'd a habit of getting halfway through before realising I'd not read something and had to substitute it or go to the shop again.

After heading to the supermarket to buy cornflour, I measured out two tablespoons, plus one tablespoon of baking powder and the flour, cinnamon and sugar. With apples from the garden I weighed out a kilo. After peeling and coring them it was clear I'd need more, so I got more, chopped them, left them to one side and mixed the flour and butter together to make the pastry, trying to roll it out on the worktop. It stuck to the rolling pin, reminding me I ought to look up how to do it properly. I was anxious to get it right, but was calm too. That was good.

I did everything in a measured manner and knew that in the event of utter fuckery, I would just figure out how to do it right next time.

I'd never been that way. I'd always given up, or tried too hard to get something right and then given up. I'd always been afraid of failure. But I was calmer now. That was good.

I knew the feeling wouldn't last into the evening, or that if it did she was there, somewhere between the carrion and cornflour, to be found, touched and discovered, but only in fantasy. That broke my heart, I must say.

I decided there would be no more whiskey dreams. What had I been thinking, trying to find her again? It wasn't her, really.

The things I sought were gone, and I was an inveterate fool for trying.

Whiskey was no cure, despite the lovely taste. I felt the sticky pastry on my fingers and the heat from the oven, now heating up nicely. No, whiskey dreams were no solution at all. I would have to try baking my problems away. That was my plan.

Only time would tell if that made me yet more of an inveterate fool.

Der Zoo, die Doughnuts

I thought about turning right, into the Starbucks just outside
Kurfürstendamm. My original plan had been to travel to
Uhlandstraße at the end of the line, but looking at my map, the
various attractions huddled together like Skittles all out of scale,
I was convinced it'd be easier to go back on myself.

That was the new plan.

It wasn't like I was short on time, but neither was I in any
sort of mood to amble, or to get lost. I'd traipsed enough cities
aimlessly in my time as it was.

Coffee was imperative, but preferably not Starbucks
coffee. They stood for everything I hated, though it hadn't
stopped me many times before.

Hypocrisy was the lifeblood of a man, and coffee got
that blood flowing in the morning. I wanted it, even if it meant
compromising my already vague and confused values. That was
called commitment to routine.

I walked on and found the entrance to the zoo, but
meandered right and back onto the main street, hoping to find a
boutique café or a tobacco shop that did coffee to go. But all I
found was a Dunkin' Donuts. That was a blast from the past.

As a fat nineteen-year-old, Dunkin's had been my daily
bread during an elongated six-week stay in Boston, when
I worked at the UMass bookstore in what proved to be an
unenjoyable stay in the Bean City.

The university was picturesque enough, very modern and
grand in an American way. It sat on the edge of Dorchester, a
blue-collar Irish district where I watched football on Saturdays
and considered trying to get served alcohol without ever having
the balls to go ahead and do it. That was cowardice.

I'd been in the States two months and was homesick
beyond belief. I should've risked deportation and asked for a
beer. That would have made for a funny story. When I began
working at the bookstore I'd expected there would be others like
me, students from back home living in America for the summer,
having fun, going to the beach, getting laid.

Like me is a relative term.

But it was late in the season. The only people I worked
with were the permanent staff and two Russian girls. The
permanent staff were invariably insane in that way people who
spend their adult lives working in libraries and bookstores
invariably become.

The Russians were nice. One didn't speak much English,
the other spoke a lot about England and how she'd like to visit
it someday. She also talked about avant-garde bands I was
too ignorant and innocent to have heard of and laughed at my

every word in a knowing, pitying way. That was so-so. We got
on well, but aside from the odd Coca-Cola at lunch, I spent
most of my time alone, comforting myself morning and night
by gormandising on sugary iced coffee and doughnuts from
Dunkin's. I didn't drink coffee back then unless it was iced and
didn't smoke either, which was just as well.

Dunkin's was a crutch, and had I been a smoker
– American cigarettes are dirt cheap – I'd have got through a
pack or two a day. Instead, iced coffee and a lot of dead poets
and writers did the trick, Twain and Poe mainly. That's what
inquisitive boys who'd be a lot less inquisitive if only they could
get laid do.

Thinking about it now, I read the entire works of Poe that
summer, buying a huge book of them in a mall somewhere in
Illinois, while shopping for jeans with my father's cousin who
I was staying with. I read every word he published and don't
remember a damn sentence.

The archaic language washed over me, and made me feel
stupid. I could read a poem just one page long and forget what
I'd read at the top of the page once I'd reached the bottom. That
was poetry for you. In short, I learned sweet fuck all. There was
a famous crow and a woman called Lenore, but it'd be a lie to
claim I remembered that from the book and not *The Simpsons*,
which parodied it one time.

At nineteen, I'd yet to start writing, except perhaps for a diary,
so aside from reading books I didn't get and stacking shelves
with others I couldn't afford (like most things in America,
education is a racket), doughnuts were all I had by way of
something to do.

There was barely a corner of Boston without a Dunkin's,
which was good for me. Visiting one of their establishments
was a moment for the senses, the thrill of a glucose kick, the
comfort of thinking for a few moments only of eating, and not
the cloying solitude that itself ate away at me, or the sense of
disappointment that my trip to America, my American dream so
full of hope, had ended in utter failure.

That's how I saw it. Failure. I had come to America to
meet girls. American girls were less shallow than British ones
– I was deluded beyond belief – and were bound to find me
charming. That's what American girls did. They found British
men charming, no matter how pasty their skin or thick their
waists or absent their social skills. That was the plan. And I
had failed. By the time I reached Boston, I'd made peace with
that failure. It was only a month 'til I went home. That was

manageable.

So I worked at the university, looking forward to lunchtime every day. It took me from the drudgery of filing library books, or directing impoverished Caribbean women to the nursing textbooks, which would indenture them to the state of America for the rest of their lives. At lunchtimes I went to the cafeteria to eat my sandwich and watch the news, which at this time was focused on the Lebanese-Israeli conflict, which no one wanted to call a war. That was an inconvenient term.

The soundbite doing the rounds – despite efforts to muffle it – implied that this was the first war that had ever taken place between two democracies. Like my success with women, that too was a relative term.

One day I saw a panellist on Fox explaining the thought process behind this categorisation, which he felt to be inaccurate.

> —Well, what you have
> to remember, John, is that these
> are the bad guys.

He was of course talking about the Lebanese. That was a given.

I was young and stupid, full to the brim with grand, idealistic and nebulous ideas. But even I had to laugh at a world where this could be said without a hint of irony. That was a gas, Debbie.

Yes, between shelving books, nudging Caribbean nurses towards penury, watching the wars on television and reading a 19th century poet I didn't understand, doughnuts were all I had. I guess I should say that was so-so, but it was pretty damn good, especially when they had raspberry in the centre.

I was staying with a young couple who had a kid, and a strange interest in *Are You Being Served*, something they expected I'd be pleased to discover. That was unfortunate. I'd seen plenty of *Are You Being Served* at my grandmother's house as a child, never quite knowing whether she laughed because she understood the euphemisms or *because* she did not. That's perhaps something I'd rather not know.

No, doughnuts it was for me and doughnuts were all I had. There was only the one time, in the whole month or month and a half (I brought my return flight to London forward but can't remember by how much) when I couldn't find a doughnutery in my hour of need.

I remember it clear as day. I was smack bang in the centre of Boston, and had been walking around for about thirty minutes

when the doughnut jitters kicked in. To shake things up a little,
I decided to go to Krispy Kreme. I was a KK virgin – among
other kinds – and there weren't so many in the city compared to
Dunkin's, with its seemingly intractable dominance. I figured
KK would be okay, if not even better, due to its boutiqueness by
comparison.

Certain I'd seen one the last time I was in town, I looked
around, but couldn't find it. I decided to ask a police officer.

—Excuse me, officer.

—Yes? he said, turning around and away from his default
position, hands on hips, exuding an air of quiet authority whilst
inwardly thanking his lucky stars he was not assigned to patrol
the bank heist-friendly streets of nearby Charlestown.

He had a stereotypical moustache, that late 19th century
Irish cop's moustache you see in comics and films, thick, bushy
and ginger, friendly, with ignorant whiskers.

His gun was holstered but stood out, and the handcuffs on
his right side looked like they'd recently been shined.

Only then did it occur to me that asking a cop for
directions to the doughnut house probably wasn't a good idea.

—Erm… I'm meeting someone at McDonald's, I said. —
Do you know where it is?

He smiled.

—Sure, he said, looking past me. —If it's the one I'm
thinking of it's just up on Tremont. A couple of blocks that way,
then left.

—Thanks.

Contretemps. If I'd known the meaning back then I'd have had
it tattooed on my forehead, a warning to anyone unfortunate
enough to bump into me. Contretemps.

That's an arse-over-tit way of saying *making a tit of
yourself*, and that's what I was: a boob. That's the American way
to say that, though, so I'll just head south and admit myself a
twat, as my English schooling would demand.

Either way, I was a specialist, never more than a stumble
from putting my foot in it. All these years later, I didn't know
if I was any less hapless or error-prone. Not much, I reckoned,
maybe a little. That was incremental progress. I didn't get
embarrassed the way I once had, easily and often, didn't feel
humiliation when a minor fuck-up occurred, perceived or

otherwise.

I'd learned to control it, the anxiousness, the way I felt in situations that might have previously embarrassed and humiliated me. I'd learned to be the keeper of it, to turn embarrassment to my advantage. I was still shy, I knew that, but years of teaching had made me more confident in myself. It was a thin and largely false confidence, but it could be put on. That was important in life.

And that was America.

*

And this was Berlin. I walked into the Dunkin's on Tauentzienstraße, and thought about Jana and the one time I'd regressed to my former self in front of her. It was dark out, mid-winter, and we were in Kaaba, where we didn't drink together often. Jana usually liked to leave as soon as she'd clocked off.

We were sat at a table near the door, one of the ones I liked to sit in because it meant I didn't take up too much room. I hated the idea the café was losing money by me sitting at a table for hours on end. People who did that drove me nuts. Who did they think they were? That was a selfish thing to do. People did it, though.

Anyway, we were sat having a beer in Kaaba. I was talking about something or other and knocked my glass. Beer spooled out across the table, onto my lap and a little on Jana's. The waiter came over, smiled, and cleaned the mess. The fact that he didn't let me clean it up myself just made things worse. When he was gone I began to twitch and asked Jana if we could leave.

—What's wrong? she said, her beautiful forehead creasing first with concern, then irritation. —It's just a bit of water.

Not to me it wasn't. I'd humiliated and made a drunken ass of myself in front of people I saw almost every day. I couldn't come back here, not now. That was Kaaba gone, my beloved Kaaba.

And it was worse than before. Before I'd just been a customer, the guy who came in with Brad to drink sometimes seven or eight beers before paying up at the till and arguing with the staff over how many beers we'd had, invariably ending on the wrong side of the argument. That was fine.

Those exchanges always embarrassed me too (they were usually Brad's doing), though never for long. I knew they

175

didn't matter all that much. But I was Jana's boyfriend now, her drunken English (there was no point in arguing about it) boyfriend, who couldn't keep a pint vertical if his life depended on it. That was terrible. I wanted to leave.

—You can't get so upset about these things, said Jana. —It's just an accident.

I began to notice people around me who'd been invisible 'til now. My attention had been completely on Jana, everything else a peripheral blur, but now I noticed every other person in the café. They continued their conversations, went on with their evenings. They hadn't noticed me spill the beer, and if they had, they thought nothing of it. But to me, it felt like I'd crossed the Rubicon, ruined everything.

—You shouldn't get so upset, said Jana. —What will you be like with something important if you get upset over that?

That was a good question, and one I'm still trying to answer. I looked down at my knees, then back up at Jana, and forced myself to smile.

—I know, I said. —I shouldn't cry over spilt milk.

I was doing my best. But the joke was lost on her. I tried to relax. Moreover, I tried to seem relaxed, but felt tense, worried about what she thought of me now. I tried hard to assure her everything was fine; I was a relaxed person who'd just slipped this one time. That man, that worried man, wasn't me.

But it wasn't working. She was certain to go off me soon now, I was sure.

Ah, what'd I done? Things had been going so well. We hadn't argued once. She'd chided me once for not speaking up for myself in a restaurant when they forgot my onion rings, but it'd blown over later that evening, when I charged around her room with my underwear bunched up my crack as high as it could go and my limbs in primatial pose.

That'd been funny and sweet too, when she told me she loved me in Czech, which always sounded sweeter.

The beer spillage was nothing, but now her eyes looked uncertain, fearful of the insecurity, instability and weakness. She could see it now. I was certain she would leave me soon. We'd only been together a few months, and I'd let slip about who I was.

There was always something to worry about. That was my life. Looking like an idiot in front of the girl, looking weak in front of the girlfriend, looking uncaring, looking mawkish. Always something.

—Promin, I said. —I am being silly.

—Yes.

When she wouldn't lighten up, I began to get frustrated.

—Jana, I'm sorry. I've apologised now.
—Yes, but it worries me, that you can get like this.
—Jana, I said I'm sorry. It is not fair to keep on like *this*.

She said nothing, and looked past me, out the window, or over to another table. Slowly, I pushed my tongue out and up towards my nose. She looked back at me and laughed, but it was more a tired snort, a little disapproving of my attempt to brush away what'd happened.

—Stop it, she said, after a few moments.

—Hu, I said, quietly.

—Yes.

—Hu?

—Yes, monkey.

Her steel began to melt. She didn't look so concerned now. She seemed as if she was forgetting my idiocy, at least the kind I didn't want her to see, remembering why she liked me.

—Hu!

Several heads turned to look at us, including Marek, the barman who'd cleared up the spilt beer, and two blonde girls I'd had my eye on (and it was only ever going to be my eye) before meeting Jana. All the eyes that'd felt like fire were welcome to look now.

—Ronan! she said, grabbing my arm. —Stop it.

It was okay. She was laughing, and I was the cause. That
was fine. It was good. It was great.

—Hu hu.

I was relaxed now, and she relaxed about me again. Everything
was okay. I'd conquered the embarrassment, regained control of
it, made a fool of myself a second time by inviting the eyes to
look upon me, but as Monkey, as Opičko.

A fool of his own making. That was fine 'n dandy.

I looked at Jana's beautiful, compassionate forehead.
Everything was fine. I'd grown in these years. I could take
embarrassment if it was on my terms, could embrace the fool so
long as people knew I'd chosen to act that way.

If I said something controversial, even at my own
expense, it was fine. I made jokes about myself all the time,
deeply embarrassing, self-deprecatory jokes. I loved to make
a clown of or humiliate myself sexually (in joke form only)
because I was in control. It was me. I was the king of my
embarrassment.

That was fine.

Now, though, alone in Berlin, the only way I was going to
be embarrassed was by falling over in the street, in which case
I'd make myself scarce. That was good, though only because
I was on my own, which wasn't so good, and never is, is it,
really?

I bought my coffee in Dunkin's. Jana would have hated it,
as she did all chain shops, particularly when it came to coffee.
She loved nature, Jana, loved to be out in the hills and the rivers
and above all else the mountains. And she loved the world that
had once been untouched by hand or head.

She hated the likes of Dunkin's because of their plastic
cups and their plastic lids. That was something she was right
about, though I was weak and often lazy and went with the
familiar when I wanted a coffee, which was more or less always.

In Prague, I often went to a Costa. Jana hated that.
For me, it was familiar, and in a city of constant, unrelenting
outsiderness, that was important. That was also a convenient,
visceral excuse which never really washed with her.

It wasn't just vague ideas of *home*, though. Costa served
their coffee in huge cups. I really did hate taking up room for
long periods of time in cafés, wary of monopolising oxygen or
space. With their garishly large cups, Costa let me justify my
presence long enough that I could read or write without fearing

the disapproving looks of staff. That was good.

It bought me time. Cafés had overheads to cover. Most people didn't realise that. I often watched people in cafés lounging around or working long after they had finished their drinks. That was unjust. Didn't they realise the café was a business? Didn't they realise they had bills to pay? That was selfish. I probably thought about it too much, maybe.

In time, Jana weaned me off Costa, never allowing me to drink too much of it in Kaaba, always laughing when I switched to beer but giving it to me nonetheless. That was fantastic.

She encouraged me to try other coffee shops in the city and that was good because they served better coffee and were generally quieter than the big chains, which were invariably full of people, mostly wankers, sometimes tourists, sometimes both together.

She'd changed my habits in a good way, yet here I was in Berlin, disposable cup in hand. And not even from Starbucks, but a chain serving even more inferior coffee. On the plus side, the menu was written in English, and I could order without looking the fool. Well, so I thought. I answered in simple German, pronouncing the 'g' in *original* as I thought a German would. That proved follicle, which for many years I thought to be another adjective form of fool to complement foolish. It turned out it was about hair. That was hirsutable. That's a little hair joke there. Unless it's the Holocaust or genocide, there's always room for a little joke. That's the god's honest truth. Important too.

Anyway, the woman behind the counter in Dunkin's smiled, asked if I wanted medium or small. She had lightly shadowed eyelids, a shade of green I didn't know. That wasn't surprising. I knew as much about colours as I did language or geography.

The woman was short and blonde. The Dunkin' Donuts polo top looked uncomfortable. I felt sorry for her, having to wear that uncomfortable-looking polo top. I paid, walked towards the zoo, ate the doughnut, and sipped on my coffee. It didn't taste as good as I remembered, and it occurred to me that I'd never had a hot coffee from Dunkin's. In America, it'd always been iced, as I didn't really drink coffee at that time.

I'd once had filter Dunkin's in Prague. The short, blonde, Republican girl had bought it for me on my birthday, along with a book of The Irish Short Story (jingoism aside, a nation that can justify a definite article in this context is a great country) and a novel about World War Two, written by one of the writers of *Game of Thrones*. That was a good book, but it's also apropos

of nothing and a digression I hope you've learned to excuse by
now.

Anyway, the short, blonde Republican girl bought me
Dunkin's. She always told me I drank too much coffee, but she
bought me it nonetheless. That was dangerously close to making
ours a proper relationship.

That week and a half when I had filter Dunkin's was great.
I drank at least a cup each morning before work, cooking it in
my Moka pot, and when it was finished, it was gone. That was
probably a good thing, or I would have impoverished myself via
the medium of Dunkin' Donuts coffee.

Back in Berlin land, I finished my disappointing filter coffee,
which was bland, near tasteless, and almost grey in colour.

I should have listened to Jana. Either that, or just gone to
Starbucks, regardless of whether they were fuckers.

Finding a bin, I threw away the cup and apologised to
Jana via the winds.

It was time for a snout. I always went back on the snouts
when travelling. The mix of having so much time to kill, the
generous pricing and the undeniable reality (which I denied to
myself) that I wanted to look like a writer in pubs and cafés –
writing, smoking, drinking – all helped me crack.

I took my pack out of my pocket, Marlboro Lites, and was
about to remove a snout when a group of kindergarten children
walked by. That was bad timing.

Moving on – it didn't feel right to light up in front of them
– I found a bench in a local square. It was there that I thought
about life a few moments.

That's a joke like the hirsutable one, but more ain't-that-
strange funny than ha-ha funny. I'm not saying the hirsutable
one *was* ha-ha funny – that's for you to decide – just that if it is
any kind of funny, it would be that sort of funny.

That's my insecurities playing themselves out there.

I always thought about life, past, future and very
occasionally present. Most certainly past more than anything.
But here I thought about it perhaps harder than usual, about
the year I arrived in Prague. I thought about the short, blonde
Republican girl, about the day I ran out of Dunkin's. My
housemate had scoured the city looking for it after seeing the
pack in my cupboard. He could've just asked me, but was too
proud. That's idiots for you.

We were in my kitchen when I asked her if she'd get me
more next time she was in America. He was there, and it dawned

on him my coffee had been imported via the short, blonde
Republican from the US of A. I'd been told by his girlfriend not
to say anything, to let him wander the city looking for it. That
was her trying to teach him a lesson in excessive self-pride.

How did I feel that morning, when it dawned on him that
he'd wasted his time? Was I happy? At ease? How did I feel the
moment his face sank? Sitting on a wall in Berlin, it was easy to
believe it'd been a simpler time. I was younger, after all.

But it wasn't easy, it never was.

That wasn't easy to admit, when on the surface life was
easy; food, shelter, love.

They were the only things you needed, yet somehow they
weren't. That was human.

I sat in that square, thinking about that time. Teaching was hard,
weekends lost in alcohol and weakness, a determination not to
be alone resulting in abandon, then regret, then determination,
then relapse. When I was younger I'd been, without realising
it at the time, as anxious as now, outside the zoo; an outwardly
calm man in a constant state of quiet chaos.

I *was* younger than now, though. That had to count for
something. I looked at the façade of the zoo walls, a mosaic of
dinosaurs from various eras. It seemed cruel on the children,
to entice them with dinosaurs, only to give them pelicans and
anteaters. That was like being promised a Magnum and being
presented with a Cornetto. It's still good, but the bathos of it
grates.

I lit my snout, took a puff, then another, and walked zoo-
ward, finishing it quickly as I walked to the ticket office.

—Eine, bitte, I said, at the entrance.
—Just zoo, or aquarium also?

I paid for the zoo only. I was in no mood for fuckery, and
aquariums revelled in it: dull, humdrum species of fish
commingling with the occasional object of interest, a shark, or
maybe a turtle. Little did I know the Berliners had put the snakes
in the aquarium. That was cheeky. Much as I love their city, it
still rankles. That is extremely cheeky of them. Had I known, I'd
have paid the extra.

I paid the woman at the ticket office and got my ticket.
She was in her late forties or early fifties, with hair that wouldn't
have looked out of place in the gaudy styles sported by Berliners
when the Wall first (and last, now I think about it) came down.
She had a narrow but noticeable gap in her teeth, but her polo

shirt looked more suited to her than the girl in Dunkin's, which
may or may not suggest I was focusing on the polo shirts too
much.

It occurred to me that the staff in various kiosks were
friendlier here than in other cities, or at least it appeared so.
Perhaps I was in cheer beneath the gloom of the last few days,
due to being on a holiday of sorts.

Jana had met someone new.

That was a detail I couldn't bring myself to write down earlier,
and for a long time after. That was a detail, but details make a
story.

The guard scanned my ticket. I walked into the zoo, past
two families, three pelicans and a stork, and decided to finally
amble about a while rather than relying on the map I'd been
given. As with all zoos, I was met initially by many varieties
of birds. I suppose it's a way of making sure you venture into
the inner recesses, rather than tucking straight into the pudding
before sodding off.

I've nothing against birds, per se, but smart zoo etiquette
demands they be given the shortest of shrift. A zoo is a big
place, and a minimum of fuckery a must.

Avians are ten a penny. How many pigeons does a man
see in a day without need for celebration? I wanted to see the
pride game first: lions, tigers, elephants and, if I were truly
lucky, the honey badger. I use the definite article intentionally.

There is only ever one per zoo, such is their insanity. That
was agonisingly alluring.

I began to amble, albeit with purpose.

And so it was.

I walked, looked ahead, yet saw nothing of what I'd done.
That was blind of me. How had I managed it?

I could have gone anywhere (within the confines of
Gatwick's low-cost airline routes), yet here I was, back in
Berlin, walking the paths of ghosts as I had been for the last two
days.

Berlin, where I'd met that man and his Scandinavian
fantasies; Berlin, where we'd enjoyed two boiling hot July days
together; Berlin, where it was so hot the Arctic Monkeys got
cut off three songs into a set, walking offstage only to return
minutes later when the electricity was back in action.

That was a blessing.

It all felt like a lifetime away, but I still had dreams like
Philipp, the Scandinavian-obsessed German, the kind that were
held in the privacy of his mind but laid out in his eyes, when he

spoke of *there*, somewhere else, a world different to his own, filled with vigour and hope and joy.

That was delusion, but it was understandable.

No, I wasn't any better than Philipp. I'd come to Berlin with ideas that something would happen; a change, that solitary moment that enervates the soul and makes you want to strive again, when something kicks you into gear. In my case, it was a wish to escape from an existence that had begun to blur like a whiskey dream.

But no, I'd merely retraced my steps. The previous day I'd walked by the Spree, seeing the very same bridge on which she'd photographed me two years earlier, running towards her, a manqué monkey in search of a cheap laugh, which I duly got. I'd stumbled across a Bavarian beer house we'd visited and couldn't resist going in. I wasn't helping myself.

She had met someone new. I was happy for her, but I was broken too. That was a good thing. Otherwise, what had it all been for?

I'd done well until now, avoiding memories of Jana. I'd steered clear of the Jewish memorial and the Brandenburg gate, hadn't set foot near Pankow. But here I was now, at the zoo, a buffoon wishing to be with her so he might act the baboon. I was sentimental. That was my problem.

About six months after leaving Prague, I visited Jana, excited amidst all the pained long-distance phone calls and Facebook messages and occasional love and hate letters that got sent in search of answers and hope.

We made love the day I returned, after a couple of hours of what felt like two strangers talking. And then we were back to normal. That was love, that.

The day after I arrived we went to Prague Zoo, a couple again, despite my geographical desertion. We sat in the zoo, opposite one another, two bison grazing about a hundred metres from a steel horse on which I'd once sat to have my photo taken a couple of years earlier, before Jana, when I was just a confused young man trying to figure out his place in the world. That would prove an ignoble and foolish cause. Had some fun, though.

We were seated beside a father and his daughter, a toddler who curled her developing fingers around five or six fries at a time, before stuffing them into her mouth. The sun was strong. It was May, and the benches looked out over Prague's poor panelak high rises and industrial areas; a factory about a mile away puffing out smoke among the best of the sights. That's the problem with building a zoo with a view: the view might not look back kindly on you. But that's all fine and dandy, too.

Yes, I miss Prague, miss the way they accepted what lay in front of them; the factories down the hill, the notion that you could have a beer in the company of your kids in a zoo without screwing them up for life. That was a breath of fresh air. Sure, they were corrupt, and apathetic. But they were loving also, and deeply cynical. That seems doubly important with every passing day.

In short, they weren't such dicks all the time. That was good.

—What will we see next? Jana asked, after we had finished our lunch.

She had come to the zoo for me. I appreciated that.

—Let's see the giraffes, I said.

I put my polystyrene plate and my plastic knife and fork in the bin. That was wasteful, and Jana hated it, but that was also the only option. Pursing my lips, I distended my ankles and acted the monkey before kissing Jana on the forehead. That was called a distraction technique.

She laughed, as did the toddler.

Six months since leaving, I could still make her laugh the same old, foolish way. It never failed, never until right before I left, when she knew in her heart I was going and going to be gone forever, something I did not. That's true, that. She always did know better than me.

We walked the long path towards the giraffes, stopping at an enclosure of African creatures. She tried to take a photo of a meerkat for her mother, but it wouldn't stand still.

I loved her. I even loved her mother, even though she drove me nuts with questions in a language I barely understood.

Jana tried once more, but the meerkat disappeared. After that we saw the giraffes, then the elephants, and then made our way towards the polar bear.

—Jooo!

I looked over. Was it a bear, or a lion, or a tiger? No, it was a dog, an everyday Labrador which she stroked with the approval of its owner.

In two hours, not lion or bear or elephant had caught her

attention the way a dog could.

I thought of the hopes I'd had in the months before I finally left; the flat we would share, alone, a place we could call home. A place. A dog. I told my mother about it, the flat, the dog. She said *no* with a definitiveness that made me feel childlike. She was right, though, knew it'd end somewhere down the line, that the demarcations of geography would rear their ugly heads in a manner that would have trenchant nationalists champing at the bit with glee.

But I was set in my dream, pigheadedly determined to stick to it. A dog would only complicate matters, when they became matters. That was the way life worked. It pissed on carefully considered plans.

But that's how I lived, repeating words of hope several times a day as if saying them would make it all come true; two parts delusion to one part reality upping the chances the former might win.

*

Back in Berlin, I walked towards the primate enclosure but sidled past when I realised there was a large group of schoolchildren and their teachers.

Instead, I went to the hippos and then to the wolves, walking around, going back on myself by mistake a few times, revisiting the rhinos with their thick hides. Earlier, one had gotten stuck under a branch he was eating, but was free now, for which I was glad. I left the zoo.

The real problem was that I was unable to cry.

That was just the way it was. It wasn't machismo or self-abasement, wasn't, so far as I knew, the result of any form of disapproval in my childhood. Indeed, I'd been raised to believe crying no bad thing. And yet, I could only remember doing so a few times in my life: after signing on, after leaving Jana the first time, and the second, following that trip which included a visit to the zoo, and also when my paternal grandmother had died years earlier, during the 1998 World Cup.

I cried the day me and my mother finally talked about my father's death twenty-four years after it'd happened, cried rivers in her lap before writing to Jana to tell her I loved her beyond belief.

I cried those times but not others, not when my mother's parents died, not at my friend's funeral, not even when Jana finally ended it all because there was no way forward.

No, even that event, which caused me to sit down and talk of life and plans and birds and zoos, did not cause me to cry. Instead, I walked around in a fug of denial, thinking of her every minute of the day. That seemed the right thing to do.

Occasionally, something triggered a memory of warmth or pain, and I would emit only a pained grunt. But tears, no.

That's just the way I was made up.

*

In a quiet restaurant, I wrote ten pages and drank a Pilsner lager. I was hungry, but had made a plan to go to Frankfurter Allen first and then find somewhere to eat before visiting the Stasi Museum. I took the U-Bahn five stops and was going to change to the S-Bahn but saw a fast food burger place called Beer and Burger and decided to stop off there for my lunch. I had a classic burger and pomme frites with a lager that didn't taste very good at all, then decided to walk all the way to the museum via Frankfurter Alles.

It looked straightforward enough.

I listened to music and felt good for five or six minutes, upbeat, like I was moving forward after months of standing still, redundant –professionally and otherwise. I walked for many, many minutes, unable to recognise anything. That was fine. There was no hurry. And there was the future to look forward to as well. Fifteen minutes passed. I soon needed the toilet, to shit and urinate too. It was fine for a while. I kept walking, certain I'd find somewhere soon. That was city life. There were toilets everywhere.

But I soon quickly got agitated. My cock was on fire, in a bad way, my stomach verging on expulsion. I felt like an idiot. Why the fuck had I ambled?

What kind of plan was that in the circumstances?

I carried on. It was all I could do in a bid to find a toilet. I listened to crashing indie-guitar rock, the sort that is trite and not particularly brilliant but makes you feel something nonetheless by pure dint of its urgency, although emotional urgency had now been displaced by that of the bowel.

After another ten minutes it became clear I'd walked too far. I must have passed the museum by now, but had seen no signs. I walked along the tram tracks and could see a juncture ahead, maybe two hundred metres away, which looked like a hub of activity. Maybe that was Frankfurter Alee.

Reaching the juncture confirmed to me I'd gone too far.

The trams were the only form of transport now, and though the museum wasn't in the centre of the city, it definitely wasn't out this far. That was not good.

I turned off my music. What an idiot! Who was I, thinking I could conquer anything. Heartbreak, memory, redundancy, life, I couldn't even conquer my bladder or bowels. I wasn't going to make it. Fuck the Stasi, I was a prisoner of my insides.

I sped up in search of a hotel, restaurant or café, but found nothing. That was harsh luck, as ten minutes previous there'd been no shortage of them. There were hardware shops and estate agents and nail bars, but no places that might have a public toilet. There were pastry shops and tobacco stores, but nowhere I could take a piss, or the increasingly likely shit.

Sometimes, when I needed one, taking a piss was a relief, and I realised I'd no need to shit after all. But this was not one such occasion. I needed a shit, and pissing in public would probably just make me shit myself. That was a quandary wrapped up in a disaster waiting to happen.

I walked fast without breaking into a run, for fear that this too would make me shit myself. The long road had failed me. It was also heading in the direction of Potsdam. That didn't bode well.

The streets were lined with more estate agents and tobacco shops. I turned left again and then – thank Christ – found a pub, a small, dingy place with only two tables and large steiner glasses hanging from the wooden bar on golden hooks. A woman looked at me.

—Toilet, bitte, I said.

She pointed left. That wasn't just good, it was heaven-sent.

I ran into the cubicle. The seat was made of the sort of cheap plastic you get on school furniture.

The plastic was cold on my skin. I looked at the thin, beige toilet paper, knowing it would be coarse and unpleasant to the touch. I didn't care, though, and breathed a sigh of relief as everything left me. Looking up at the frosted window and sunlight outside, I could have cried with happiness.

The world felt good again. I'd avoided disaster. The world, devoid of hope just moments ago, held the promise of goodness. I wiped my arse, cleaned my hands, and returned to the bar, where I found the woman talking to a large, barrel-chested man.

—Erm, eine bier, bitte, I said.

                              —Nein, she said, waving
                    dismissively. —Es ist fein.

So I left, walking out the door feeling like a new man and a fool
all rolled into one. I'd nearly shat myself through my inability to
read maps. But I hadn't.
      That was important to remember. I hadn't shat myself.
      Should you ever come close to shitting yourself, but
successfully do otherwise, through luck or ardour, always
remember that.
      I walked back towards the tram stop. The distances
became shorter, now that I wasn't on the verge of soiling myself.
I jumped on a tram, and within ten minutes was back to the
burger restaurant where I'd had lunch.
      Halfway there, I saw the junction I should have turned left
at, which would have taken me towards the museum. I decided
to go somewhere else in the city and write for a while, to have a
beer, to not think about it all; the foolishness and the memories
and the notions of conquering it all, of feeling better, of feeling
anything other than the pain, which I'd no choice but to feel.
      I decided I'd just take a beer at a down-at-heel bar if
I could find one, and write in my notepads and not think too
much, if at all. That was good.

THATCHER

The air was cold and bitter as it always was in Prague at this time of year. She wrapped her thick cotton cardigan around herself, knowing full well it would do little to make her warm. It was her cheeks that were cold, which only compounded the feeling of coldness, which compounded the loneliness, which compounded the reality of being alone again now.

Although it was so cold, she didn't want to go home. It was Saturday morning. She'd started doing things – better things than before – with her weekends. She'd done what anyone would do at first; drink, not alone but with friends, out in bars and clubs 'til the early hours, which felt good until she slept and awful the rest of the following day.

But she didn't do that so much now. She went to the mountains with her friend Bláža, she got out of the city, out into the nature, as she loved to do; and it did help, it helped a great deal. Occasionally, if there was a big party, she would drink and smoke copiously and wouldn't feel much guilt about it because it was rare and – though unhealthy – no longer characterised her weekends. She visited her parents more often than she had in the last couple of years and that helped too, although it was forever twinned with the thought that she ought to be somewhere else, with him.

But it was a place of calm and relative relaxation and, although her mother asked too many questions and her father was loud without trying to be, it was away from the city and, more importantly, the flat.

She picked a twig from the floor. It was an innate action, like something she'd do at her parents' place while walking Barnabaš, her dog. But he wasn't here now, and she realised she was just a woman walking in the park, picking up twigs for no apparent reason. It made her laugh.

Maybe she was going insane. The park was quiet, even for a Saturday morning. There were a few dog walkers and one jogger she recognised from previous walks or the few occasions when she went jogging. It was rare for her to be in the park, or even up, at this time. If she had gone out she'd be sleeping now, and if she was out of the city she would have been up earlier and halfway to the mountains.

Her plans for the weekend had fallen through at the last minute when Bláža cancelled their plans to head south for the weekend. It was a pity. Bláža could be flaky, but on this occasion it was forgivable.

Her uncle was unwell and she knew how close Bláža was – and it was clear it would soon become *had been* – to her uncle.

She walked back on herself, past the children's park, which was empty, and the beer garden. She reached the brow of the hill and saw the Sokolovna where the students trained for track events and gymnastics, and, more importantly, she saw the benches on the top of the hill and just over, overlooking the small beer garden below, nestled under a number of trees.

She realised that all these places were as loaded with memories of him as the flat and decided she might as well go back there. It was warm at least.

It was ridiculous, the way everything reminded her not only of him, but of them, that period when they had been an entity, intertwined and inextricable. It seemed ridiculous that it had ever been the case, just as now it seemed ridiculous that it wasn't. He had cut and run.

She couldn't hate him, except for small pockets of moments when she could, and she both savoured them and was terrified by the strength of feeling they stirred within her, mostly because they resembled the love she'd felt more closely than any other feeling she'd had over the past year.

She walked back towards the flat. It irritated her, the way everything was so filled with memory. It felt infantile and childlike, but the reality was that these things reminded her of him.

She walked past The Tavern, a half-Czech half-American burger place where they'd eaten several times.She remembered the way he had gone off to the toilets and come back in an inexplicably sullen mood. It emerged he'd seen some people from his past he hadn't wanted to, and although they didn't talk, it stirred feelings of bitterness in him. He was entertaining and frustrating that way, forever unable to voice his opinions and emotions, only capable of stewing in them, like the apples in the pulled pork burger he'd once vomited after a big night out, when he had gone overboard while she was away.

He told her all about the girls who had betrayed his friend and how bad they were and shook with a quiet rage she couldn't understand. It was amusing. It was baffling. It was him.

She passed the recycling bins. They held no memory. That was good.

She walked past the potraviny, towards the flat, and opened the door with the same key she had thrown down to him on several occasions, wrapped in a sock so as not to risk it falling on and damaging the cars below.

She walked into the hall and a gust of acrid air hit her nostrils from the bins at the entrance, and that too brought a

memory. She climbed the stairs quickly, so as not to think of all
the times they'd ascended and descended them and, yes, made
love on them, his trousers round his ankles, his boyish smile as
he realised they might be caught and became coy in his English
manner.

She turned the key and walked into the flat. There was no
one else in. The others were away for various reasons. She had
it to herself, which had appealed, and now seemed like the worst
thing possible.

When he left he left suddenly, and as a result had left lots of
things behind. She wondered if he ever thought about that.

Although she'd done it before and had left the flat early in
the hope of not doing it again, she decided to look at his things,
an innate desire she was unable to fight.

Instead of walking to her bedroom – she still considered
it *theirs* – she walked into Vincent's room. She opened the
cupboard door where there was a bicycle that took up much
space, but also several coats and jackets belonging to all of the
flat's occupants.

And then there was his blue denim jacket which he'd
loved so much. She knew he'd only left it behind because he
was forgetful and, in the state of his mind when he had left,
wouldn't have remembered where it was, not in the depths of
winter, so close to Christmas.

She felt the coarse material and remembered him wearing
it on one or two summer days, but couldn't say for sure when
they'd been. She held the sleeve in her hand for a few moments
before recognising the cloying emptiness of Vincent's room
and the musty smell it gave off due to all the old bric-a-brac he
collected from various bazaars around the city.

She left the room and walked to her own. The tiny
hallway seemed ever smaller. The coats on the hooks were piled
up so heavily, leaving little space for manoeuvre. The tiles were
cold against her feet, even with socks on, and there was barely
any natural light coming in through the frosted windows of the
bedroom. But when she entered her own room, which looked
out onto the street below, it seemed no more light or airy than
that narrow hallway.

He'd left remnants of himself. Not intentionally, not with
reason, but he had, and they were there.

The books were the worst.

All his books, piled on the shelf, half of which he'd never
read. A couple he had talked to her about at great length, as he
would sometimes do when he really enjoyed one. Some of these

were the ones he'd left, which confused her more than anything. She picked one off the shelf: *J.* She leafed through it without purpose, placed it back and picked another: *The Van.*

She realised why he'd left these books behind and not others. There was a simple explanation and it was that these books were bulky and he had been in a hurry to leave and had done so with as little physical baggage as he could possibly manage. And now he had left her to deal with the excess that was lined on the shelves and in the cupboards and elsewhere.

She picked up another. A biography of Thatcher. He'd occasionally ranted about her in a near nonsensical way. She never understood what he was saying but was attracted by his passion and amused by his utter lack of conviction or insight.

He never read the book, as far as she remembered, even though he'd asked for and received it from his brother for the last birthday he'd had while living in Prague.

It was huge, seven hundred pages or so. She understood why it remained here, but didn't know what to do with it. It felt a crime to throw it away and at the same time an act of cathartic purgation.

She opened the cupboard they'd bought and brought home together, back to this, their flat, which they shared with others. They had carried it up the stairs with the help of one of her friends.

The bottom drawer was broken now. Every time she fixed it she reminded herself not to use the drawer any longer, as it put the whole cupboard off kilter. But after a month or two she always forgot in a fugue of trying not to think of him, and would break it all over again.

She opened the main door of the cupboard carefully and felt the woollen cardigan he'd left behind.

—I want you to have it, he had said.
—It's going to be cold this winter and it's my warmest jumper.

She floated her eyes towards his suitcase.
—And your biggest.

He looked hurt, and she was glad that he looked hurt. She wondered now whether he really had done it to keep her warm, to care for her, to say sorry to her.

She felt the wool a few more moments, then closed the cupboard. Even the latching of the lock reminded her of him, when he had been good, running and jumping about the room;

Opičko, the monkey man.

Back when he would wake her in the morning, far too early, crashing and banging, never more so than when he tried to make little noise.

The last months came to her mind now, when he began taking days off work because he couldn't get out of bed; and finally, the hollow feeling as she helped him pack so he could leave her, not intentionally forever, but forever nonetheless. She knew in her heart what was lost on him.

She decided to leave the house once again. Even the things that held no connection suddenly had a connection because they reminded her of him with their counterpoint, the knowledge that they were of the time before she'd known and loved him, which her life resembled now. And so they were *of* him in their own way.

She descended the stairs with their memories and passed the balcony with its memories of both beauty and angst and left the flat, remembering times walked together hand in hand or at the beginning of bike trips which he'd hated. She walked back to the park. It was her second visit in one day and it wasn't yet nine in the morning. She felt a cloying emptiness and, worse, an anxiety, not knowing how many times she would repeat this today, or what else she could do to avoid his ghost.

Walking past the beer garden, her hope was that it would remind her of the bits of him she didn't like: his drinking, his almost-religious love of football which had threatened to mar the summer of 2014. But the memories didn't bring up hate or even bitterness. They were just pieces of a man gone without a trace.

She walked on, towards the hill, and looked out upon the city, something she never did. She stared out at Prague from the hill and thought about the one New Year's Eve they'd shared amidst the fireworks set off by teenagers and the popping of champagne corks and children running around and away from their parents.

But as always, memory returned to the flat. For reasons she didn't understand, the memory was bittersweetly sweet.

—Hu?

It could only have been eight in the morning. There was sleep in her eyes. One was shut, the other half shut.

—Hu, she replied, not sure if she was really amused at being woken on a Saturday morning, but not quite able to muster frustration.

—Huuuuuu!

She laughed, and he kissed her on the temple.

—Jo, she said, embracing the warmth.

—Hu, he repeated.

His apeisms were best in the mornings, when he wasn't worn out or ground down and was at his most determined to entertain. She nodded.

—Hu, Opičko.

They made love, she climbing on top of him – he was too lazy for legwork.
They lay perspiring after, and he returned to his childish impressions, which for some reason didn't jar with the lovemaking of minutes earlier.

—Hu, hu, hu, he said, curling his fingers, scratching the top of his head and then pretending to remove ticks from her hair.

She laughed again as he turned himself on his back and began to pat his arse in imitation of a baboon.He scrunched his body into a shell and began to pat his feet up and down on the bed.

—What are you doing?
— Nevím, he replied, still acting the fool. —I don't know.
He stopped.
—Máš hlad?
She nodded.
—I will make breakfast, he said.

He left the room. After a few moments, maybe even a minute, she sensed an odd presence. She looked over to the door. His head and the tops of his eyes were peeping around, waiting for her to clock him.

—Opičko!
—Hu!

He disappeared from view. She didn't understand why, but
in his bouts of zooanthropy, he loved pretending to fear her.

— Opičko, she said again. —Pod' jsem.

She called him to her.
He returned, but still acted the monkey. He was wearing
only his underpants, and pulled up the material to expose his
arse again.
He jumped into the sofa they had in their bedroom and
bounced up and down.

—Hu. Hu. Hu!!!!

She burst into laughter, and when he took an empty
cup and put it on his head, she laughed more as droplets of
yesterday's green tea ran down his forehead. She couldn't
remember the name of it now, but his routine had come from
some English comedy he'd liked.
He would do it whenever he felt the need to make her
laugh, whether it be to mask some ill feeling or sadness or just
for the sheer sake of it, the sakeness of fun, of laughter, of joy.
This was him, Opičko, the sad and comic monkey.

—Miluju tě, Opičko.

—Miluju tě víc, he said, in a purposefully guttural voice.

—Ne, she said. —I love
you more.

He looked at her for a moment with his lips distended and
brow arched, before running over while dragging his knuckles
on the ground. He kissed her on the forehead several times.

—Ne, ne, ne. Hu, hu, hu, he said, and jumped off the bed
and away towards the kitchen.

For many minutes she could hear him crashing and banging as
he always did when cooking. She knew he would have started
with coffee for himself, as he always did, safe in his belief that it

was impossible to function without it.

She heard the kettle boil and hoped that he had made her tea, which he usually did. After some minutes he returned with a plate on the palm of his hand, his feet angled out as if he had rickets, still monkeying around.

—Jooo, she crooned, realising that he had made pancakes. —Miluju tě.

She said it again, as if it were new, and it was. It was a new love, a moment's love, from the sight of pancakes and the monkey with the plate, refusing to break character.

—Ty víc, he said.

He scrambled off to get his coffee and more or less remained in character throughout breakfast, nibbling on his pancakes, emitting guttural noises when she spoke to him. After breakfast he nestled himself in her lap and began to wipe his nose on her thick grey cardigan for warmth. They began to watch the news online, together.

That was then, though parts of it remain a part of now, I believe.

And that's important, I think.

Gdansk

I always liked *Self-Portrait*, didn't care what people said. Maybe it was a bad album, but I still liked it, especially 'Alberta #2'.

At least when I die, the music at my funeral won't fall victim to cliché. That's something to look forward to.

I was less obsessed with time, some of the time.

Just a few months on and that assertion already rang hollow.

The week had started so well. On the Wednesday I wrote, albeit badly. I knew it, even then. Sometimes it was better to give up. I was no Steinbeck, couldn't flog a horse 'til it came out galloping. It had to feel right at the tip of the finger. It could be rusty; as long as there was a kernel of promise, I continued. But there were times when it was just shit: the themes flaky, the dialogue desperate, the whole thing near unreadable. Wednesday was one of those times. That was bad.

I first tried in the morning, at Cable Café, a small place near Oval station where no two chairs were the same. They would scrape along the concrete floor in tune with the constant wushing of the coffee machine and the clatter of cups and plates. It was extremely loud there. They had no dishwasher. That was authentic, but in being authentic, extremely loud. That was the price of authenticity, I suppose. I sat drinking my coffee and eating a piece of walnut cake when distraction arrived in the form of an attractive Scandinavian girl beside me. She was short, blonde and pretty.

Short, blonde and pretty girls aside, why I still work in cafés is a mystery, the notion of them as places of calm and focus an illusion: no smoky cloisters of quiet ardour, no ashtrays spilling over with the fag ends of productivity, no jazz, no red wine-stained tables. I don't like jazz, but it suits the environment. That's an inconvenient truth.

Nowadays it's pushchairs, prams and ladies who lunch; Skype calls home or for business, the loud chattering of four students sharing one pot of herbal tea and friends catching up over homemade cake that may or may not really be homemade. That's nice, at least. Cake always is. Catching up with friends too, for the most part. Still, for whatever reason, call it hope, call it nostalgia, I always return to cafés. That's a bad habit.

The Cable Café, with its concrete floor and proximity to salubrious parts of London, was a serial offender, embodying the worst traits of modern cafés. But it was the closest thing I could find to Prague, and Kaaba, so I came often, a sucker for memories.

The Scandi was pouring water when I caught her eye.

She lifted the jug, which had three lemon slices and four orange
slices, plus a lot of mint, and poured a glass into a large tumbler.
Lifting it to her lips, she missed her mouth and spilt water on the
floor. She looked around and, upon catching my eye, began to
laugh, as did I. The Scandi ordered a coffee, and then sat next to
me.

—Don't worry, I said. —I'm a waiter, I do it all the time.

What that meant I've no idea, and neither did she. After a brief
smile we returned to our separate computer screens, lives,
bagatelles and concerns. It was true, I was a waiter, but what that
had to do with spilling water was unclear. After returning from
Germany, I'd come to realise that a new job mightn't be around
the corner.

Low on money and with a meagre redundancy pay out, I
returned to a place I'd been so many times before: the bar. That
was that, for now at least.

I worked around four or five shifts a week, day and night,
and usually Saturdays and Sundays. Having not worked in a
bar since my early twenties, it felt like a regression. I'd never
planned on doing bar work again, but here I was, almost thirty,
barworking.

That was funny if you were me, ha-ha funny if you were
an outsider with a cruel sense of humour, tragic if you were a
customer looking for service with a smile.

I was considering coming off my Fluoxetine full time. I'd
tired of that green and white skirt. The thrill had gone; I was
unfaithful, there one day, gone the next. We were in a bi-daily
relationship now and it seemed a good idea to call it quits, even
if I wasn't doing too well, or perhaps because I wasn't doing too
well. We'd grown apart, or far too used to each other.

That was clear.

The girl was working on an essay of some sort. I
recognised the language as Scandinavian, but wasn't sure which
one. That seemed wrong. There were several, I should have been
able to distinguish which one it was. I needed a Scandinavian
girlfriend, I decided. Then I'd be able to tell the difference. That
said, I'd lived in Prague nearly four years and never grasped the
difference between Slovak and Czech, even though many of my
students came from Slovakia.

They had softer, sing-song accents I imagined to be a little
like the Aran Isles, and when students asked me if I could tell
the difference I said yes, but it was a lie. I couldn't tell a Slovak

from a Bohemian from a Moravian, not until I'd been told. Only then did the softer voice become evident. All the Slovaks I knew were women and all of them were lithe and beautiful. Of course, this isn't true. Memory tricks me. They weren't all beautiful, and they weren't all women. It's simply that I choose to remember the beautiful ones.

When I force myself to think about it, there were many who don't fit my skewed, convenient image. One girl I taught stands out. Šárka was a short, plump woman who joined my Mondelez class shortly before I left the country. Mondelez is an offshoot of Kraft Foods. It is also Russian slang for blowjob. They spent millions preparing the launch of Mondelez. Nobody thought to check what it meant elsewhere. Let's just hope the Russians like blowjobs as much as they like chocolate, or vice versa. That would be good.

Šárka had large, protruding ears and a coarse laugh of rustic, rural fervour. She planned to return to the Slovak countryside one day, and was engaged to a boy from a city not far from her own. She planned to save some money and move home, where she would buy a house in a village, have several children, and play the role first of doting maminka and, later, adored babička, loved for her svíčková, guláš and – only after she had died – coarse laugh. That was her plan.

Only in forcing myself to remember Šárka is it possible to accept my flawed memory. That takes some doing.

Still, despite all that, the Slovak women I knew were mostly beautiful, fun and immensely unobtainable. That much was true.

Now, I couldn't concentrate on my writing, not with the attractive Scandi beside me. I was wearing an old brown T-shirt that was short at the sleeve, and hoped that maybe she'd ask about the tattoo on my left arm.

If I angled my arm right, maybe the Scandi would ask about it. I hoped so, because I knew I'd never strike up a conversation, much as I wanted to. I'd never been that way, not even with Jana. The first time we spoke, it's likely I tried to say as much as possible in the space of a few seconds, desperate to get across some semblance of personality, desperate to know her. Or maybe I just said hi.

That's likely.

*

I wrote out of a desire that the world might take notice of me, but on the few occasions it happened, it scared me and I'd furrow

203

my brow, burying my head into the screen, afraid of what might happen if I engaged with it. I needed the world to read my work, wanted the recognition, but the risk of engaging with it was too big. What if I was terrible? What if I didn't deserve to be noticed? That was too risky. That was also what they call a self-fulfilling prophecy.

Nowadays, I wrote not to be noticed, but through necessity.

After everything that'd come and gone, I still wrote, still needed to. That was just about the only thing about it that felt good. I'd no intention of impressing the Scandi with my writing or an air of mystique I once thought sitting hunched over my laptop might have had. I just wanted to talk to her. If she would only start a conversation, I'd be fine; I was good at talking, able to speak volubly when in the swing of things.

But striking up the conversation? That was anathema to me.

Unsurprisingly, the Scandi said nothing, and with disappointment, I continued with my work. After a while, she started to hum as she looked over her essay.

I hated hummers. But she was short, blonde and pretty, so I forgave it. That was typical.

Then she started a Skype call. I hated this even more. It was incredibly rude. But she was short, blonde and pretty, so my annoyance was diluted. What would I have felt had it been my Slovakian student from yesteryear? What if it had been a man? I'd have wanted to punch him. It was pathetic, but that's what it was.

And it stopped me from working. After forty minutes or so – she was still on Skype – I left, walking towards home, blaming myself for being unable to work.

I was flying to Gdansk the following afternoon and wanted to print off my boarding pass. I'd booked the flight two weeks earlier, and was pleased with my uncharacteristic level of organisation. I still had a little of the redundancy money left, and the flights had been dirt cheap. With nothing happening on the work front, I figured it was a good chance to get away, and to write.

That morning, before the Cable Café and the Scandi, I'd tried to check my transfer from Stockwell to Gatwick, only to realise I'd never booked one. That seemed odd.

But at least I'd spotted it. I booked a return ticket to Gatwick, downloaded the boarding pass and the recently purchased bus ticket, and put them on a flash disk. I was in my room, which was growing smaller by the day.

It was April now and I'd moved into the room in October. I hadn't hoovered once, and it was filthy.

I left the house, turned left, and meandered towards the library, where I'd recently registered with the intention of working outside my small room at least two afternoons of the week. But after arriving, I discovered most of the library boarded up with MDF.

—The main library is permanently closed, said the librarian.

She pointed towards a small workspace behind me, with two computers and two elderly men.

—That's all that's open now.

And that was that when it came to working in the library two to three times a week. I remembered now seeing flyers advertising a protest against the library's closure, which I'd failed to attend. I should have gone, but it was too late now.

That's called having principles in principle.

Back home, my room remained in a state of chaos.

A bedroom should be a space for rest or play, but for me it was neither of those things. It was my home and refuge, but also my cage and office. I was there too often, bitter even though I told myself not to be bitter, lonely because I had to be lonely.

Right now, recalling all this, I sit in Kitchen & Bar at Luton Airport (I'll explain shortly), where the chairs are cheap and scrape harshly on the floor, which is not concrete but a cheap type of laminate that makes the sound all the harsher.

It shouldn't upset me. When I leave, my chair will scrape no matter how hard I try to avoid it. Even with my best efforts, I'd have to lift the chair while standing to enjoy any hope of not scraping it against the floor. Even then, it's near certain that for a split second the chair and the surface of the floor will collide, resulting in a shrill, discordant sound echoing around the high-ceilinged room. I should worry less. That's wishful thinking.

I'd a grandfather once, two actually.

But this first one died before I was born, so I guess you could say I never had him at all. Still, he existed, small imprints of that existence trickling towards me like driftwood. That's a simile. I don't use them often because they're not my strength, you might argue they're an Achilles heel even. That's a weakness. Anyway, my grandfather used to say a thing, and that thing was this:

You have to listen to thunder.

That much was true, certainly. Thing is, though, he was speaking about people, the noise around, the racket.
He wasn't thinking of the storm inside, the carousel tempest. That was my problem.

I am just a thing within it.

Yes, it was true, I was just a thing in the world, but what did that mean? Did it stop me feeling the things that happened, or mourning the losses? Not in the slightest. Did it give me perspective? Did it prevent me from repeating my mistakes? Did it preclude me bedding my thoughts in rhetoric? Clearly no.
The world still baffled me at every turn. Things happened, things that made me want the world to stop turning, just for a moment or two, as if by way of apology for all it had done. I was angry with it. I'd lost Jana. That's what I was the most angry about. I'd lost Prague too, one way or another, when I got so sick and came home. I was angry that no matter what I tried to do I landed on my peachy monkey buttocks instead of my feet. I was angry at that. It was a nice arse, a monkey's arse, a playful arse, and did not deserve to be landed on, but patted and caressed and enjoyed for its aesthetic qualities and the bouncy timbre it produced when slapped.
That would have been nice.
Perhaps I wasn't just a thing in it, perhaps the people of the world truly were different from the seas and mountains and animals and everything else. We knew anger. That seemed important. Sometimes, all a person wants is to punch the world in the face. That'd be nice, that, fun too, cathartic to boot.

I was stagnating and knew it; writing, yes, but enervating with every day spent behind the bar, something which left me feeling as if I'd fallen back into an earlier form of myself I'd never planned on returning to. Bar work was fine, but it felt as if I wasn't moving forward, something that never seemed important before, but did now. In Prague, I'd lived with no plan, was almost proud of the fact. Writing was the closest thing I had to one. That seemed good.
Occasionally, I worried about the future, but it was rare. Writing was my only concern, finishing the book my obsession.

Yes, that was linked to my dissatisfaction with life and who I was, but at times it was possible to enjoy those pockets of days where I just wrote, good or bad, and felt contented enough in that.

Now I wrote, perhaps more than in Prague. It felt important, after losing it all, to be at the very least moving forward in some manner. That was in itself odd. I was terrified of death like never before, terrified of the passing of time, the wasting of it, now that my days were elongated and filled with nothingness; neither the ardour of satisfying work, nor the blank fug of full-time drunkenness. That was a mouthful of morbid for you there.

Apologies.

I'd taken the road less travelled by, and now I served lattes. That was fine, but only in a stoic way. In reality, that sucked, as Brad would have said, it was god-awful, much like that Czech bread. That is a rhyme.

*

I texted my boss to ask if I could use his computer before starting my shift. After that, I began tidying my room. I'd work to do and still hadn't written, but it was impossible to get anything done in this mess. I looked at my phone. It was one o'clock.

Unbelievable.

Time raced when I was at home, trying to fit in as much as possible before the days and nights working at the pub, where time trickled, each glass rinsed or plate served just another in a sea of glasses and plates and puddings and desserts and pints and wine measurements of 125ml or 175ml or, most commonly, 250ml. I was more obsessed with time than ever before. That was not good at all.

Of all the things I wanted to fit into my day, cleaning was at the bottom of the list, but now, in the immediacy of the dust and dirt and grime and strewn papers everywhere, the camel's back was well and truly broken. I couldn't live with it anymore. The dirt aside, there was a plastic wrapper from the business cards I'd had made a month or so back, a screwed up crème egg wrapper from about three days prior to Easter when I'd embraced the resurrection, a number of cables, a book, two NHS prescriptions – I visited the doctor often – and more. It needed to be dealt with.

The shelves remained chaotic and disorganised. As always, only Jana's Hemingway collage stood with any pride or distinction, with the possible addition of a stuffed toy turtle I'd picked up in Abu Dhabi in October, convincing myself at the time that it would all be okay, numbed as I was by what'd happened, unable to feel pain or sadness, or to allow the valley of tears that was so very popular these days in its catharsis to seep from my manqué monkey lids, which were sallow rather than sad now, through tiredness and weariness. That, admittedly, is another mouthful of morbid for you, verging on the digressional.

I'd gone through the trip trying not to think about it all and had done a fairly good job amidst the lagoons and sand and men in white robes, and Indian coolie workers behind buffet carts and Nigerian prostitutes outside the grand hotels. I did well not to think about it all for a great while. That wasn't good either, but it was better than thinking about it, no matter what anyone said.

The turtle sat on the edge, staring at the door attentively like an adoring, domesticated hound. There were many magazines, which I'd picked up here and there in the hope of one day working for them. But as things stood, they were merely scraping away at the already limited space the room had to offer. So I walked downstairs and took the hoover from the space between the stairs, which was cluttered with Christmas decorations and cleaning products and a number of other items. I took the hoover into the living room-cum-kitchen, and plugged it in.

The blind was down and the room dark.I'd always been confused as to why my housemates left the blind down, even on weekends. But I wasn't anymore.

After spending a month or so at home more or less daily, I'd developed cabin fever in my room, what with the cramped space and wrappers and ever growing stack of magazines. So to extricate myself from it, I decamped downstairs, only to notice each and every passerby.

The flat was beside a main road, opposite a health centre and close to a small supermarket. It backed onto a rundown estate where the forgotten lived and mental illness thrived like bacteria in a petri dish. That was the reality of it.

The poor and insane wandered without purpose, to and fro past the flat, and I began to feel as if I were being watched.

One local mad woman knocked on our door every two days or so. The first time it happened, I nearly jumped out of my skin. She slammed the letterbox once, a single, shrill clatter. I opened the door. She was elderly, or looked it. She may have been riddled by alcohol and god knows what else; I'd seen her walking around town holding a black plastic bag swollen with cans.

The woman had elephantiasis and I couldn't understand a word she said. Scared, I closed the door, ashamed for spitting on whatever mix of Catholic and Irish and just plain good manners I'd been raised to believe in. I was ashamed too, for being scared at all.

I was twenty-nine.

What was there to be scared of? Still, whenever she was around, I pretended no one was in.

Now, I kept the blind down, took the hoover upstairs, plugged it in and felt the suction. It was weak. So I began to take the hoover apart. The filter was clogged with a thick mat of dust. I peeled it off, put it in the bin and banged the filter against my jeans. A cloud of dust rose into the air, making me cough and sneeze a while.

I reassembled the hoover but the suction was still poor, and I realised the body of it was filled with dust and detritus that would need to be emptied from the hoover's carcass.

I did this, but was then unable to reassemble the machine, the pieces refusing to slide back into place, not by force or encouragement or wheedling or rage.

There was an orange lever which clearly held the key, but no matter what angle looked at or perspective taken, that orange lever wouldn't fit. I pumped my fists on the ground with a monkey-like rage like never before, not even in the days of Opičko, for when I was Opičko the Monkey there had only been playful displays of stupidity on couches, feigned removal of ticks, unabashed waltzes in public with my legs distended, and hu and hu and hu. That had been very good, that.

Now, there was only rage and frustration. I spent several minutes trying to put the shell back into place, to no avail. I pressed and pushed and prodded and poked but the hoover wouldn't yield.

—Do prdele!

Even now, eighteen months later, I still swore in Czech.

Sometimes English words simply didn't do justice to my frustration. Without a doubt English swearing was the best there is, yet at times its diversity, uniqueness and flexibility fail, times when something earthier and more simplistic are needed. That's a plain and clear fact.

At this particular juncture, with the hoover redolent of a life that sucked, I needed a simple way of airing this frustration.

And yet, just when all hope was lost, when the chips were down, when the gig was up and all the clichés were worn and through, I realised where the solution to my problem lay: the lip of the hoover's plastic upper half.

All I needed was to clamp it down and slot it into the lower section. Quite literally, everything fell into place. She sucked like a dream.

Within two minutes the floor, for so long a haven of dust and dirt, was spotless. I took two of the badly organised books from the shelf, lifted the bed and placed them underneath; the first *A Song of Ice and Fire*, the second *The Chymical Master*, both of which I chose due to their size and bulk. If I'd thought the floor around the bed was bad, the dark, cavernous space underneath was far worse, home to various things I'd pushed underneath lazily in order to make or retain space over the months.

I cleaned up the pens that had rolled under and the paper pads I'd kicked under, and three empty suppository wrappers that had been allowed to disappear with good reason, much like their erstwhile contents. After this, I hoovered the skirting boards, discovering a layer of dust thick as an addict's line. And then, the room was finally clean.

I put my shoes on a wooden rack and hung up my shirts and jackets with some hangers I'd discovered while cleaning out the cupboard. The only messy place now was the bed, which was strewn with books and papers, and the shelves, which I'd decided to do tomorrow. But at least my room was tidy. I could begin packing. Later.

First, I had to write, to prioritise it now that cleaning was done. That was ideal.

With laptop, pens and pads in tow, I made my way to Brixton. The high street was busy (as always), so I turned left and walked to the Duke of Edinburgh in search of hops and peace and quiet. It was closed. I walked back to the Craft Beer Pub, which was also closed. Brixton had been ruined. Those who'd made it expensive were in offices and the businesses that relied on them were shut for the afternoon, and yet it was still as busy as hell with the rustle and bustle of H&M bags and Poundland bags and McDonald's paper bags, unrecyclable in their grease-laden state post-use.

Yes, Brixton, despite its prices and charm, was still a hub of activity in the daytime, busy mothers rushing through a busy town in hunt for the cheapest clothes and the cheapest and most frozen of foods because choice, choice was not something available to everyone. That was a fact. There wasn't a thing aspiration or delusion or filter or clarity or the right kind of face or accent was going to do about that.

As the Duke of Edinburgh was shut and the Craft Beer Pub was closed, I decided to venture into the Prince of Wales, where I bought a pint of Guinness and sat down to write. I'd three hours 'til work.

Those lucky enough to have travelled for something other than work – and it is luck – will understand the intense feeling of anticipation and restlessness that comes the night before leaving.

At once, there's elation in knowing that in just nth hours, you'll be on a train/plane/boat, or in a car. It's the knowledge of not only being somewhere different, but being different also, for to travel is to live a different *you*.

That's not to say it changes you, or if it does it mightn't be for the better. The Western world is awash with ignorant, well-travelled idiots. Look at Parliament. Or the White House. Or the media. Or literature. Or the Premier League.

Still, there's something to love about travelling for the sake of travelling. Enjoying all of it, from the walk to the bus station, the buckling of belts, the beer at the airport, on the plane, in the first hotel or bar at the destination.

And the night before Gdansk, I possessed a niveous, virginal glow of pure delight, even though I had to go to work.

Deciding to take the biggest bag possible to Gdansk, I packed my DVD player, various cables, chargers, an adapter, my phone, books and two pairs of shoes. I always over-packed, unable to leave anything to chance. That was called paranoia.

Work was quiet. There were a few people, mostly couples or small groups of friends.

The busiest table consisted of five, including a portly, gay, Falstaffian Scotsman who made many innuendos with warm cliché before I could finally convince his group to order some food.

   —I'll have a cheeseburger. Medium rare. Sweet
 potato fries, please.

I turned to the next person.

—I'll have the same, but medium.

And the next.

    —I'll have the burger, medium rare, but with cheese and Brie. And mac and cheese on the side.

    And the one after him.

    —Oh, that's a good idea. I'll have the same but with blue cheese instead of the Brie.

    And then I turned to the final person, who just so happened to be the portly, gay, Falstaffian Scotsman.

    —I'll have the cheeseburger. With blue cheese. Brie. And-
He ran his finger up and down the sides.
    —Mac and cheese.

The others gasped. That was a decadent order. But then, the PGFS was a portly man, a look he wore well, I might add.
It seems only fair that I refer to him as the PGFS so as not to fill your mouths with yet more superfluous words. It's a digression, but one you have earned. The PGFS's appetite shouldn't have been a huge surprise. I appreciated his boldness and honesty, and after taking the order, repeated it back to the table to ensure everything was correct, before asking if they wanted drinks, namely booze.

    —Yes, please,
said the PGFS.

Instead of telling me what he wanted, he held an empty bottle of wine, stroked the shaft, and smiled at me.In the process, I recognised the wine as Malbec from the alcohol content, and in many ways understood why he stroked the shaft with lusty ardour, even if it did make me feel ill at ease.

    —It's hard to tell with you stroking that bottle of wine, sir, I said, for the sake of clarity. —Does that mean you'd like Malbec again?

    —Yes, please.

    I turned to walk back to the bar, but stopped when he

lifted his hand in the air.

—Ooh, sorry, I forgot. And a Becks for this man.
He pointed at his friend, who had his back to me,
and grinned.
—In a straight glass.

It was obvious from the corners of the man's mouth that he'd
winced, and I went to get their drinks, enjoying the good mood
I was in, only a few hours now 'til I was *there*, such that being
here didn't seem so bad, as it often had since I'd got the job.

Tonight, through sheer boredom, my colleague had also
made the two of us Old Fashioneds. That was delightful.

*

When I'd gotten ill in Prague, *there* had become London. And
then when I was in London, Prague became *there* (and remains
so, if I'm honest). Yes, it was an unattractive way to be, a grass
is always greener, not-happy-with-your-lot kind of way of
leading your life. But it wasn't a choice. It wasn't such a stark
not-choice as that of the women in Brixton with their plastic
bags and Maccy D's, but it was a not-choice nonetheless. I'd left
Prague never wanting to return. That was the truth.

I wasn't so sick as not to know that this was just how I felt
at the time, not necessarily how I *would* always feel.

I'd hopes that I might return, but getting on that plane,
when I left her and the city, *there* was still very much England
and *here* was Prague, a place unliveable. That much was true.

But right now, in Oval, *there* was a different kind of there,
a temporary escape, nothing more. I held no illusions that I
might go to Gdansk and want to stay, knew that if I did it was an
illusion based on pleasure and the picturesque medieval illusions
of an Eastern European city centre.

I was reading *The Tin Drum* and looked forward to that
illusion, as imagined by Günter Grass, but knew it for what it
was and would be, a brief escape, an escapade laden with hops
drunk rather than served for a change. That was good.

My evening was one of calm verging on serenity. The queries
and demands of customers didn't bother me; in fact, they
seemed – almost without exception – perfectly reasonable (there
were times when I'd happily imagine killing customers for the
crime of demanding cutlery).

I even enjoyed conversing with customers, knowing that

in just a few hours I'd be on the way, travelling, on the road, *there*. A few more customers came and left but the restaurant remained mostly quiet, save for the table of five, who were loud without being unreasonable, full of well-earned post-work cheer. That's an overuse of hyphens.

After about an hour, the PGFS asked for the bill. I went to the iPad we used at the bar to keep tabs on people's drinks and food orders, searched for table 20, and pressed *Print Bill and Save*. The bill chook-chook-chooked out of the printer. I put it on a small metal dish, and gave it to them. The PGFS placed four debit cards on the dish.

> —We'll do four times 46.20 on these, please,
> he said, pointing to each of his colleagues. —And
> then I'll cover whatever's left after that.

What was left was 83.20. Gratuity was included, as it always was on tables of five or more, and he paid it without batting an eyelid.

I printed his receipt, handed it to him, and asked if he needed anything else. I even meant it.

They'd been a nice group, polite, rude and fun all at once. Besides, the tip was included whether they liked it or not. That was the benefit of things coming in fives. There was a glint in the PGFS's eyes.

> —Just your number for this gentleman, he said,
> pointing to the man with his back turned to me.

L'esprit de l'escalier. That's a French phrase which translates as 'staircase wit'. That's a thing where you think of a comeback much later than you would have liked, i.e. not immediately. I don't speak French. That's one last digression.

At around ten, ten-thirty that night I thought of three witty comebacks and four pithy remarks. That was typically unquick-witted of me. At the time, however, I drew a blank, opting instead for a childish blush followed by a mumbled comment that I couldn't remember my number off by heart. The PGFS winked.

> —So it's an 0800 number then?

That's how to be quick-witted.

Sadly, the only thing quick about me was my about-turn to the bar. Even that turn of phrase came off the back of a rewrite.

I envied the PGFS with his easy, ribald humour. I had jokes like that in me, thousands of them, but they never saw the light of day.

That was a pity.

I thought myself a man of easy wit and charm, but when it came to it, I was far too insecure and slow to be like that. I'd had moments over the years, but that was all they were, moments of brief glory: a stunning comeback, a great turn of phrase, a shocking ejaculation, as it were.

But in general, as with my fantasies of playing Glastonbury or winning the FA Cup or saving a damsel in the stressiest of distresses, it remained there, in my mind, nothing but a perverse notion.

That was okay, though. Fantasy was a part of me. I knew that. I'd more awareness than before, and those moments when I was witty and charming usually came about while drunk or working towards it, when I liked myself and the person I was. That was dangerous, because it wasn't true, and was important to remember.

The rest of the evening passed without incident. I closed the bar, putting the chairs on the tables, cleaning the coffee machine, restocking the fridges, pulling in the awning with the grey remote control. That was my shift.

*

In the morning it felt like all the shit of life had washed away. I knew it wouldn't last, that in less than three days I'd be back behind the bar, in Oval, living the same life as before. But for now, I was free. I'd packed, and gone out for coffee, stopping in on the way home to get a haircut at Michael's. Perhaps it was foolish of me to worry about the length of my hair instead of checking my tickets.

That's hindsight for you, though.

But just as I felt the last time I'd gone to Michael, long hair brought chaos to my being, and it was something I needed to fix before presenting myself to the Polish nation.

Hairs cut, I checked my things once more and left the house, with my laptop and books and cables all in the lower compartment of a large Nike bag. Thirty paces down the street, I checked everything again, even though it was impossible that anything might have fallen out or left the bag of its own accord since I'd walked those thirty paces from the door.

I'd always been this way, checking, rummaging through my pockets to ensure my wallet was there even when I could feel it, knowing it couldn't have disappeared. Oh, if only I really had been Opičko, with no need for pockets or wallets or money or driving licences or anything of that ilk at all.

Though it might seem like it, that wasn't another digression, rather an overdue bit of exposition or explanation on the precipice of denouement. That's an overuse of big words. And that is a digression once more despite the promises.

So apologies from me, to you.

As expected, everything was in the wallet. I reached St John the Divine and, as if by divination, realised I'd forgotten something after all: my pills. I returned home to get them, one for the following day, one for Monday, with one skipped on Sunday. As I said, me and Fluoxetine were on a one-day-on, one-day-off thing right now and it was working okay for both parties, even though I'd asked my doctor if I could stop seeing her completely. She'd cautioned not to cut ties so fast, but I lived in the hope that, sometime soon, I'd be down to no days at all.

That seemed like a good plan.

I didn't want to be on pills my whole life, not the red and yellow suit kind or the green and white kind that were like a skirt or Celtic's football kit. I didn't want to be a bhoy forever.

The pills were exactly where I'd left them, on the shelf beside my bed, which had been home to ill-advised bottles of red wine, the bottle of whiskey that had pre-cursed the return of the whiskey dreams and a medal my father won in a rowing competition in Dingle, back in the mid-seventies.

I'd worn it round my neck for years but the leather strap had broken months ago. I intended to replace the leather strap soon, but of course, it never quite happened. That was life. Life was walking and waking and shitting and eating and doing stuff too, though. That was important to remember. And so I walked to Stockwell station, stopping in at a nearby café, not to shit, but to get coffee.

Life was also coffee, thankfully.

With my pills and my coffee and all my boarding cards and baggage, I got to the bus stop fifteen minutes early and waited. Time passed. The bus didn't come. More time passed. At 11:44 there was still no bus. 12:15 came.

I looked up how to get to Gatwick by train and took photos of the bus stop to prove to easyJet down the line that I'd been there, waiting. That was a very middle class thing to do. Eventually, it showed up. I got on and showed the driver my ticket.

—I was waiting for the 11:44, I said. —It didn't come.

He peered up, with the resigned look of a man who has had to repeat himself over and over.

—This is it. We're running a little behind schedule.

That was what happened when men like Mussolini didn't run your transport system. That, though, was a good thing. I smiled, and got on.

—No worries.

I was on my way, and took out *The Tin Drum*, which I was enjoying a great deal.

I'd wanted to read Grass for years now, but never got round to it. For that reason, I was worried that it might be several years before I got round to replacing the leather strap for my father's medal, that medal I'd worn around my neck for many years, partly to remember him in some manner, partly in the hope that someone might ask me what was that medal around my neck; a question, an inquiry, an interest.

I read for around twenty minutes. Even though the bus had arrived late, I was still going to be early. That was good. South London, and then the bit just south of South London, drifted in and out of view as I looked up from the page every few minutes.

Wizz Air.

I'd not flown with them for a while, not since the days when I'd travelled back and forth between Prague for Christian holidays and one time the Christian funeral for the very unchrist-like death of a friend.

I always flew from Luton, but here I was on the way to Gatwick, flicking through the pages, dismissing the thought slowly creeping into my mind. Wizz Air must have started a new route from Gatwick. Why else would I be heading there?

The lines on the old, yellow pages began to grow blurry. I couldn't concentrate on Oscar and his drum or any of the various descriptions of places I was going to visit (the novel was set in Gdansk).

Check the ticket, I told myself. Put your mind at ease. And so I slowly closed the book, put it to one side, and pulled out my ticket, which was filed with my passport in a see-through plastic sleeve, everything well organised and filed appropriately, everything still going according to plan.

The 15:00 flight to Gdansk, 1G581, departed from Luton Airport.

That was the that of the that of that plan. I immediately understood why I'd not booked a bus transfer in the first place. I understood too that, from this point forward, I would never again be able to laugh at anyone who had made a similar flight-related fuck-up in years gone by.

I understood that I was utterly incapable, and a fool to boot, that I was an idiot, a waste of carbon and oxygen and whatever else it was that made up me; things I'd never understood in science class because I was a fucking cretin and a fool, who couldn't even get himself to the right airport.

A deep sense of self-loathing enveloped me, and I sat in a state of numbness for several moments, unsure what to feel, let alone do.

By the time the bus reached Sutton, I was ready to give up.

I deserved everything that had happened to me. What kind of person goes to the wrong airport? I couldn't organise a piss up in a brewery, or perhaps that was just about all I could organise, a damn, dirty drunk fool of a man.

I wasn't in the best of sorts. That much was clear.

I sat on the hard National Express seat stewing in my own self-loathing. All these months of struggle and strife, of trying to get on my feet again, over Jana and back into work, all of it was encapsulated in this moment. What an idiot I was!

It wasn't just that I'd gone to the wrong airport. I'd been kidding myself ever since January, ever since December 2014 even, when I'd left Prague, thinking maybe things would get better if I just sorted my head out a little, thinking I could leave and somehow magically find a way back, a way forward for the two of us, so very similar and different people.

I'd been a fool to think I'd be okay when it was over. I'd been a fool when I'd taken her to Ireland in the hope it could be home. I'd been a fool when I'd gone to Michael's instead of checking my tickets and I'd been a fool when I'd tried to bake my blues away or find her again through Irish liquor. I'd been a fool.

Each time it seemed I was moving forward was actually just me setting myself several inexorable steps back; shuffling with the childishness of MJ, if not the style, nor the high-pitched voice. It was mid-April, and I was no better off than I'd been in the depths of winter, when it all began, or in September, when

Jana had been brave enough to do what I couldn't.

Life was a circle of folly and resolve, hope and despair. How blind I'd been to think it would get better, to think I would get better, be better, be happier and more capable, at ease with myself, the world and, of course, the memories. It never got better. That's called a low ebb, which is a metaphor from the sea.

That's where most of our metaphors come from, because we are the Island, and god don't we know it.

*

Through depressed eyes, I looked out of the window. We had just pulled into Sutton. Was there still time? No, it was futile. I was more likely to make it to Luton in time from Gatwick than I was from here. I pulled out my phone and rang my mother. I couldn't think what else to do. I told her what I'd done.

—I'm such an idiot, I said. —I'll probably just come back to Harrow.
—Well, she said slowly, knowing my predisposition for self-loathing.
—Consider your options before you make any decision. It's not necessarily insuperable. Is there another flight you can get?

I'd never heard my mother say the word insuperable before. That came as a surprise. As did the fact that in the midst of the self-loathing and regret, I'd somehow checked flight times.

—There is one at eight-thirty from Luton. But it'll be too late. My host expects me at six.

—Have a look into it, you never know.

—Okay. But I'll probably be home later.
I hung up. My immediate plan was to go to the house I'd grown up in, where I could be a sullen fool swaddled in the comforts of home. I couldn't handle a whole weekend in Oval, not when I'd planned to be abroad. If I was going to stare out of windows bitterly, I wanted them to be large ones. I sat wondering what to do. I could tell by my mother's tone she was desperate for me to find a solution, knowing full well what I was like.

219

And she was right.

No, I said, possibly out loud. Not this time. Cinderella
will go to the ball, I thought to myself, in a manner of speaking.
Cinderella. That's a story that doesn't come from one place, it
comes from all over, though many claim it as their own. That's the
world for you.

There are two sorts of men in the world: those who love
themselves too much, and those who love themselves too little.
I was of the latter, though I imagine pointing that out now is
something approaching a digression, or just plain obvious.

Such men blame themselves for the things that happen,
even in a world where a plan is about as reliable as a job or
a government or a whiskey dream or an ideal or a love or a
country or a parent or a child or a sea or a sail. These men blame
themselves for the missed flights, the failed relationships, the
grand shitzem of life. That was the kind of man I was. But not
today, I said to myself.

Just for once, I was going to do things differently. That
was a plan *worth* planning. I took my phone out again. Much
as I maligned the modern world for its attention deficit disorder
writ large, I needed it now, and it was there when I needed it.
That was the reality of technology for you.

Within a minute, I was a step closer to resolving the
situation. I found the Wizz Air website, booked another flight
like money weren't a thing, even though on this occasion it was
a thing, seventy of them to be precise. I sent a message to Ewa,
my host, telling her I was going to be very late, and that I'd find
a hotel. I was going to Gdansk come hell or high water.

*

When I arrived at Gatwick, I ate a simple but overpriced lunch. I
received a message from Ewa. She said she'd wait up. That was
kind, on my wallet as well as my soul.

After eating the simple and overpriced lunch, I set about
getting myself to Luton. The train ticket was expensive, twenty-
seven notes, but it had to be done. What would I do if I didn't
make it? I could picture myself, lying on my bed all weekend,
beating myself up. No, I couldn't let that happen.

Arriving at Luton four and a half hours early for flight
number two, I went to the grotty pub beside Burger King and
bought a pint of Heineken. After that I went through security,
which was easy, taking less than five minutes. With four hours
to kill, I got another beer and wrote two thousand words for

a travel blog I'd started, before starting a new, handwritten short story. I had another beer and then queued for the plane extremely early, so as not to leave anything to chance. That was smart.

On board, I sat next to a slender blonde with an unfortunate wedding ring, and flicked through the inflight magazine. I decided to borrow it, so I could pitch the editor. I borrowed a Benelux brochure as well. It was well written, considering it was translated from French. There were some mistakes, however, and I hoped to maybe help them out in exchange for money.

The flight was smooth, but they were out of beer, which shouldn't have bothered me but did. By the time we landed I was too exhausted to care anymore. I'd been up a long time. I should have been in Gdansk hours ago, but as we touched asphalt, something clicked in me. I was here, I'd made it. It mightn't sound like an achievement – idiocy was still, undeniably, the dish of the day – but in a way it was. I'd overcome myself.

I got through passport control sharpish, and went straight out onto the airport forecourt and hailed a cab. The driver said hello in English, but it was clear he couldn't speak much of it. Polish and Czech weren't dissimilar, so I thought I would try Czech.

—Potřebuju tento adresa, I said, pointing to where I needed to go.
—This is street, he said. —I need number.

There was a number beside the street name, but it appeared to be incorrect. He asked me something in Polish. I didn't understand. I replied in Czech, which he didn't understand.

—Deutsch? he asked.
—Ne. English.

He shook his head, and looked ahead, wondering what to do.

—Universita, I said. —To je fajn.

He nodded. I figured I could find my way from the university. As we sailed past the drab airport surroundings, lit only with billboards and the occasional bar, I sent Ewa a message about the apartment number. Once more, technology was my saving grace, and she soon came back with the exact number.

—Aha! I said. —Dvacet sedm.

The driver nodded enthusiastically, and repeated the number, slightly different in Polish, but close enough to get us there. We were on our way.

After ten minutes, he pointed to an apartment block on the opposite side of the long road we were on, and told me it was the address I was looking for.

He did a U-turn at the first opportunity, and dropped me off outside. I handed him eighty zloty, twenty of which was tip – I was extremely grateful to him.

The large, communist-era building was nondescript, which may explain why he waited in the car until my host arrived, perhaps bemused by the sight of an English man, who clearly couldn't speak the lingo, hanging around at midnight. But Ewa's husband – I'd not realised this when booking – soon showed up and let me in.

—Welcome to Gdansk.
—Thank you, I said. —Sorry for keeping you awake so late.
—It's no problem.

He handed me a guidebook to the city, and we walked up the stairs. The apartment smelt of fresh paint and wood, and looked like it had been put together hastily and cheaply. That's not to do it a disservice.

There was a bright, new bathroom with a power shower, Formica worktops and a knock-off espresso machine. More importantly, there was a bed for a night. I was in Gdansk. I handed him a bottle of wine.

—To say thank you, I said. —For staying awake for me.

I made no mention that I'd expected it to be Ewa I'd be thanking with – and sharing – the bottle of wine. I think he could tell. He nodded.

—Thank you.

And then he left. Fuck it. I didn't care if he was the husband. Hats off to them. That was smart thinking. They'd clearly thought out their Airbnb ad in order to rope in schmucks like me.

I'd be lying if I said the greyscale, studio-quality photo of Ewa hadn't played a huge role in me choosing that apartment over the other options available, some of which were in the city centre.

I slept like a baby.

*

In the morning, I got dressed and prepared for the day. Laptop, books, phone charger.

My thought process – clearer now – was that I'd head to the beachfront to get coffee and a pastry.

After that I'd head into the city centre. That seemed like a good idea. I walked down the stairs, and was met by an old woman. She stared at me for several seconds.

—Vy jste okay? I said.

She smiled, and said she was waiting for me to pass. She was old, and patient, and wanted me to go in case she held me up with her slow steps. I smiled back, walked down and turned left, as Mikel the Husband instructed, towards the waterfront. That was the plan.

It was early. A few cars passed to and fro, and the road ahead didn't look particularly scenic. So I turned back on myself, and walked towards the train station. I would visit the beach later. That was the new plan, and for once I didn't mind diverging in such a cavalier manner. That was good.

Near the station was a kiosk selling cigarettes – I wasn't going to buy any – sweets, magazines and tickets. It was tightly packed. Every window corner had a magazine or a sample of the various things they sold.

It was just like in the Prague, which had had the same kiosks, always manned or womanned by someone of at least forty-five, if not a lot more. They usually had a radio on in the background, a tabloid beneath their eyes and a cigarette of one of the cheaper brands – such as Winston's – in hand.

The Prague.

I laughed to myself.

In all my years of teaching, no matter how hard I tried, my

223

students and lovers – plural, yes, if only just – never got it right. They always inserted articles where they didn't belong, omitted them where they did. That was Czechs for you.

It worried me at first. In time, I realised it was the same for every teacher. Articles were either embedded in or impenetrable to languages. That's just the way they were.

The Czechs didn't have a hope. I might as well have tried to tell them English food was nice or gypsies were not lazy or football was better than hockey. There are truths out there just not worth saying. That much is true.

I once argued with a woman about which had more words, English or Czech. It's English.

A little research will prove it, a simple dictionary sufficient as evidence. It didn't matter, though. No matter what I said, she refused to believe me. She'd been taught from a young age that hers was a rich and beautiful language. That may or may not be true (subjectivity has its merits), but there aren't more words in the Czech language than in English. That woman drove me nuts. I'm not telling you who she was. That's a mystery for you.

I told you about haemorrhoids and wanking and how I sometimes dream I'm saving the day because the day is so very insignificant, like me, and I told you about trying to bake away and buy away and travel away and drink away depression, and I told you all about my travels including this little trip to Poland (which, let's face it, was probably all too proximous to the Prague), but I will not tell you who that woman was. That's called having your secrets, just a few of them.

That's actually a good thing, boys and girls.

I walked up to the kiosk, peered into the small, dark window and asked for a normal ticket. The train came after a minute, Gdansk gliding into view. I stared at Grass's city, famed for its promenades and churches.

It was the green cranes of the shipyard that stood out, though, like mourning herons, forever bowed in solemn reverence to the revolution they'd borne in the '70s.

The city was sleepy. It was only 8:46. It was picturesque. The central square was pretty. There were lots of tourists, and hawkers of tat which the tourists bought in droves: fridge magnets, children's toys that bore no relation to the city we were in, and other trinkets, such as knock-off Barcelona FC merchandise, including a wooden Lionel Messi model which appeared to be suffering from the Zika virus. That was global recognition for you.

Despite the time, people were already sipping beers in

restaurants beside the cobbled paths. I ate a buffet breakfast in a local restaurant, watched the BBC World Service on a large widescreen television and cracked, knowing full well that I was going to buy those cigarettes, which I did.

That was the first failed plan of the day, and there had always been an air of inevitability about it.

Something about traveling to foreign cities did that to me. I think it was the routine of it: walk, do something, smoke, see something, drink a beer, smoke or, if writing, drink a beer, write, smoke, write, smoke and so forth. That wasn't good, but it was a routine, and routine was a good, good thing.

I decided not to get a beer until later, after seeing a little of the city. That was saintly of me. As it transpired, there wasn't a whole lot to see. The waterfront was pretty, but the main street was all dug up and fenced up for refurbishment by a construction company. That was bad timing, though good for the city, I guess, because building was a sign of progress, was it not?

Much of the harbour was closed, and the view was better from the other side of the water than it was from the waterfront, where many tourists were sat with coffees, admiring the view of JCB diggers and dug-up earth and other detritus. That was ha-ha funny to me, if not to them, though they didn't look overly disappointed.

I got a beer at around eleven and wrote thirteen hundred words on my computer about my trip, explaining the disaster of the previous day. The waiter didn't understand me when I asked for an ashtray using the Czech word, and I decided then to stop kidding myself and just revert to English for the remainder of the weekend.

I thought of Jana then, how I'd both relied on and resented her in my desperation to learn Czech, to understand her parents and the world around me.

That's what's called being careful what you wish for.

Jana did her best with me, teaching and otherwise. She wasn't a great teacher, didn't have the patience for it, but she did her best. That's all anyone can do.

Unless you have money, in which case trying can be diluted by roughly the same ratio as you'd dilute Robinsons cordial.

I took a cigarette out of my pack, lit up, and laid my arms across the bridge across the Gdansk River, or sea, or whatever the fuck it was.

At that moment, I remembered going for a walk in Jana's village with her dog, a huge poodle who barked often but was extremely gentle. We walked past the small children's playground on the edge of the village where we had taken her nephew Petr to play. We walked up a small hill to say hi to her neighbour. His dog came to greet us, an ageing sausage dog which rolled on its back, encouraging Jana to rub his belly. The neighbour shook my hand, said hello, then turned to Jana.

—Chce pivo?

For once, I understood what someone around me had said. Did I want a beer? Was it rude to say yes, or rude to say no?

Of course I wanted a beer. We were in the countryside; what the hell else was there to do except climb the tree in Jana's back garden or try to keep her poodle entertained?

I wasn't bored, though. I was restless. I was in the calmest place in the world and couldn't have felt less at ease. Why? I needed fire, I needed life. I needed excitement. And when I was in the city with the fire and the excitement and the life, I would crave the quiet and solace of the country.

That was man.

*

And so I left. I left because I couldn't understand, couldn't speak to the people around me, couldn't understand the conversations that for years had filtered through in a pleasant, meaningless fuzz.

They had suddenly taken on meaning; 'til Jana, they had been welcome in their incomprehensible nature.

I could write around them, sitting with headphones in my ears, enjoying the sound of humans talking without distraction. But at some point I needed to understand and thought I never would because I'd not the nous or strength of character to learn her language.

And so I left. Now, living in the country where I was born, I understand more or less every word that hits my ears. And without sounding melodramatic (I prefer slow rise to drama), I understand even less than I did before.

Ha fuck you very fucking ha.

After all was said and done, I'd wasted a lot of time over the last few months, fixating on things done and said or the reverse, to no avail. I'd created wild realities in my mind about injustices done to me, by editors, by friends, even by Jana.

I had reverted to fantasy, because reality, well, reality had become just too absurd.

It had all just happened, not because of any effort or

226

ineffort on my behalf, just because.

It all just *was*, and for that reason plans seemed ineffectual and at times downright foolish. There was no closure. And without closure there was room for anger and pain and delusion to foment, to become twisted and deluded and toxic.

There was no finality, no apology on my part for causing the pain and sadness and loss I inflicted on Jana and myself, no end to the reality that I had been the keeper of tears and the architect of broken dreams. That was the that of the that of the that.

There is never closure, just an ongoing sea.

You wake up good one day and vile the next, earnest one moment, another resigned. You are sober then drunk, determined then defeated; and the only constant is the anger, the unmarshalled, un-understood, aimless anger: at that cunt editor or city, that cunt company, that cunt circumstance.

That cunt inbox, that cunt newsreel, that cunt loneliness, that cunt the past. That cunt you, with his ideas and ideals, compromised on repeat by the bottom of a glass. But that's just how it *is*.

*

I stood on the banks of the river or the sea and looked out upon the water with one highly prevalent thought rushing through my mind.

I would like, preferably soon, not to be insane.

I wanted to leave behind the Fluoxetine and her green and white skirt, the manic thoughts, and the role-plays of mind. I wanted to leave behind the imagined anger, to start making plans I could stick to, plans that were not so important that if they went wrong it threw my whole existence out of whack. Or to make no plans whatsoever. Mainly, I just wanted not to feel insane anymore.

I lit up a snout and thought of her, about how very sweet it had all been, of a time. That was good.

I sucked in a puff of smoke, and that was good, no matter what anyone said about it. I exhaled and that was good too, and I thought about the good times with her and the bad, and that was, as you might expect, both good, and bad.

And as I stood there on the bank, one more truth stuck out with more lucidity than any of my wild fantasies or longings for recognition or self-loathing or wishes not to be insane or broken or hopeful or alone or wedded to the bottom of a glass, and that thought stood out like fire.

Despite it all, it is so very good to be alive.

Despite the loss and the pain and injustice and ignorings and chaos and forgettings.

Between the losing of the job and the baking of bread and drinking of whiskey and the trying, just trying to be okay.

Between the fish and chips and red wine, between the accusations and forgivenesses. Between cleaning glasses in a dirty sink on a night rather than writing, just writing as you would rather.

Between the cigarettes and loneliness and the silent staring at computer screens, hoping to be whisked away.

Between the whiskey dreams and kneaded pain, between missing flights because the mind was too foggy to read a ticket, between it all. Between Jana, the having of her.

The losing of her, the cuntery of circumstance.

Between the manqué monkey and Opičko, the loyal, loving, sad monkey man with his impressions and hopes and dreams that never quite could come to fruition. Between it all, it was so very good to be alive. That was true.

Doubtlessly (hate adverbs as I do, they have their place), that was overly (see) earnest, but damn it, that was true.

*

On the first full evening of my stay I ate an opulent dinner: half a duck, with potatoes that were poorly cooked, espresso, two cigarettes and red wine.

That was divine.

I went back to my apartment and was lonely, so I invested in a bottle opener and a bottle of red wine. That was probably not very good, but it wasn't so bad either.

I tried to watch a film called *Omar* on a DVD I'd brought with me and had got for Christmas for no reason other than I couldn't think of something to ask for as a present. The DVD player didn't work, so I watched two episodes of *The Walking Dead* – which I hadn't watched for some time – and drank the red wine.

In the morning, I chided myself for it all, and promised I'd do things differently that night.

I visited a maritime museum and walked the ghosts of my father, who had been a sailor. I went back to the sea later that day, just to watch it a moment.

And I found a bar, where I watched Tottenham Hotspur in their last great performance before they capitulated that season. That, when that came to happen, was ha-ha funny, unless you were a completely humourless human being.

She had been wonderful to me. That much I knew. She had been reading *Kafka on the Shore* the last time I'd seen her and would ask me to clarify the meaning of words. She often gave me cake for free in Kaaba, though only after I'd overcome my shyness and spoken to her. She often came into the bathroom and hugged me while I was brushing my teeth, an action I never thought could be layered with love and vulnerability and the feeling that you really did mean something quite special to another human being, but there in the plastic and foamed paste, that feeling would stand out. She'd been wonderful to me.

In the evening I ate a meal in a traditional restaurant and went home and went to sleep early.

In the morning, I went for breakfast, then directly to the airport, and waited to go home and continue with it all.

It was good to be alive.

That was good.

Acknowledgements

Thank you to my editor Cara Quinlan for her eagle eye, suggestions and amendments, and Mike Gibson and JJ for reading through sections of the book in an earlier form. Thanks to Tim Parks for his frank, vital feedback in previous years and kind encouragement in those more recent.

A huge amount of gratitude must go to Bobby Saunders and Alex Pitt for their generosity and time during the book's design.

I'm especially grateful to my illustrator Gary Ogden for his patient work on the book's artwork and willingness to tolerate my flighty indecision. Special thanks must go to my siblings, aunts, uncles and cousins for encouraging me to write at ebbs both low and high; lending me resilience during the former, grounded focus the latter.

Thank you to Jamie, for giving me the time, space and freedom to write this book. I am eternally grateful to John Johnson for every pint bought me, considered ear lent me and second of time granted me as I made my way through the difficult years that culminated in *Bad Bread, Good Blues*.

Finally, I am forever indebted to my mother, for her love, encouragement and support in the face of my mistakes, knock-backs, heartbreaks and hardships. In gratitude, I would promise not to get any more tattoos, but unlike my plans, promises are something I like to stick to. That much is true.

Author's Note

The text in *Bad Bread, Good Blues* was written in an atypical style. The unusualities in both prose and dialogue are intentional, as are the discrepancies in spacing.

Space is good, for both the eyes and the soul. As for the bits in between, that's for you to decide.

*

Thank you for reading this book. Please leave a review on Amazon or Good Reads.

About the Author

Ronan J. O'Shea is a writer and journalist. After living in Prague for several years, he returned to London, where he now lives.

Learn more at *ronanjoshea.com*

www.ingramcontent.com/pod-product-compliance
Lightning Source LLC
Chambersburg PA
CBHW050846190726
48286CB00007B/2250